BLOOD
AND
STONE

BLOOD AND STONE

ELIAS KARO

Kravitz & Sons

INNOVATORS IN PUBLISHING, MARKETING AND ADVERTISING

Kravitz and Sons LLC
1301 Farmville Blvd, Suite 104
Greenville, NC 27834

Published by Kravitz and Sons LLC.

ISBN: 979-8-89639-226-2 (sc)
ISBN: 979-8-89639-227-9 (e)

Because of the dynamic nature of the Internet, any web addresses or links contained in this book may have changed since publication and may no longer be valid. The views expressed in this work are solely those of the author and do not necessarily reflect the views of the publisher, and the publisher hereby disclaims any responsibility for them.

PART I

PROLOGUE

Scattered throughout the Hrefn Sea, just north of the Kingdom of Aethel, lay the Free Isles of Fjell. Founded independently at various points throughout the Twilight Age, it was eventually determined that the island city-states would benefit from forming a coalition. But among the Free Isles, few were as isolationist as Edelheim, and of the ruling houses, few were as enigmatic as the Drakes.

King Regnant Sagramor Drake had ruled Edelheim for thirty-five years with minimal interaction with the rest of the Isles, but his health had deteriorated in the succeeding years, so his sons and advisors had largely been ruling in his stead.

The eldest of his sons, Prince Percival Alarch Drake, had been groomed since birth to rule Edelheim. He had been trained in statecraft since he could walk and had felt the pressure of the crown for just as long. His brothers—Meliodas, Bedivere, and Elyan—had also been trained as competent noblemen, but it was an unquestioned fact that Percival would succeed their father.

~~~

Percival was sitting in his father's study, poring over various political documents. Usually, Chamberlain Wigan would be the one to take care of this kind of work, but he had been called away on family business. The light of the candle flickered, and Percy felt his eyes begin to glaze over, his eyelids becoming leaden and heavy.

Just a bit of sleep can't hurt, he thought, resting his cheek on his hand.

"Your Highness!"

He shot up, the weariness washing away as he hurried to the door. He threw it open to see a thin man in a green cloak, panting and out
~~~

of breath. The king's study was at the top of a high tower, and it seemed the poor man had run the whole way up.

"A missive for you, sir."

Percy raised an eyebrow. "It's the middle of the night. Couldn't it have waited until morning?"

The courier shook his head and cleared his throat. "No, Your Highness. It's from High Cleric Ascena."

Percy's eyes widened, and he quickly snatched the missive from the courier. Indeed, it held the insignia of the Covenant of Light: two golden rings intersecting. He tore open the seal and quickly skimmed through the letter. He looked back up at the courier and stood up straighter, brushing a stray hair from his eye.

"Summon my father's privy council at once."

The messenger nodded and then dashed back down the stairs.

Once every ten years, every kingdom on the continent would send a representative to a conference, which is usually hosted by the Covenant of Light. For the last century and a half, Edelheim had been excluded from these conferences—until this year, if this missive signed by the High Cleric's hand was to be believed.

"It's an insult!" The king's most trusted advisor, Lord Escanor, slapped his palm on the table, causing the light from the candles to waver slightly.

"Now, now, let's not jump to conclusions." Lord Pernam sighed. He was the oldest member of the privy council and had served under Percival's grandfather, King Demetrus, shortly before his death and had been on the council longer than anyone in living memory.

"Pernam is right." Lord Tristam, the final member of the council given Wigan's absence, crossed his arms. "This could be an olive branch. The High Cleric is not a vindictive woman, and the Covenant gains nothing from the humiliation of Edelheim or the Drakes."

Tristam was the youngest in the council, only a few years older than Percy, but was also the only one among them who had any experience outside of Edelheim. He had spent six years in the Empire of Valmera, serving as an advisor to Empress Élisabette D'Mer's half-brother, Duke Despereaux.

"Your Highness, you are regent in your father's absence. What say you?" Pernam folded his hands, his large eyebrows falling so low over his dark eyes they were almost completely hidden.

Percy hesitated. The Covenant had never given a reason for excluding Edelheim from the negotiations, nor were they under any obligation to do so.

Technically based in Aethel, the Covenant of Light was independent from any one country's jurisdiction, answering to no one but the Gods themselves. This meant denying them would be tantamount to denying the Gods. Furthermore, the High Cleric was the Gods' direct emissary on earth, which made denying the high cleric exponentially more offensive.

Percy glanced at the creased piece of paper in the center of the table, the black ink shining in the candlelight.

"The High Cleric asked for me by name." Percy cleared his throat. "I don't see any way that we can refuse such a request without insulting the Covenant and the Gods."

Tristam nodded. "Of course, Your Highness."

Escanor didn't look happy, but the old man never looked happy. Pernam looked content, but at that age, he had figured out how to turn nearly every scenario to his advantage. The one person Percy had never learned how to read was Tristam. There was a twinkle in his eyes, like he always knew more than he let on, and he had a vulpine smile that made Percy's stomach churn. There was something off about Tristam, something under his waistcoat and perfectly pressed lapel.

Percy dismissed the privy council and returned to his father's study. As he began penning a letter to Meliodas, the cawing of the ravens outside his window welcomed the rising dawn.

CHAPTER ONE

Percival was scared. He was big enough to admit that. At twenty-five years of age, he had seldom left the confines of the palace grounds, let alone travel all the way across the Beorht Strait to Aethel. He had only been to Aethel once before as a young child, and now here he was, on the way to that place once more. Within the hold of a ship, he was surrounded by other nobles and their processions.

He had been more conservative with his entourage; he couldn't afford not to be. Just two trusted guards whom he'd known nearly his whole life and whom he knew would defend him to their last breath. Andrea Poole was only a few years older than him, and he had his suspicions that she might fancy him just a bit. He did not return her affections but found it charming nonetheless. The second guard was a man named Sir Janus Eyre. He was getting up there in age but was still as fit as he had been in his twenties, or so he said.

Before joining the Drakes' court, Janus had been a member of the Dragonguard, a group of men and women dedicated to protecting Nymor from threats both magical and mundane. He had practically raised Percy, being far more of a father to him than the king. Janus had taught the young prince how to fight despite his mother's protests that he should focus on statecraft and leave the warfare to his younger brothers. As the eldest prince, Percy had dozens of tutors to teach him how to be a good ruler. But Janus taught him how to be a good person, and for that, he was eternally grateful.

At this moment, however, his trusted guard and friend didn't look as distinguished as he usually did. Janus leaned against the side of the hull, clenching his fists and closing his eyes as if he was trying very hard to concentrate on something.

"Looking a little green around the gills there, old man." Andrea laughed, patting the older man heartily on the back.

"Poole, I swear to the Gods," Janus grunted through clenched teeth, "if you don't shut your fat gob, I'll wring your skinny neck right here."

That shut the poor girl up, and now she was looking nearly as pale as the man who seemed quite close to losing his lunch.

Percy sighed, looking up at the man from his place on the floor where he'd situated himself. "Janus, if you're not feeling well, I'm sure we can find a healer to—"

"It will pass, Your Highness." Janus waved his hand dismissively. "You needn't worry yourself with an old man's woes."

"Nonsense. I need you in fighting form if you're to protect me! Who knows what kind of beasts or brigands could ambush us on the way to the Temple!" Smiling playfully, Percy uncrossed his legs and lifted himself from the ground in one fluid motion.

"Thank you, Your Highness, truly." Janus forced a smile, cringing slightly from the effort.

"Andrea, stay here and make sure no one tries to snoop through my things. Some of my

mother's imported quills are in there, and you *know* how cross Father would be if I lost them."

She nodded, standing to attention—perhaps a bit too enthusiastically, as she whacked her head on the low ceiling of the ship's hold as she did so.

As Percy wandered around the ship, he didn't recognize anyone there. That wasn't a surprise, of course. When the royalty of Eastwell or Velhaven held galas, no one ever thought to invite Edelheim. He half suspected that most of them wouldn't even be able to point to it on a map—if they even knew it existed at all. He couldn't help but notice the way many of them were dressed. They were all draped in silks and drenched in jewels, as if asking to be robbed. But perhaps with a company of nearly a dozen guards and two dozen servants, they'd be safer than most.

Percy didn't think he'd be able to find a sorcerer on board, but perhaps there might be an herbalist. Surely one of the visiting dignitaries from all over the Free Isles had brought someone with medicinal knowledge. Percy dreaded the thought of returning to Janus and Andrea empty-handed, so he pressed on. By the time he reached the room housing one of the three ruling families of Eastwell, he was getting quite tired of getting no answers, which was perhaps why he was a bit impatient with them.

"My friend is ill. Are any of you healers?"

The Suncrests looked up at him, clearly annoyed that he had interrupted their apparently very important conversation. They were a small family, unlike most royals in the Free Isles, and much tighter-knit than most as well. All of them had distinctive dark skin and pale eyes, a striking appearance that set them apart from the common folk of Eastwell, most of whom were as pale as Fjell's winter storms.

"And you are?" A man with a strong chin and a weak nose glared at him.

"I'm in a bit of a hurry. Now, are any of you herbalists? Alchemists?" Percy tapped his foot impatiently, scanning the group for any recognition.

"I am." A small woman nestled in the very back of the group spoke up.

She was dressed in a long dark cloak that covered her entire form, and her long black hair was tied in a braid behind her head, although a few strands hung loose.

"Tessia, no." An older woman, presumably Tessia's mother or governess, grabbed her arm roughly, trying to stop her from standing up.

Tessia's pale green eyes softened, and she kissed the woman on the forehead. "Don't worry, Mom. I'll be careful."

Reluctantly, the woman released her arm from her grasp.

Tessia turned to Percy. "Now, can you show me to your friend?"

When the two returned to Janus and Andrea, the old man was looking much worse for wear. He was sitting on the ground now, his head propped up on a board, and Andrea was frantically patting his sweat-soaked forehead with a piece of cloth.

Percy gasped, rushing to his side. "Andrea! What happened? Is he all right?"

"I . . . I don't know, sir. I was watching your things like you asked, and he just . . . collapsed!"

"Oh my." The color drained from the healer's face, and her eyes went wide.

"Well? Don't just stand there! Help him!" Percy ordered roughly, although the fear in his voice did lessen the authority he intended to project. Still, Tessia nodded and got onto her knees next to the man.

"I'm going to need you to stand back." She closed her eyes, moving her hands to hover over the man's quivering form.

"What're you doing? Where are your herbs? Your potions?" Percy looked frantically between her and Janus.

"I don't need them. Now, don't make me tell you again."

There was the authority Percy was looking for. He nodded, took a few steps back, and motioned for Andrea to do the same.

Tessia closed her eyes, beckoning the strength she needed. Her hands surged with energy and then gradually began to glow with divine light. The light pulsed slightly but didn't increase beyond the intensity of a candle's flame, so nobody else in the ship's hold noticed the display of sorcery. Beads of sweat rolled down Tessia's face and onto Janus's chest, but soon his breathing evened out, and the shaking that wracked his body ceased.

A small smile graced Tessia's lips before she collapsed, falling into something soft and warm—Percy's arms, as it turned out. But she didn't know that.

~~~

Tessia awoke in her quarters on the ship, surrounded by familiar faces looking down on her with concern. As soon as the haze over her vision cleared, she felt the familiar sensation of an open-palmed hand on her cheek.

"That was incredibly foolish, young lady," Senior Magus Agatha scolded her. "Do you even know anything about that man? His family works in dark magic, child. You should not have helped him."

Her memory was hazy for a moment while she tried to remember what she'd been doing. Then it returned to her.

"That man! I need to tell him something!" She tried to sit up but was pushed back onto the bed by strong yet boney fingers.

"Not on my watch, young lady. You need to rest!" She sighed, brushing hair away from Tessia's brow. "You know you can't be doing magic like that, especially not so soon after your Awakening.
~~~

The Arcane College and your parents sent me to watch over you, and I won't have you overexerting yourself with reckless magic!"

"But, Master—" Tessia protested.

"No buts. Now you will stay in that bed until we reach Aethel, or I will tie you to it."

Tessia wanted to fight her, but she knew that she'd lose, so she resigned herself to her comfortable prison. Surely, she'd see the man again after they'd docked, and then she could share her suspicions. The thing that ailed his friend was no ordinary seasickness; if her suspicions were correct, it was no sickness at all. There was something arcane about it. He had been poisoned.

~~~

As it turned out, Tessia did not run into Percy again once they docked. Janus was still feeling slightly under the weather by that point, so the group decided it would be wise for them to rent a few horses to take them up the long road to the small mountain village of Sanctuary. There, at the end of the road and hidden deep within the heart of the Bulwark Mountains, was the Temple of Last Rest.

According to legend, it had been built by the first followers of the Covenant of Light in the middle of the Black Age and was the Nameless Prophet's final resting place. The Nameless Prophet was a slave in the Empire of Wyveria who went against her master's dragon-worship to preach a marriage between the two most prevalent deities: Tyr and Astraea.

Tyr, also called the Old Man of the Forest and the Blind Hunter, was worshiped by the ancient orcs of Orcanum, some of the clans of Dejar, and the lowlander tribes of Aethel. Astraea, also called the Wayfinder and the Starchild, was worshiped by the northern tribes of Fjell, the southern peoples of Valmera, and the mountain tribes of Aethel.

It was the Nameless Prophet who formed the Covenant of Light and brought the disparate human and orc groups together, eventually toppling the Empire of Wyveria. It was with her blessing that the Temple was built. Over the intervening centuries leading up to the Sun Age, the location of the Temple was lost until it was rediscovered ten years prior by a caravan of Valmeran merchants who'd been stranded in the mountains.
~~~

The Temple was a massive complex, befitting the final resting place of the Covenant's prophet. As they made their way toward the massive doors, Percy couldn't help but marvel at all the diversity. There were dwarves and elves from all over the continent and even a few hired orc mercenaries. He'd never seen so many nonhumans in his entire life.

His palace had a few elven servants, but here, there were real-life fair-folk, elves who still followed the Old Ways of nature spirits and ancestor worship. Also, in the past, he'd only ever seen dwarves from afar when merchant caravans would stop on Edelheim on their way from Velhaven to Windhollow in the north.

As for orcs, he'd only heard of disparate groups traveling through Aethel but had never seen one in person. They were massive people, most of them at least seven feet tall. The color of their skin ranged from pale olive green to a deep viridian, and most of them were adorned with intricate tattoos the likes of which he'd only ever seen in illustrations. Orcs followed a strict philosophy of order and self-control, as was evident from their uniform posture. They were some of the best fighters in Nymor for a reason and were highly valued by mercenary companies when they left their homeland of Orcanum.

Percy doubted there'd been such a diverse congregation of people such as this for the entirety of the Sun Age.

As Percy and his companions stood before the wooden doors of the Temple, they felt welcoming and warm, and a sense of security fell over him.

Chapter Two

Tessia Suncrest was found unconscious at the epicenter of the explosion. She was not dead, but she might as well have been. In her moments of wakefulness, she could do nothing else except scream until her throat was raw, at which point she would fall once more into the inky blackness of unconsciousness. During these violent fits, she would lash out not only by thrashing violently with her body but also with her magic. Pillars of flame and ice shot from her cell at least once an hour, more if she was having an especially bad night terror.

The only one that could soothe her was a renegade sorcerer who had found himself in Sanctuary during the commotion. He was an elven man who seemed to hold himself as someone older than he was—although how old that actually was, was debatable. His name was Hawthorn, but that was practically all anyone knew about him. He used magic that the other sorcerers weren't familiar with to calm Tessia's troubled mind long enough to treat her injuries, most of which had been sustained after the explosion.

For nearly three full days, Hawthorn was the only one allowed in Tessia's chamber so that she would have time to rest and heal. The second prisoner that the temple guards had apprehended, however, was not so lucky.

~~~

Percy's hands were bound, and his mouth was gagged. Andrea was dead, Janus was gone, and now he was trapped in a dark cell beneath Sanctuary. His throat was dry from repeating the same story a hundred times to his incompetent interrogators: "I told you what I saw. Why won't any of you believe me?"
~~~

He didn't have the answers they wanted, and the answers he gave only made them angrier. Someone had killed the High Cleric and the emissaries from nearly every power on Nymor in a massacre that rivaled even the last Cataclysm in terms of body count from a single event. The Covenant of Light was leaderless and shattered, and new sects were already starting to crop up all over Valmera and Aethel. People were rapidly losing trust in the Covenant's authority, which was a recipe for chaos. The people of Sanctuary were rattled; they wanted revenge. Percy couldn't blame them, really. Grief made people do crazy things. But he was grieving too.

The other prisoner, whom he didn't know, had woken up. The commotion outside of his cell could tell him that much. Everyone's attention was on the other prisoner, and he knew he wouldn't get a chance like this again. The shackles on his wrists were loose (not eating for three days would do that for you), so he quickly slipped out of them. He untied the blindfold around his eyes and looked down at his bare feet.

Shit.

They had taken his thick leather boots along with the rest of his belongings after he'd been arrested. If he didn't find something to keep warm before the guards returned, he was more likely to die in the wilderness than succeed in his daring attempt to escape. His cell was completely empty save for the well-used pile of straw he had been forced to sleep on for the last three nights.

"Oh, how the mighty have fallen," Percy whispered miserably, lifting himself up from the ground as silently as he could manage.

His legs ached from the hours of sitting in odd positions and lying on the cold hard floor, and he silently cursed himself for neglecting to go on all those camping trips Janus had invited him to. Maybe then he'd be at least a little more used to living like an animal.

He heard voices coming from the cell at the end of the hall. One of them sounded familiar in some way, although Percy couldn't quite place it. Maybe someone he had run into during the conference? Whoever they were, they were on their own in this mess.

Someone in that room, a voice he recognized as one of his interrogators, raised her voice at the prisoner, yelling incoherently. And Percy took his chance. He scrambled to the door as quietly as he could and began feeling around in the straw and dirt for a sliver of wood or metal. He never thought learning how to pick locks would actually ever help him in life, besides the original intention, which was to irritate his parents. He wasn't exactly glad to have been proven wrong.

His fingers hit something hard in the dark, and he lifted it to examine it. It was a sliver of wood, maybe from a board or door. One more and he'd been that much closer to freedom. His pace quickened as he heard the rustling of chains and the sound of feet being dragged across stone. The other prisoner was being moved. Percy pulled away as quickly as he could, pressing his body flush against the wall next to the door. He held his breath, silently praying his fluttering heartbeat wouldn't give him away. And, Wayfinder be praised, it didn't.

The footsteps moved past his cell door and up the stairs into the main temple building. He waited in that position for a moment until the footsteps completely faded from earshot and he was sure he was alone. He half-hoped that maybe they'd forgotten him in the excitement of whatever the other prisoner had told them, but he wasn't willing to take that chance. The lock was laughably easy to pick, and Percy wondered if it had ever been used at all before him. He didn't have time to look this particular gift horse in the mouth and silently snuck out of the cell.

He was unable to locate anything even remotely suitable for what he had planned in the dungeon, so he made his way up the stairs in hopes of finding some appropriate footwear in the main temple. At the top of the stairs, he spotted three Covenant sisters near the front of the building, along with Wayfinder knew how many pilgrims just outside. He'd have to find a back exit. He stayed close to the wall as he moved, staying in the shadows the best he could. Out of the corner of his eye, Percy spotted the flickering of light through a just barely cracked doorway. He listened for voices or footsteps or even so much as a breath, and once he was satisfied that the room was empty, he pushed open the door.

It was a bedroom with three beds and a dresser pushed up against the wall. Below the third bed was a pair of slim leather boots with a simple yet elegant embroidered trim.

Perfect. He slipped them over his already chilly toes, and immediately his confidence spiked. *Maybe I can actually get away with this.*

He poked his head outside the door to make sure the coast was clear, and that was when he saw it—his key to freedom, more accurately his *door* to freedom. He felt the cold draft on his face and saw the disused door swinging slightly on its hinges. There was just one thing in his way, a young boy no older than ten sitting idly on the ground and playing with a fake sword. Percy had no idea why a little boy would be left alone in an empty temple, but that was for the sisters to worry about. He had to figure out a way to get around him.

"Hi, sir, why are you hiding?"

Shit.

"Oh, um, hello, little boy." Percy stood up slightly, waving at him.

"My name's Mallory. Are you one of the bad men, sir?" The boy's eyes narrowed, and he pointed his "sword" at him.

"What? No, of course not! I'm with the good guys. I'm on a secret mission." Percy slowly stepped toward the boy, his hands out in front of him in surrender.

Mallory's eyes widened. "Really? Are you working with the Lady Paladin?"

Paladins were soldiers of the Covenant, so it made sense why one would be involved in all this. Their stated purpose was to safeguard the sorcerers at the Arcane Colleges who were learning to harness their abilities, but it all too often devolved into abuse, with the college becoming more of a prison than a place of learning.

Percy nodded. "Yes! The paladin needs me to go out that door and get her something very secret and very important."

The boy's face became very serious. "All right, sir, but you've got to be careful. My mother says there's wolves in the forest!"

"Right, well, thank you, young man." Percy stepped around him, waving slightly as he slipped through the door and into the freezing cold morning.

~~~

As the creature fell with a screech, Tessia's staff was still pulsing with blue-green energy. The massacre at the Temple had drawn
~~~

enough chaotic energy to make it possible for portals between the realms to form. Nightmares from the ephemeral realm of Phantasma surged forth to torment the living.

She panted heavily, clutching her side with her free hand. Up until this point, the entire journey up to the summit had been a blur for Tessia, but the pain in her stomach brought everything sharply into focus.

Her chaperone sheathed her blade, wiping the sweat from her brow. She was a formidable woman, at least six feet tall and orcish by the green-grey of her skin and the intricate tattoos tracing up her arms. Her hair was white, with other colors of hair braided into it, a symbol of prestige in orcish culture. Her name was Dame Nestra Casterly, a member of one of the few orcish families who held a title outside of Orcanum. She was also a paladin but had abandoned the Covenant over philosophical disagreements on the treatment of sorcerers.

At the moment, Dame Nestra was busy conversing with the elf who'd been battling the Nightmares before they arrived. His skin was snow-white, as if he hadn't seen the sun in ages, and his eyes were a deep violet-red. The color was not entirely uncommon for elves, but it still caught Tessia off guard. When he spoke, she paused, something about it stirring something in her memory.

"I'm sorry," she interrupted whatever the elf was saying. "Have we met before?"

He looked at her with a puzzled expression. "Yes, I watched over you, I suppose. I hadn't imagined you were lucid enough to remember me, however."

She chuckled lightly, then offered him her hand to shake it. "I remember your voice. I think it helped me with the night terrors. I feel I should thank you for that."

"No thanks necessary. I would have done it for anyone." He bowed his head slightly and handed her a healing potion.

"Well, thank you, nonetheless." She gratefully took it.

"We need to meet Isadora at the forward camp." Dame Nestra turned to her. "Suncrest, do you feel fit enough to make the journey?"

Tessia hesitated. "I . . . Yes, I can do it. Let's go."

~~~
~~~

Percy had barely made it a foot out of the door when he was met with the point of a blade to his throat. The blade was connected to an arm, and the arm was connected to a man. Percy had never been one for the company of others, and men and women back home preferred his brothers to him, especially the charming and introspective Bedivere or the gallant and handsome Meliodas. But even he, in his inexperience, could admit that this man was attractive. His hair was golden blond, and there was a scar tracing up his face from the right side of his mouth. Percy half-considered inviting him to join him on his escape attempt. Then he noticed the sigil on the man's cuirass: two swords crossed over a burning star. He was a paladin.

Fuck!

"Fuck," he said aloud.

"I know you." The paladin narrowed his eyes, pressing the sword ever so slightly into his throat. "You're the one they found outside the Temple after the explosion. You're the one who . . ." His face flushed with anger, and he took a step forward, turning his blade to press it lengthwise against Percy. "Nearly every noble patriarch and matriarch was in attendance. Do you have *any idea* what level of destruction you've caused? I can't kill the other woman. She's got information the legion needs. But *you* . . ."

As he got closer, Percy noticed his eyes were bloodshot and had heavy bags under them. It must've been weeks since the man had slept, and his hands were shaking, however much he tried to hide it.

"Why'd you do it then? You're just some Fjellian noble. What could you possibly gain from chaos in Nymor?" the paladin asked, his breath ragged.

"Like I told everyone else who's already asked me that damn question, *I didn't do it*," Percy answered through gritted teeth, trying his best not to twitch against the paladin's blade. It was just barely avoiding cutting him, and it told him that even in his state of unrest, the paladin was a trained killer, a soldier who knew how to use a sword as an extension of himself. "Now get off me, and I'll get out of your hair. I promise you'll never see me again."

The paladin smirked slightly. "Nice try, but even if I don't kill you right now, you're still a prisoner of the legion."

Percy grimaced slightly, quickly glancing down at the sword. "Well then, why don't you? Kill me, I mean. If you're so convinced I'm guilty, why not carry out your *justice*? Although I would like to at least know the name of my executioner, just so I know whom to condemn when I meet the Gods."

The paladin's grip on his blade tightened, and Percy noticed how his breath caught in his throat. He smiled to himself. That got to him. So he was a religious man then?

"I would not be condemned for killing the man who *murdered* the High Cleric of the Covenant of Light."

"And if I didn't do it?"

The paladin paused, and he loosened his grip on Percy.

"Are you so sure of your convictions that you would risk killing an innocent?"

~~~

Despite the snowy landscape, the sun beat down heavily on the bridge, where the woman with dark eyes and hair like fire waited with bated breath.

Isadora was still shaken up, though she was loath to admit it. Hundreds of people, including some she considered dear friends, had been murdered, and now the fate of the world rested in the hands of the person who might've been responsible. She trusted Dame Nestra, though, even if the prisoner wasn't willing to help of her own volition, Dame Nestra would convince her. She had a certain affinity with people that Isadora lacked, and stronger fists.

As if on cue, a messenger approached her and informed her that the prisoner had managed to defeat the Nightmares and close the portal behind them and was on her way to the forward camp along with the paladin, the elven renegade. Isadora didn't trust the elf, not one bit. As far as she had been able to find in the last few days, he hadn't existed before he approached Dame Nestra with an offer to help. It was entirely possible that he truly was just from an extremely remote village. But Isadora was a naturally suspicious woman, and her instincts hadn't failed her yet.

The massive gate at the end of the bridge swung open, and Isadora let out a sigh of relief when she saw Dame Nestra was safe. She knew that Dame Nestra was a formidable warrior and could handle herself,
~~~

but Isadora considered her a friend and was glad to see she wasn't hurt.

"You made it," Isadora said, sighing in relief.

Her eyes flashed to the prisoner, who truly looked out of her depth, and any doubts about her innocence vanished in an instant. Isadora turned to the sorcerer, whose eyes were almost brimming with tears.

"Tessia, wasn't it? I'm glad you're all right."

Tessia smiled slightly and wiped her eyes, seemingly soothed by her words.

There was some discussion of what route should be taken to reach the ruins of the Temple. Eventually, they decided to take the more direct path through the valley and to send some of the soldiers ahead of them to clear the way. Before they had even reached the camp, they heard the sounds of violence rolling over the valley and prepared for battle.

~~~

Even with a sword at his throat, Percy had convinced the paladin to not kill him, but now he had to convince the man that he wasn't a threat.

"I can help you."

"You?" the paladin scoffed. "How? Your family has abandoned you, as have your noble allies."

Ouch. That was news to him.

Percy just hoped the stress from the whole ordeal hadn't pushed his father closer to the grave. He hid his shock well, however, and continued, "I wasn't talking about allies. I can fight."

The paladin looked as if he was trying to hold in a laugh. "Sure, and I'm the queen of Orcanum."

Percy gritted his teeth. "Just take me with you. You're armored for battle, so I can only assume your plan is to make your way to wherever the other prisoner was taken. If I can't handle myself, I'll be killed, and your conscience will be clear."

The paladin considered it for a moment. Then he sheathed his blade and drew a short sword from his other hip.

He held it out for Percy to take. "Fine, but I'll be watching you, Drake."
~~~

Percy smiled. "Wouldn't have it any other way."

Percy had never fought Nightmares before. Actually, he had never fought *anything* before. He understood the theory, of course, but putting it into practice was a different story altogether. He didn't inform the paladin of this fact, of course. The combination of adrenaline and pure animal instinct had protected them both thus far.

The paladin still hadn't told Percy his name, and his earlier deflection hadn't escaped his notice. Percy wasn't personally invested in the subject, and he decided he'd indulge his curiosity once their lives weren't in danger. He still needed something to shout in the heat of battle other than "Hey, you!" so he had started calling him "Sir Paladin." The paladin didn't seem to like it very much but didn't correct him either.

The valley was absolutely overrun with Nightmares. Being locked up since the explosion had denied Percy the opportunity to truly grasp the scale of everything. The explosion had completely shattered the surrounding region, leaving it little more than a blasted heath. He knew the effects of this would reverberate all over Nymor. Percy momentarily wondered if it would reach the Free Isles, but he quickly pushed the thought from his mind. He couldn't think about that right now, about his family, of them abandoning him. He had already lost so much in the last few days. He couldn't consider how he'd lost them too.

The pair cut through the mountains, Sir Paladin following a barely defined path it seemed he'd followed a hundred times before. Seemingly hearing the question Percy had only spoken in his mind, he answered.

"After the explosion, I made a lot of trips to the ruins to . . . think. And to be alone." And then he was silent again.

The pair reached the Temple before the other paladin and the prisoner. But the way for them to advance was blocked by a jagged portal hovering in the air. It hurt to look at it, like it wasn't quite there but at the same time was painfully there. They decided not to think about it and to focus on killing as many Nightmares as they could.

Their efforts seemed entirely futile. Every time they would strike one down, two more Nightmares would erupt from the ground in a flash of iridescent light. Percy was getting tired, and he could tell Sir

Paladin was too. Sweat gleamed on his forehead as his blade clashed against the carapace of a Nightmare.

Percy crouched over with his hands on his knees, trying to catch his breath. He looked up just in time to see a heavily armored shade with its claws raised and ready to strike. He didn't even have time to react before a dagger buried itself in the creature's eye, flying deftly through the holes in its helmet. The thing fell back, crumbling into a heap, and dissolved into a pile of ash. He craned his neck to see where the blade came from.

Standing on the crumbling battlements was an orcish paladin, her white hair wiping in the wind. Close behind her was an elf, staff gleaming with crystalizing ice energy. And finally . . . Percy's breath caught in his throat as his eyes fell upon the final person. With her black hair hanging loosely around her shoulders and her green eyes gleaming with determination, Tessia made eye contact with him, and her demeanor immediately changed. She quickly rushed down the steps, skipping the last couple to reach him more quickly.

"You're here!"

"You're alive," Percy breathed, only barely daring to believe it.

Tessia glanced behind him at the battle. "It's good to see someone else survived, but listen . . ." She quickly drew her staff, which began to crackle with lightning magic. "We need to talk after this. There's something you should know."

Without another word, Tessia charged off to find high ground. Percy sighed and cracked his neck. Then he followed her lead.

Chapter Three

Percy couldn't get the sound of Tessia's screams out of his mind, the way her face twisted in complete agony, and the look of terror in her eyes as the Nightmare behemoth struck her, a final death flail of a creature not of this world. And now she was unconscious. Again. She could've died.

Percy was furious at how flippant they'd been with her life. So he didn't leave her side the entire time she was out. He didn't even know Tessia that well, but he felt a connection with her. They had been the sole survivors of an event that had killed hundreds. That was something very few people could relate to.

Tessia opened her eyes groggily. "Hey." She smiled weakly.

"Tessia!" He sat up, wrapping his arms around her neck. He quickly pulled back, his face flushed. "I . . . I'm sorry. I know you don't really know me. I just . . . I'm glad you're all right."

"No, no, it's fine. I'm glad someone else made it out too."

"Dame Nestra's waiting for you in the temple. It sounded important."

"Thank you. You know, I never actually asked you your name." She laughed airily.

"Percival."

"Thank you, Percival." She sat up, then paused. "Before I go, you should know. Your friend? The one I helped? I don't believe he was ill. He was poisoned."

The next days passed quickly as the Legion of the Gods was built from the ground up. Sir Paladin, who had still refused to reveal his name to Percy, had been made the commander of the legion's measly forces. A woman called Isadora had been made the spymaster, and from Percy's momentary interactions with her, it seemed a well-earned title.

The last member of the legion's tribunal was a noblewoman named Lucrezia Alcàntara, who was from the Dejari capital city of Calal. She was in charge of ensuring that the legion's relations with the outside world remained cordial. Given that the legion was an upstart religious cult that seemed to opportunistically rise in the High Cleric's absence, Percy thought having such a diplomat would be useful—not that anyone cared to hear his opinion, obviously.

He had been thinking mostly and training when he could. It felt good to hit something. The last thing Janus had eaten before he'd fallen ill was the food Percy had packed from home. Someone in their own household had tried to poison Percy, and Janus would've died if not for Tessia's intervention. She had left a couple of days ago to retrieve an ally from the Greenwood of western Aethel, something about a group of Covenant sisters with some political connection or another.

Percy didn't know most of the details. He was still being kept under watch. Tessia had proven her innocence to the gathered pilgrims at Sanctuary, recounting a vision of being rescued from the blast by an aspect of Tyr. Percy had no such good fortune.

The legion was in a complicated predicament with him. On the one hand, sending him to the capital of Valmera and the home of the Covenant, Arc-en-Ciel, to stand trial would undermine their authority and almost certainly end in his execution, regardless of his guilt. On the other hand, the legion didn't have the resources or the time to have a formal trial. So he was stuck in an uncomfortable grey area between innocent and guilty.

No one trusted him, and even Tessia was somewhat wary of him. That hurt more than he expected. He hadn't been able to leave Sanctuary without an escort and had only been given wooden or dull iron swords to train with. It was mildly humiliating. Percy was completely on his own.

Every letter he had sent home had gone unanswered. The only thing he had received was a notice from his father's privy council informing him that he had been removed from the line of succession and was no longer welcome in Edelheim.

The frigid air was crisp on his skin as he swung his legs off the side of the pier, nursing the bottle in his lap. It was some kind of orcish brandy he'd managed to steal from Laila, the owner of the tavern in Sanctuary, where the legion was stationed. If he was going to be stuck here, he might as well enjoy it. He wasn't technically supposed to be alone like this, but he thought the guards must've taken pity on him.

He *hated* it—their pity. He also hated the way they looked at him, like he was a kicked dog or, worse still, the way they looked at him with disdain, like he'd kicked *their* dog. It made him want to scream, made him want to grab their dagger and show them who deserved their fucking *pity*. He hadn't felt this kind of rage in a while, hadn't allowed himself to feel it.

With Tessia's wariness of him, his imprisonment, and now his own fucking family abandoning him, he felt that familiar satisfying heat rising in his chest. He wanted to break something. He wanted to make someone fucking *bleed*. He stood to his feet and screamed, hurling the bottle at the ice, where it shattered into a million pieces. It didn't do much to assuage his anger, but it helped. A little.

"Wayfinder, you look like shit."

Percy spun around to see Sir Paladin standing there in simple brown trousers and a dark brown jacket. His arms were crossed over his chest, and he was smirking at him.

"Fuck off," Percy slurred, wiping the brandy from his lips.

"Hard to believe you were ever a noble," he scoffed.

How dare he? Percy growled and lunged at him but missed as the man stepped out of the way.

"That was sloppy," Sir Paladin scolded. Then he tossed Percy a sword from his side. "Try again."

The sword landed in the snow in front of him, and he stared at it for a moment, then back up to the paladin. He raised an eyebrow and picked it up, holding it in both hands as he readied himself to attack. Sir Paladin smiled and drew his own blade. His stance was precise and practiced. What else could Percy expect from a seasoned warrior, a paladin no less?

Percy lunged again, more carefully this time. Despite his inebriated state, he even managed to land a hit on the paladin's side.

He had sparred enough with Janus to know how to hit light enough to not cause any harm, but even still, he was surprised when he drew no blood. Before he had time to congratulate himself, however, Sir Paladin had disarmed him once more, sending his sword flying at least ten feet this time.

"Well done." He smiled, bemused.

Percy turned to retrieve his weapon. "Oh, shove it," he grumbled, kneeling over and pulling the sword from the snow.

He brushed the white powder aside and noticed something on the sword he hadn't before. It looked like an engraving. He couldn't quite make it out, though. The sword had clearly seen some action, and the carving had become faded and illegible. Percy heard the snow crunch behind him, and he turned to see the paladin making his way toward him, hands on his hips.

"Having fun playing in the snow, are we?" he teased before noticing what he was looking at. "Ah, yes." He sighed. "It was a gift from my sister before I joined the paladins. The engravings say, 'To Safeguard the Light.'"

Percy frowned and stood up. "And you still have it? Most paladins join very young."

The paladin shrugged. "I was older than most, and besides, it's a good sword—for those who know how to use it," he added cheekily.

Percy rolled his eyes and fought back a smile. He hated it when the paladin did that, when he acted so . . . *normal*, acted like *he* was normal. Percy hated how it made him feel; worse still, he hated how he loved how it made him feel. It was deeply confusing.

"So . . ." Sir Paladin cleared his throat, looking almost sheepish. "Do you have any of that brandy left?"

Percy rolled his eyes again. "If you're going to berate me for stealing from the legion's stores, don't bother. I know I'm getting an earful from Laila later anyhow."

"No, that's not what I . . ." The paladin sighed, rubbing the back of his neck bashfully. "Honestly, I could use a drink."

Percy's eyes widened at that, but when the paladin didn't explain, he relented. "Yes, fine, but I don't have it with me. They're back at my cell—" He corrected himself spitefully. "Sorry, my *room*."

Sir Paladin's face fell, a reaction Percy very much didn't expect. "I am genuinely sorry for the treatment you've received. Everyone's on edge. They need to have someone to blame, even if that someone is innocent."

Percy looked at him in surprise. "You believe I'm innocent? Why?"

"I was . . . brash when we first met—frustrated, scared, confused. There had been so much death, and I needed someone to blame, someone to . . . *punish*. You reminded me too much of people I've known before—Saddler and Helaena, people I trusted. And then . . ." He clenched his fists, causing Percy to instinctively tighten his grip on his sword. "You—Edelheim—you have nothing to gain from the death of the High Cleric and all the others. This chaos benefits no one, least of all Edelheim. I don't know you well—that much is true—but I can see you are no fanatic intent on sewing chaos."

Percy nodded, trying to ignore the slight feeling of warmth blooming in his chest. It was probably just the booze. "Right, well . . . thanks." Percy cleared his throat. "Drinks? Let's go get drinks."

He mechanically handed his weapon back to the paladin, then turned on his heel, marching toward Sanctuary and praying to the Wayfinder and anyone else who was listening that the paladin hadn't seen the blush on his cheeks.

"It's Edric, by the way," the paladin said, smiling at Percy softly over the mug of ale Laila had just poured him.

Percy stopped sipping his own drink and looked at him, confused. "What?'

"My name," Edric clarified. "It's Edric Royce. You were going to find out sooner or later.

Best it be from me. Besides"—he shrugged—"it was childish of me to hide it from you anyhow."

There it was again, that warmth. "Oh, well . . . thank you, I suppose." Percy frowned. "Why are you telling me all these things anyways? Not that I don't appreciate not being treated like some wild animal. I just . . ." He trailed off then shrugged.

"Honestly?" Edric looked away, avoiding eye contact. "Lady Suncrest asked someone to look after you, to keep you company. I volunteered."

Percy felt his heart fall. Of course, why had he expected any different? What did he think, that Edric *fancied* him? That simply didn't happen to Percival Drake. And he was fine with that, happy even. Romance just got in the way. It only led to pain. Like he didn't have enough of that already.

Edric was just doing a favor for Lady Suncrest, watching over their poor little prisoner. If he hadn't already cried enough tears to last a lifetime, they might come now. But none reared their ugly heads, and he remained composed and stoic. Percy downed his drink in one long gulp and stood up, wiping his mouth with the back of his palm.

"Right, well, this has been lovely, Commander Royce. But it's almost my curfew, so I must take my leave." It wasn't entirely a lie. He did have a curfew. It just wasn't for a few hours.

Edric frowned and opened his mouth as if to say something, but Percy was out the door before he even got the chance.

Percy stared at himself in the mirror. It was old and cloudy, but he could still make out his reflection. Why had Edric's rejection stung so badly? Why did it make him want to tear his skin from his bones? It wasn't the first time he'd been rejected or even the first time he'd been rejected by a man. So why did it feel so raw this time?

He examined his face, scrutinizing every possible flaw or insecurity. His grey eyes were lifeless and sat too close together. His face was too angular and bird-like, and his flat ashy hair was thin and dull and hung too low past his ears. A hundred things ran through his mind—everything wrong with him, everything unlovable. His own family couldn't even love him. Why would a practical stranger? He cursed himself for his naivety, for thinking that just this once the Wayfinder was throwing him a bone. But no, the Wayfinder expected him to starve, cracking open bone after bone only to find them all empty of marrow.

Percy considered running away. The guards had grown laxer as of late, and he could likely slip out without notice. It wasn't like he had anything keeping him in Sanctuary. Then again, he didn't have anyone to turn to outside either. He was entirely alone, and *Gods*, was that terrifying! He didn't notice he was shaking until his hand slipped and he knocked a glass vase off the desk in front of the mirror. He cursed under his breath, then leaned down to pick up the pieces, but he stood up too fast and smacked his head against the underside of the table.

"Fuck!"

He dropped the shards again but didn't bother to pick them up this time. He just sat down on the floor, holding his legs to his chest. Gods, he was pathetic. He hated feeling like this, hated feeling *anything*. His hands were shaking. He needed to hit something. He needed to get out of there. He couldn't *breathe*. He huffed and focused on his breath—in, out, in, out. When he felt solid enough to stand on his own two feet, he wiped his eyes, though no tears had come.

He stood to his feet, swaying slightly, and grabbed his fur-lined cloak from its hook by the door. It was one of his few personal belongings that had survived the explosion and one of the fewer that had been returned to him. That hadn't even given him his mother's quills, claiming he could use them to stab someone. Percy hadn't considered that option until it was suggested. Now he would very much like to stab someone.

The things that filled his tiny room were just that—*things*. There were a few cloaks and waistcoats he hadn't planned to wear in the first place, a horsehair brush too coarse for his thin hair, a bottle of Valmeran perfume that smelled like his grandmother. He took the perfume, stuffing it into a satchel along with a few slacks and shirts the legion had deigned to give him. It wouldn't be enough to keep him warm for long, so he had to pray he'd find warmer lands soon. He grabbed a tinderbox, a waterskin, and a few strips of fabric from his torn-up blanket.

Fuck.

He was actually doing this! The more he packed, the more his confidence grew, and the higher the moon rose over the horizon. The only thing he was missing was a weapon. He'd at least need some sort of bow to hunt, but a blade would be nice too. He didn't like the idea of having to fight bandits or, the Gods forbid, Nightmares, but such things were often impossible to avoid. And he had no idea how to use a bow in a combat situation.

Percy swung his knapsack over his shoulder and peeked out the window. It was dark, judging by the position of the moon around one in the morning.

Perfect.

It would be the changing of the guards, which would leave Sanctuary largely empty for the next fifteen minutes or so. The next thing that caught Percy's eye was the stand of the merchant Bardin. It was empty, obviously, and he'd just left all his wares on display for anyone to just walk past and grab. Bardin was well known for overcharging and underdelivering, especially for the villagers of Sanctuary just barely scraping by after the attack at the Temple. Bardin stole from the village, so Percy didn't feel sorry at the idea of stealing from him. The amount he was ripping everyone else off for would certainly make up for it. His hand pressed against the door, and it swung open noiselessly.

One of the Gods' little blessings, he thought.

He stepped out the door, careful to not leave tracks in the already-melting snow. With any luck, any tracks he did leave would be gone by morning, but Percy rarely had such luck. He reached Bardin's stand easily enough and noticed a wide selection of weapons. He quickly grabbed a simple scout's bow and a quiver of thirty arrows. They looked solid enough to spear a rabbit, and that was all he really needed from them. That was when he noticed an ornate onyx longsword locked in a glass case behind the rest of Bardin's wares. He took a step toward it and ran his hand along the glass.

"How did that little weasel get ahold of something like *you*?" he purred at it, gazing at the blade with reverence.

Percy glanced around, looking for any guards or sleepless villagers. He was alone, so he crouched down and began fiddling with the lock. Once again, the Gods smiled upon him, as Bardin had elected to store his lock-picking wares just next to the glass case. The lock opened with a *click*, and Percy rose to his feet. Now that the scuffed and stained glass had been removed, he could get a proper look at the blade. It was carved with runic lettering he didn't understand and had a jagged, serrated edge. The most striking aspect of it, however, was the faint red mist that drifted off it and the red gems inlaid into the hilt that seemed to pulse with a slight glow.

"Gods . . ." he murmured quietly.

It reminded him of the pictures in the books he'd read as a child, the books his parents tried to hide from him, the ones Janus would bring him after the servants had gone to bed, the ones about the Dragonguard and, more relevant, the Draugar. The Draugar were a race of undead monsters that rose from the earth once every five hundred years in an event called a Cataclysm, where they would wreak havoc upon Nymor. The longsword was the blade of one of these undead, and it was in Bardin's shitty shop!

His mouth watered slightly. The blade was beautiful, and it should've been a *crime* for someone like that merchant to have it. He didn't hesitate a moment longer and wrapped his fist around the hilt. He didn't know what he was expecting, but it wasn't nothing. Yet that was exactly what happened—nothing. He didn't burst into flames. His hand didn't rot and fall from his arm. Just nothing. He couldn't tell if he was relieved or disappointed.

Percy lifted the sword out of the display case and marveled at how well it was balanced, how snuggly it fit in his hand. It almost felt like it was *made* for him. He twirled it in front of him, the blade whistling slightly as it sliced smoothly through the crisp evening air. He grinned to himself and strapped the blade to his belt, leaving the bow and arrows on his back.

He could hear people beginning to stir, so he quickly made his way to the front gate, slipping out without notice. There were a few guards outside, but all of them either didn't notice or didn't care about him leaving. He looked around, quickly deciding his best bet would be the gate just to his right. The closer he got, the better he felt about his odds. He'd be a fugitive of both the Legion of the Gods and every country who'd lost someone in the explosion, but and the dark irony did not escape him. They all had much bigger things to worry about than one escaped prisoner with a couple of stolen weapons.

Finally, he reached the massive wooden door, smiling to himself. He was finally going to escape the fucking monotony that had been his existence for the last eternity. Even before he was a prisoner of the legion, he was a prisoner of the crown's expectations of him as the heir, a prisoner of his father's expectations of him as a man, a prisoner of that damned manor in the center of Edelheim's acropolis, his gilded cage.

He placed his hand flat on the wood and prepared to push. But his luck had finally run dry.

He was interrupted by the sound of clattering armor.

"Stop right there!" It was a man's voice.

Fuck.

Percy raised his arms and turned slowly to face the man. His fingers itched for his blade, itched to make this man *bleed*. He was a young man, too young, barely more than a boy. He reminded Percy of Andrea, and he almost faltered.

"Just let me be on my way. I don't want any trouble," he said carefully.

The boy snarled, "You're that prisoner, the one they found in the Temple of Last Rest!" Then he said accusingly, "You killed the High Cleric! You probably tried to kill Lady Suncrest too!"

Shit, he's getting loud.

Someone would be drawn to the commotion soon. He needed to shut him up. Percy began lowering his arms slowly, and the soldier drew his sword. His hand was shaking.

"D-don't move!" he stammered, his voice shrill as he shrugged to keep it level. Gods, that boy was scared.

Percy continued lowering his arms. "Please, just let me go," he pleaded.

The boy stood up straighter, and his hand stopped shaking. "Surrender now, or else I'll—"

The blade flashed across the boy's throat, and he gasped, clutching his neck as he crumpled lifelessly to the ground. Percy's face was splattered with his blood, the hot spray coating his eyes and mouth. He wiped his hand across his face, smearing the boy's blood over his eyes. He let out a shaky breath and brushed his fingers through his hair, leaving streaks of red in his sandy-blond hair. His throat bobbed, and he turned back to the door, ignoring the heat that now pulsed from the tenebrous blade on his hip.

~~~

Tessia's return to Sanctuary after gaining the assistance of the Sisters of Threnody was not the victorious homecoming she, and most others, had hoped it would be. She returned to find Sanctuary in utter chaos. A prisoner had gone missing, an artifact from the First Cataclysm had been stolen, and a soldier had been murdered. All fingers pointed to the escaped prisoner, the former Fjellian prince.
~~~

Tessia had hardly known the man, but he seemed nice enough, if a bit troubled. But this was . . . this was *brutal*. The victim's throat had been slit. Then all the blood had been drained from his body. According to the scout who found him the following morning, he hadn't even had a chance to draw his blade. The commander seemed especially troubled by the events. It made sense, of course. The boy was one of his recruits.

Tessia asked Isadora about it, but she just told her to talk to Edric. So she did. She found him in the tavern, staring at his untouched glass of ale.

"Commander Royce?" She approached him, and he looked up at her with a faraway look in his eye. "Edric?" she called out again.

"Hmm? Oh, hello, my lady. Something I can help you with? I'm off duty, actually." He gestured vaguely to the tavern.

"Oh, no, it's not work-related." She shook her head, scolding herself for avoiding the actual reason she was there. "I just wanted to talk to you about the boy that was murdered."

"Jaime," he said simply. "What?"

"That was his name—Jaime Bakker. He was from Darkwater in the Free Isles. He joined up shortly after I did." Edric shook his head. "He was barely twenty."

She sat down next to him and placed her hand on his arm comfortingly. She opened her mouth to speak, but he interrupted before she could.

"I just . . . I just don't know how I didn't see it!" He threw his hands up, causing Tessia to flinch slightly.

"Edric, what're you—"

"Drake! I don't understand how I didn't see this coming. I should've kept a closer eye on him. I should've . . . I should've had Isadora keeping tabs on him or . . ." He threw his hands up, a growl of frustration bubbling up from the back of his throat.

"He had us all fooled. Even I—" She stopped herself. "It doesn't matter now. What matters is what we're going to *do* about it."

Edric looked at her, and he looked dreadful. There were heavy bags under his eyes, his hair was mussed and tangled, and his cheeks were gaunt. The stress was clearly getting to him, and she worried he would burn himself out if he kept pushing himself as he was. The guilt was killing him. She just hoped it'd take its sweet time.

"So, Commander?" She looked him in the eye. "What's the plan?"

Chapter Four

Aethel was cold. By Astraea and Tyr, it was cold. The Isles could get cold, of course, but *fuck*, Aethel was *cold*. Percy made a mental note to move somewhere up north, maybe Orcanum. It was supposed to be warm there, wasn't it? He hugged himself tightly, teeth chattering violently. He needed to find shelter, and soon. He shot a look up at the sky, white with the swirling snow around him.

"Fuck, Goddess! If you're still in the rescuing mood, I could really use an assist."

He wasn't answered by anything except the whistling of the wind. He didn't expect to be answered, of course, but he bitterly wondered what Tessia had done to deserve Tyr's mercy, probably not killing a young man, probably not that. Percy felt his stomach churn when he thought of the boy, his blood sullied on his clothes, his gaunt face skeletal.

Wait. When did he look like that?

As Percy's blade pulsed warmly, his head throbbed. He thought about something else.

A couple of hours passed, but they felt like days in the freezing mountain. Percy was starting to think he'd escaped the legion only to die in the cold when he caught sight of something through the snow. It was a light, a gently flickering flame. As he drew closer, he was able to make out a shape, something brown and large. A house? Gods! Maybe Astraea really had heard his prayers. He felt his stomach fill with butterflies. *Hope*—he hadn't felt that in a long while. But wait. Ah, yes, he was still covered in blood. That could be problematic.

Percy dropped his knapsack into the snow and grabbed a shirt. His pants and cloak were dark enough that the blood couldn't be seen, but his white shirt was far from it. He briskly unclasped his cloak and laid it gently in the snow. He then pulled the clean shirt over the soiled one, then donned his cloak once more. His face was likely still covered in blood, but he didn't want to risk trying to clean himself off with the snow.

Letting out a shaky breath, he approached the house, walked to the door, and knocked. "Hello? Is there anyone there? I've . . . I've been out in the cold. If I could just have a few minutes next to your fire, I could—"

The door swung open, and he was met with a middle-aged woman. She was short and lithe and had pale pink eyes and hair the color of flour. By the look of her ears and the intricate tattoos on her face, she was a fair-folk elf.

She cursed in elvish, shaking her head. "Spirits, you're a mess! Come in, come in. Hearthmother knows I won't leave someone out in the cold."

Hearthmother was the elven spirit of fire and warmth, if Percy remembered correctly. She was one of the elven spirits that was a manifestation of Astraea, according to the Covenant of Light.

Percy nodded in relief and entered the small home. It was quaint and filled with herbs and animal hides. There were also multiple different bows displayed on the wall. The elf must've been a hunter. The home had a comforting feeling to it, like the house itself was inviting him to kick off his boots and rest awhile.

"Well? Have a seat. Take off those dirty boots of yours." The elf put her hands on her hips and gestured to a chair next to the fire.

Percy nodded gratefully and obeyed the strange woman's command. He removed his cloak and hung it over the back of the chair before sitting down. He stretched his toes and rubbed his hands together over the fire. He let out a pleased sigh and leaned back.

"Thank you, Miss . . . ?"

She shook her head and chuckled. "It's just Karya if you please. No 'Miss' necessary."

"Nice to meet you, I'm—" He stopped. He couldn't use his real name. There would be people looking for Percival Alarch Drake. He couldn't be Percy anymore either. He needed something different. He needed a fresh start.

"What's wrong, dear? Wildcat got your tongue?"

He shook his head. "No, sorry, it's . . ." He blanked out for a moment, then said the first word that came to his mind, "Raven." He thought back to the birds that used to gather on the trees outside his window back in Edelheim, how he envied their ability to fly away whenever they wished.

"Raven?" Karya's brow cocked skeptically. "Strange name for a human." Then she shrugged. "But considering my own parents wanted to call me Nethanyal, who am I to judge?" She laughed jovially. "What brings you out here? We're quite far from any civilization, and if you don't mind me saying, you looked rather . . . ragged."

He chuckled and nodded. "I was part of a merchant caravan heading to Sanctuary. We were attacked by wolves, and I got separated from the rest of my group." He didn't like how easily the lie came to him.

"Oh, you poor dear. Well, take as long as you like here. Spirits know I've supplies to share."

It felt strange having this woman treating him so . . . normally. At Sanctuary, they treated him like an animal, a murderer (which he supposed he now was). Before that, he was treated like something fragile, a porcelain doll too delicate to be taken out of its glass case. It felt nice not to be Percival Alarch Drake, heir to Edelheim, or Percival the murderer and just be treated as Percy—or Raven now, he supposed.

A small part of him wanted to stay here forever, to live with Karya and help her however he was able, but a louder part knew he had to keep moving. He wasn't far enough away from Sanctuary yet, and though his tracks had been covered by the blizzard, any sufficiently skilled hound could track his scent out here. He might be able to stay a few hours, though, at least until the blizzard died down.

"Thank you, Karya. I don't know how I can repay your kindness."

She waved her hand dismissively. "No payment necessary. It's just nice to have a conversation with someone aside from that old wolfhound for once."

Percival—no, *Raven* (he'd have to get used to using that name in his head if he wanted to use it convincingly with other people) hadn't seen a dog in the small house or anything resembling a dog for that matter. He was about to ask about it, but Karya changed the subject.

"Would you like some tea? I just put the kettle on."

The kettle whistled, and Raven nodded.

Raven's entire body felt like it was wrapped in a warm blanket, floating in a bed of downy feathers. He sighed and cuddled closer to the warmth, not wanting to open his eyes for fear of breaking the drowsy spell that had been placed upon him. Eventually, though, the warmth faded slightly, and he opened his eyes.

It was dark, far darker than he thought it should've been. He frowned and pushed the blanket off. It was his cloak, and it was slightly moist. It took his eyes a moment to adjust, but once they did, his confusion only increased. The house was empty, completely empty. The fire was dead. It didn't even look like there had been a fire in the first place. The only furniture he could see was the chair he was seated on.

How long had he been asleep? He stood up, stumbling slightly as he did so. He sniffed and frowned. Something smelled like meat—rotting meat. It was wet and sweet and rancid. He was shaking. Why was he shaking? Why couldn't he remember falling asleep?

"Karya?" he called out weakly.

No answer came, just silence and the wind whistling through the draughty roof. He swallowed and took a step forward. There was a kitchen farther into the house. He considered if maybe Karya would be there. Instinctively, he grabbed his blade, the warmth of the hilt filling him with enough self-assurance to continue.

"Hello?"

He peeked into the kitchen, but just like the rest of the house, it was devoid of life. But it wasn't empty. In the corner of the room, its head cracked open, sat the long-dead body of a woman. She was far too decayed for anyone to make out any distinguishing features, except for the point of her one remaining ear.

The corpse's finger twitched, and Raven acted instinctually, severing the thing's head with a clean slice. It didn't move again. Raven let out a shaky breath. And then the house seemed to flicker. One moment it was the dark shack; the next, it was the warm cottage he remembered. And then it was back to the shack.

He looked down at his shirt. He was covered in blood again. He spun around, frantically looking for the source, but when he turned back, he was standing over Karya's bed, holding her decapitated head in his hand. He screamed and dropped it. It landed with a wet *crack* on the floor, and Raven stumbled back. His knuckles were white as he clutched his blade, and it pulsed dully, seeming to hum slightly, a tune he couldn't quite pinpoint.

It soothed him slightly, reminding him of a lullaby his mother had sung to him. It felt familiar somewhat. Had he heard it before? He almost forgot the carnage before him as he hummed along but was quickly brought back to reality by the sound of the door being slammed open by the force of the wind.

Raven jumped and then glanced back at Karya.

He felt sick but, paradoxically, hungry as well. A low grumble in his stomach communicated that he hadn't had a proper meal in days, maybe weeks. Raven sheathed his blade and walked out of the room and back to the kitchen. He moved through the house like a ghost, blood-covered fingers gently glancing across Karya's pristine counters.

He wondered what whoever found the place would think of the scene. He almost laughed imagining their confusion. The elf didn't have much food that would last a trip, but the flatbread and dried venison would have to be enough. He stuffed his bag with all he could carry. Then he caught sight of a small bag of coins. He knew he *should* feel bad, evil even, but every time his mind turned too far, his sword sang to him and soothed him.

It wasn't right. He *knew* it wasn't right. But he *felt* . . . nothing. Not anything, really. Karya wouldn't have any use for the gold. He needed it more than a dead woman. He pushed away his apprehension and grabbed it. Despite the weather, when Raven stepped outside, he felt warm and renewed. He felt strong. He didn't question it; he didn't want to. He was fine with believing it was another of Astraea's blessings. He knew he didn't deserve it.

CHAPTER FIVE

It took him a little over a week to reach Oisin's Watch, a large settlement on the edge of the Sea of Shadows in northwestern Aethel. By that point, he was hungry, thirsty, and filthy. Raven hadn't been able to take a proper bath in all that time, and he hadn't trusted himself to stay anywhere long enough to get a proper meal. He'd stretched Karya's rations as far as he could, and now he was penniless.

When he saw the buildings from afar, he didn't even care if the legion had plastered wanted posters bearing his likeness all across the town; he just needed a hot meal. He certainly got a few strange looks as he made his way through the town but nothing that would lead him to believe they saw him as a criminal. If anything, most of them looked vaguely put off, scrunching up their noses when he walked past. Raven was aware he probably smelled foul, but he'd worry about that after he'd had something to eat.

The settlement's inn was at the top of a small hill just in front of the temple. He'd have to make a stop there too. Gods know he had much to atone for. The interior of the inn was warm and homey, but Raven couldn't help feeling on edge when he walked in. His hand rested firmly on his blade. He did not have the intention to use it, but the leather of the hilt felt comforting in the overwhelming environment. He made his way to the front, finding a stout man wiping down the counter.

"Hello?"

The man looked up at Raven, his expression shifting quickly from annoyed disinterest to blatant disgust. "Gods, you smell like shit!" he spat at Raven.

Raven felt the place just behind his ears growing warm. The sword on his hip hummed slightly louder, but he ignored it. "I just need something to eat and a room. I'll have a bath after I've eaten." He gritted his teeth.

The man scoffed, "I don't do charity here. If you want a free meal, you can try the temple."

Karya's bag of coins clattered loudly as Raven dropped them onto the counter. He glared icily at the man, who at this point was staring wide-eyed at the one or two gold coins that had spilled out of the pouch.

"I can pay."

Raven's room was small, and there was barely enough room for the small rigid bed and wash basin. Despite that, it was almost as soon as he entered that he felt a great deal of the tension leave his body. He splashed a bit of water on his face, doing his best to wash the dirt and dried blood out of his hair. There was a small mirror on the wall, and when he looked into it, he didn't recognize himself.

He thought back to the portraits his parents had commissioned of him. He was always donned in too-tight waistcoats that made his arms and chest look bigger than they were and heavy decorative medals commemorating fictional achievements that pierced the fabric and riddled his skin with tiny pinpricks. But *Gods*, could those artists make him look regal, like a man who actually *deserved* his station? They always added a bit more blush to his cheeks, making him look livelier. They added a curl to his flat, straight hair that he could never achieve himself and made the color a warmer blond, almost gold. They added an intensity to his eyes that reminded him of his father. It never looked quite right, but it made his mother happy.

He always looked more confident in those portraits than he felt. Now, though, he looked *exactly* how he felt. His eyes were dry and bloodshot, and his hair had grown longer so that it now hung almost to his shoulders. Despite his best efforts, it was tangled and matted, clinging to his scalp like fleas on a dog. He splashed more water on his face, but while he was able to wipe the dirt away with his hand, the tiny specks of blood scattered across his face like freckles were far more stubborn. He scrubbed his face until it was raw, then scrubbed some more. But the small red dots near his eyes refused to fade.

Raven growled irritably and tossed the wash rag to the ground. It landed with a wet *splat*, and he couldn't stop the image of Karya's decapitated head from entering his mind. He punched the mirror, and it splintered, tiny shards digging into his fist. He cursed and stepped back, staring down at his bloodied fist disdainfully. He looked at his knapsack on the floor. Some of his clothes were spilling out, and most noticeably, his grandmother's perfume was lying on the ground on its side. His face softened, and he bent over and picked it up. It smelled floral and earthy, just like he remembered.

Raven shook his head and set the bottle down carefully on the table. He needed to speak to someone before this feeling consumed him.

The wooden box was small and cramped, and the air felt heavy in his lungs. Maybe that was intentional. Were people more likely to confess their sins in claustrophobic situations? Or was this box meant to simulate dying?

Or maybe I'm overthinking it, and it's just an uncomfortable box because the temple can't afford anything better, Raven thought.

"Be not afraid, my son. What is said here stays between you, me, Father Tyr, and Mother Astraea." The mother's voice was soft and comforting, her strange accent giving it an almost sing-song quality. Was it Dejari? It might be.

"Thank you, Mother. I just feel so . . . *angry* so often. I don't understand where this comes from."

The mother hummed. "Anger is a curse many of us struggle with. What has this anger wrought, my child?"

Raven bit his lip. "I hurt people. I . . . I didn't want to at the time. I was scared, and they . . ." He trailed off. "And I hurt them."

She was quiet for a moment. "Did you enjoy hurting them?"

Raven didn't know how to answer that. At the time? *Yes*, Gods, it had felt good. But after? It was harder to say. It made him feel good to kill that soldier. It made him feel good to kill Karya. But did he enjoy it?

"I don't know, Mother."

"Are you worried you'll hurt people again?"

"Yes," he responded quickly, maybe too quickly. But it was true. He was worried he'd hurt people again. He was worried he'd kill again.

"Might I make a suggestion?"

Raven nodded, hoping the small *hmm* would articulate his agreement.

"I suggest you take some time to be away from those you could hurt. Live in solitude until you understand your anger and how to control it."

"Thank you, Mother. You've given me . . . much to consider."

The mother hummed appreciatively, and Raven stood up from the uncomfortable wooden chair. He pushed open the door of the booth to the rest of the temple and let out a sigh. Now he had a purpose of some kind, a direction. He wasn't sure where he'd find the solitude the mother spoke, but he knew it wasn't in Oisin's Watch. He'd have to leave, and by the sounds of whispers of Lady Suncrest coming to meet with some of the remaining Covenant officials who'd congregated in Oisin's Watch, it would have to be soon.

Raven walked up to the small shelf holding candles for the fallen. He lit four—one for Karya, one for the soldier, one for Andrea, and a final one for Janus. His memories of that night were still fuzzy, but the look of Janus's blank face hadn't left him. He wasn't dead—at least not the last Raven saw him—but he wasn't himself either. Something had happened to Janus, twisted him into a mindless husk following the whims of whoever had orchestrated the attack on the Temple. Raven didn't know what had happened to Janus, but part of him knew that if they met again, he'd have to kill him. The candle he was lighting for Janus was preemptive, but he was certain it would be necessary.

The last of Raven's coin was spent on acquiring proper clothes and rations—a leather tunic with a proper strap for his bow, a sturdy belt with a sheath for his blade, a few pouches for healing elixirs should he come across any on his journey, and a sturdier knapsack than his linen one, which was already starting to tear at the seams. He hoped the rations would last him until he reached wherever he was going. But he wasn't counting on it, so he made sure to practice with his bow before he left. When he did leave, it was just in the nick of time.

He was making his way down the road from Oisin's Watch when suddenly there was a loud *crack*. He spun around and saw an iridescent portal hanging in the air. His eyes widened, and Nightmares started pouring from the portal.

Shit! he thought.

"Shit!" he cursed aloud.

Just then, he heard footsteps approaching from behind, and he quickly dashed off the road to hide from whoever it was. Of course, since the Gods seemed to have a sense of humor, it was Tessia, along with some people he didn't recognize—a blonde elf with a bow, the orcish paladin from Sanctuary, and the elf from the Temple. Tessia herself looked good, as much as Raven didn't want to admit it. Her dark hair was pulled into a tight ponytail behind her head, and her face was painted with a determination he didn't often see on one so elegantly composed. There was also mud on her face, but somehow, she made it work.

"Shit, T!" the elf said. She had a rough accent and skidded to a stop as she stared at the portal.

Once again, Raven felt that familiar itch—the itch for battle, the itch for bloodshed. His vision seemed to close in on the Nightmare closest to him, a weaker one if he remembered correctly from fighting in the valley with . . .

He stopped that train of thought before it got too far, before he did something reckless. The elven sorcerer waved his staff in the air and shattered the shade. Clearly, Tessia's team had it covered. He took his hand off his blade. When had he grabbed it? He couldn't remember. Raven stepped away, praying to the Gods and all of Karya's spirits that Tessia was too distracted with the Nightmares to notice him sneaking away.

Once more, the dice rolled in his favor, and he disappeared into the Greenwood.

CHAPTER SIX

No one had heard anything of Percival since the murder in the woods. A fair-folk woman, a hunter it looked like, was killed in her bed, and then Percival had robbed her. Tessia wouldn't have believed it if the hounds hadn't tracked him there by his scent. The scene was much more brutal than Jaime's murder. The elf had been *decapitated* and then once again drained of her blood. Tessia felt sick just looking at it.

"By the Gods." Edric surveyed the scene, his eyes the size of dinner plates. "How? *Why?*

Why didn't Percival just rob her? Why would he do . . . *this*?"

"He can't be well." Tessia shook her head. "No sane person would do something like this. He must be mad or possessed."

The commander gritted his teeth. "Or maybe he's just evil." "No such thing," she responded quickly.

But looking down at the elf's gaunt face, she wasn't sure if she believed that anymore. She always held that people were neither good nor evil, that they were just people who were capable of good or evil things. She'd seen paladins take pleasure in the needless torment of the sorcerers, but they weren't evil. Saying they were simply *evil* would absolve them of their crimes. They were just as capable of kindness as they were of cruelty, and they *chose* cruelty.

Edric rested his hand on the blade. "Mad or no, he must be brought to justice. And this . . . If he were a sorcerer, I'd suggest he be sundered from his magic, but I can't see any justice for this aside from death."

Her nose curled in disgust. "Do not speak to me of Sundering, *Commander*," she spat venomously. "I have lost many friends to that, nor do I think death is the only option. Do not pretend you are innocent. Lord Chaplain Helaena's abuses were an open secret among the Arcane Colleges."

His lips were sealed, and Tessia turned away, storming off. The way he could be so callous sometimes infuriated her. It was as if he was a hapless associate of Lord Chaplain Helaena and not her *right-hand man*. The Rite of Sundering was a cruel practice where a sorcerer's connection with magic was shattered entirely, leaving them a mindless husk unable to cast spells or do anything aside from following simple instructions and performing manual labor. The Covenant called it a necessary evil. Tessia called it slavery.

Edric had done cruel things—Tessia had heard of them from sorcerers who'd had firsthand experience—and he seemed to think simply serving the Legion of the Gods was enough to atone for that. It was like it didn't matter whom he had hurt as long as he was doing something now. Then he had the audacity to suggest execution. She couldn't deny that it was an option, especially if, when she was caught Percival, he showed no remorse for his actions. But the *only* option? If Percival wasn't worthy of redemption, how could she be?

~~~

It was the night before her Awakening, the ceremony where a sorcerer discovered their magical aptitude, and the entirety of the Eastwell Arcane College was abuzz with excitement. Tessia had made many friends in her time at the College, although many were only interested in the influence her family held in Fjellian politics. She didn't mind, of course. She was used to having people who wanted to get close to her to get close to her family ever since she was a child, before her magic manifested.

She was wringing her hands and pacing her room, which she shared with the one woman she considered a true friend—Liara. She was an orphan from Windhollow who had been left to die on the streets until she was found by a group of paladins. Unlike most sorcerers, she viewed the College as her salvation from the streets and was grateful for the security it gave her. Tessia didn't always understand her, but she was glad to have a friend that didn't care about her noble birth.
~~~

"Stop pacing, Tessia. You're going to give me a headache!" Liara moaned, clutching her forehead dramatically.

"Easy for *you* to say. You've already had your Awakening! And you won't even tell me what it entails!" Tessia glared at her friend.

Liara shrugged. "Sorry. Rules are rules."

Tessia groaned. "You're awful."

"You love me." Liara laughed.

Just before sunset, Tessia was approached by the Administrator, who was flanked by two armored paladins. Usually, while within the walls of the College, the paladins wore simple leather fatigues, but now they wore heavy enchanted plate mail and full-faced helmets, concealing their identities. It was what they wore when a mage was sundered, so if they lashed out with their magic, they'd have no one to direct their anger at. But Tessia wasn't scared. She knew how much coin her family had put into Eastwell College, and she knew they couldn't afford to lose that support. She wasn't particularly powerful, and she'd never been any more rebellious than any of the other apprentices.

So when they led her up the stairs into the Administrator's office, then through a small hidden door behind a bookshelf, she wasn't afraid. Even as they continued to move up the tower, up and up, farther than the outside geometry of the tower should've allowed, her footfalls did not falter.

She had been preparing for this test her entire life, ever since she'd set her governess's hair alight at the dinner table as a child and the paladins had stood outside the manor door, framed by the storm and lightning that characterized the climate of Eastwell, come to take her to the College and away from everything she'd ever known. This was the fate of all sorcerers if they did not wish to become apostates of the Covenant. The Awakening was her final test, and she would not fail.

Eventually, they reached a large wooden door. It was carved with intricate runes, some of which she understood, most of which she didn't. There were runes of the ancient Aethic mountain tribes. Some were from the long-dead dragon-worshiping Empire of Wyveria, and some of them, though she didn't recognize them at the time, were in the language of the Draugar.

The Administrator stepped ahead of the group and placed his hands on the door. His hands began to glow with iridescent energy, a magic Tessia had never seen until that point, the magic of Phantasma. He began chanting in a language she couldn't understand, and then the door shattered. Tessia had seen magical doors open before—all of the College's professors and officials' offices had them—but she had never seen anything like this. The very space around the door seemed to fold into itself, break into fractal shapes, and then warp away in a brilliant flash of rainbow-colored light. And then they were standing in front of a dark entryway devoid of light and sound and feeling.

Tessia felt her hands begin to crackle with elemental energy, and she stepped forward.

Her sleep that night was restless, wrought with night terrors and visions of horrible things. They were things she begged not to see but was shown nonetheless—Liara's dead body staring up at her with a look of utter betrayal, the entire Arcane College burned to the ground, the deep and rough chuckle of a Nightmare . . . She whirled around, desperately trying to locate the source.

"Show yourself!" she cried, hoping she didn't sound as small as she felt.

The chuckling grew louder, and she felt a form manifest behind her. She squeaked and whirled around, coming face to face with a massive Nightmare. It was at least twice her height, and its mouth curled into a cruel grin.

"Hello, little mouse," it growled.

She swallowed. Her throat felt very dry. "L-leave me alone, creature!" Her voice was meek and not nearly as authoritative as she'd hoped.

It let out a roaring laugh. "You truly are pathetic, aren't you?" It looked down at her and narrowed its six eyes. "But you don't have to be, little mouse. I can make you strong!"

She shook her head vigorously, like a small child trying to banish a night terror by pretending it didn't exist.

"No, please," she whimpered.

It laughed again, a booming noise that made her ears ring and bleed.

"No, no, no, no," she begged, continuing to shake her head.

The laughter only grew until it reached a crescendo.

"I said *no!*" she roared this time, her voice echoing with something else, something farther away and closer all at once.

In a flash of light, the Nightmare vanished, and Tessia shot awake, coated in sweat with her hand wrapped around Liara's throat. She gasped and released her vice grip, but Liara didn't stir. Her face was purple, and her eyes were wide open.

"Liara? Oh no, oh no! Liara, *no!*" Tessia sobbed, backing away slowly.

She was shaking her head, not wanting to believe the sight in front of her, so she didn't notice when she backed into her bed. She tumbled over it and landed on the stone floor with a *crack*. And everything went dark.

Tessia wasn't suspected of Liara's murder. For one, Tessia's injury implied that she had been attacked as well, and for another, her family's influence made sure to steer the investigation away from her as much as possible. She never spoke of the "attack" to anyone, and most assumed she or Liara had been raped. She couldn't admit to being a murderer, let alone one influenced by a Nightmare. It wouldn't matter how much her family had contributed to the College; she'd be killed or, worse, sundered. And she would deserve it. So she sat with her guilt, lived with it, and tried to become a woman worthy of forgiveness in the eyes of the Gods.

~~~

Lady Suncrest was drinking. She hated the taste of alcohol, but she needed to medicate. It was late, and the tavern was empty of most of its rowdier patrons. It was just her, the barmaid Laila, and an elven girl called Minthe. Minthe was a strange girl. Born in Stronghold, she'd lost her mother when the Draugar breached the gates during the last Cataclysm. Despite that, her golden-amber eyes never seemed to lose their luster or their sense of mischief. Tessia swirled the copper-colored liquid in her glass, staring at the way the ice clinked against the walls of the cup. Gods, was she always this easily entertained?

"You look terrible." Minthe slid into the seat across from her, cocking an eyebrow and crossing her arms.

Tessia shrugged. "I *feel* terrible."
~~~

Minthe nodded. "Oh, yeah. I heard about the lady in the woods—messy business."

Tessia shook her head. "No, it's not that. Well, it is a bit. I'm just . . ." She groaned. "Everyone expects me to know what to do! They expect me to know how to be a messiah, how to live by the prophet's example, but I . . ." She buried her face in her hands. "I have *no idea* what I'm doing, Minthe. I have no idea how to lead or how to protect people. I know Tyr saved me from the explosion at the Temple, but I'm worried he made the wrong choice."

Minthe frowned. "You sound tired, Tess."

Tessia laughed. "I am. I am very tired, Minthe. I need a break."

The elf bit her lip, a look of mischief creeping across her face that said, "I have an idea." Then Minthe took her by the hand and gave it a little squeeze. "C'mon, I want to show you something."

Tessia felt a lightness in her stomach, something she hadn't felt since before her Awakening, and she nodded in hesitant acceptance.

By the time they had finished, Isadora's maps had been hidden around Sanctuary, Lucrezia's books had been reorganized by color, and Edric's shield had been painted bright red with a picture of Minthe shooting arrows into paladins' faces.

It was a much-needed reprieve from leading the legion. It felt nice to just spend time with Minthe and do stupid bullshit. It gave her a new appreciation for her often-blasé attitude. Sometimes raging against the dying of the light was sticking your tongue out at it and blowing raspberry.

"Thanks, Minthe. That was . . . That was good. Thank you." Tessia laughed, slightly out of breath from running from Edric after he'd discovered their masterpiece.

"I'm surprised you had fun, Tess. I thought you'd be some stuffy stuck-up pompy. You really are just a girl when it comes down to it, aren't you?" Minthe laughed, kicking her legs off the side of the roof of the temple.

"That's what I've been trying to tell everyone." Tessia shrugged.

Minthe smiled. Gods, she had a nice smile—and nice eyes.

Wait, what?

Tessia looked away, blushing. She wasn't supposed to feel this way about another woman, was she? She'd never heard it explicitly condemned, but all the stories she'd read were about men and women. Wasn't that normal?

"You all right?"

Tessia bit her lip and looked back at Minthe. "I don't know."

"Is there something I can do?"

Tessia thought for a moment, then nodded. "Can I kiss you?"

Minthe looked taken aback, and Tessia was almost worried she'd overstepped, that there really *was* something wrong with her, until Minthe leaned over and put her arm around her neck. Tessia let out a small gasp and then melted into the kiss. Her lips were chapped and rough, but they tasted like honey. Minthe's fingers on her neck tickled, and she would've laughed if not for fear that breaking the kiss would bring her back to reality, to a world where something that felt so right could possibly be wrong. Minthe broke the kiss first, and Tessia couldn't help the small whine that escaped her lips.

"Spirits, have you even kissed *anyone* before?"

Tessia's face turned tomato red, and she shook her head bashfully.

Minthe laughed. Every time she laughed, Tessia liked it more. "Well, let's catch up on lost time." She pounced, and Tessia squeaked, almost rolling off the roof.

"Let's get off the roof first?" Tessia stared at the ground worriedly.

Minthe sighed. "Yeah, you're probably right." She pressed a quick kiss to Tessia's lips. "Race you to the bottom!"

She nimbly leapt from the roof, and Tessia groaned and followed after. Once she reached the bottom, however, she was stopped by a breathless young man, one of Isadora's runners by the closed-eye symbol on his cuirass.

"What is it, agent?" She crossed her arms, glowering despite herself.

"Sorry to interrupt, Your Eminence, but it's urgent. It's a missive from someone calling himself the Harbinger."

"Well? What is it?"

The runner swallowed. "He . . . he wishes to claim responsibility for the attack on the Temple of Last Rest, and he wants you to know he's not stopping there."

CHAPTER SEVEN

It took Raven two and a half weeks to reach the region of the Mirewoods in northern Aethel. Well, at least it wasn't cold. It was wet and cloudy and full of walking corpses, but hey, it wasn't cold. And whether he liked it or not, it was exactly what he was looking for. The mountains surrounding the small village of Caer Deaglan were all but abandoned. The villagers had fled to the safety of the town once the undead appeared. Said undead also supplied ample opportunity for Raven to vent his frustration in a semi-productive way. In theory, it was perfect—"in theory" being the operative term.

On his first day there, he was chased off and nearly killed by a pack of wolves. They didn't get him, but they did make off with a considerable amount of the venison he'd bought in Oisin's Watch. On the second day, a group of bandits attempted to rob him. They didn't succeed. So much for avoiding unnecessary bloodshed. At least he got a new bow out of it and some coin. On the third day, he got caught in the rain and got sick. It was awful. He couldn't stop shivering and coughing.

He wanted to give it a few days, hoping it would just go away so he could avoid any more human interactions. That was until the night terrors began. He was staying in a small dank cave at the time, and there wasn't a night when he didn't wake up in a cold sweat, feeling the need to vomit. He never remembered the night terrors; of that at least he was grateful.

He went into Caer Deaglan on his sixth day in the area. Once again, he found that the legion hadn't plastered his face all over the walls. And he had been bathing in the rivers so he wasn't as filthy as when he entered Oisin's Watch, so no one paid him any mind. Well, that wasn't true.

He was approached by a small woman with mousy brown hair and eyes the color of turquoise. She hid her ears under her hair, but the gemstone eyes were enough to indicate she was at least of elven blood. The woman had noticed how ill Raven looked and had offered him a cup of tea. He didn't want to accept. What if he hurt her too? But the idea of a warm drink was simply too tempting, and Raven was so very tired.

Hesperia, as the woman was called, was a healer, not a sorcerer, though that didn't surprise him given the remote location of Caer Deaglan. Additionally, she was, in fact, quite a skilled alchemist. The tea she made was floral and sweet, and it felt like it warmed his entire body.

"Thank you." He sipped the tea. "You really must let me repay you. I have some coin." Granted, it was the coin he'd gotten off those bandits, but he felt far less guilty about that than using Karya's coin.

Hesperia waved her hand dismissively. "Nonsense. Times like these, with the continent trying to tear itself apart and the dead rising to torment the living, we need to stick together, outsiders too."

"At least let me gather some herbs for you to replenish your store."

She shook her head and sighed. "Fine. If you see any redroot or elf-flower, you can bring it to me. But don't you go putting yourself in danger, understand?"

Raven nodded excitedly. Finally, there was something he could do for someone. Finally, there was something he could do to *attempt* to atone for his crimes. He only hoped that the Gods would appreciate his efforts, even if it was for naught.

Where the *fuck* was the redroot? He'd found dozens of elf-flowers, maybe hundreds judging off the weight in his satchel. He'd found exactly one redroot, but that one was dead. He was starting to think Hesperia was some sort of spirit of mischief, sending him on a wild goose chase to find a plant that didn't even exist.

Raven grumbled and kicked the grass, sending a clump of dirt rolling down the hill. He followed it with his eyes until they landed on a procession of people in heavy armor. Paladins? They looked like paladins. They wore the paladin emblem on their cuirasses. But there was something wrong with them. Did paladins usually glow like that? Raven didn't have much experience with them—Edelheim having no Arcane College and all—but he was fairly certain they weren't supposed to glow. And by the Gods, what was that thing following after them? It looked like a homunculus from the pictures his father had shown him to scare him away from magic (it hadn't worked). But it was pitch black, and it was massive. It was at least three times the height of the heavily armored soldiers.

The leader of the group held up his hand, and they all froze, including the hulking behemoth at the back. Raven quickly ducked behind a bush, and almost simultaneously, the leader turned his head toward him. Raven was sure he was hidden, but he couldn't shake the feeling he was being watched.

After a few moments, he heard the shuffling of metal boots, and it seemed they'd started moving again. He let out a sigh of relief, then felt the point of a blade against the back of his neck.

Shit.

Crack!

A leather-gloved fist hit Raven's face. He spat blood at the man, as well as a tooth.

"Answer me! The Harbinger demands to know where you got your blade!"

"Fuck you," Raven groaned, his entire body throbbing in pain.

He didn't even know why he was hiding it. What did he care if he knew it was from the legion? Maybe it was spite, or maybe there was just something about being knocked out and dragged into a cave in the middle of nowhere that made him feel uncooperative. The blade his captor spoke of was leaning up against the cave wall, humming softly. Raven didn't know if the paladin could hear it too. By the rage that appeared on his face when he started swaying to the music, he guessed no.

The paladin hit him across the face again. Raven's vision tunneled, and he felt his brain was rattling against the inside of his skull. That wasn't normal, probably. It felt like something was broken, maybe his nose. It was hard to tell when everything was spinning like that. The paladin glowered and stepped away. He turned to another man, his superior judging by how tall his helmet was. Usually, the person who had the biggest hat was the one in charge.

Raven almost chuckled, but the shooting agony in his jaw stopped that train of thought. Then he paused. The one in charge looked wrong. His armor was the wrong shape, the wrong color, even though color and shape were hard to make out in the dark. And it was hard to think. His memories were fuzzy, hard to make out. It was like trying to read a water-damaged book in a dream.

"Bring him and the blade to Saddler. The general will get something out of him," the one in charge ordered gruffly.

Raven almost felt like he recognized that voice. It was gruff with a subtle Valmeran flavor. Once again, though, it slipped away, the pages of his memories dissolving in the salty waves of what was almost certainly a concussion.

That name, though. Saddler. Someone in the legion mentioned that name, right? A paladin . . . or ex-paladin? Edric . . . Edric mentioned him. But why did he mentioned that name? Memories. . . difficult.

"Yes, Sir Dragonguard." The shorter one nodded and bowed.

The Dragonguard leaned over Raven, and even though his face was covered with his helmet, the sneer in his voice was almost audible. Raven opened his mouth. To defend himself? To ask him why he seemed so familiar? To curse him out? Whatever his plan, he never got the chance.

The Dragonguard's fist connected with Raven's cheek. It was a metal-clad fist. Raven's jaw shattered, and his mouth immediately filled with blood. He tried to scream, but the Dragonguard grabbed him by the face and held tight. The blood trickled down his throat, and he started to choke.

"You deserve worse than that for your crimes. You're lucky you have information," the Dragonguard spat and then threw Raven's head back into the chair. Then the Dragonguard turned on his heel and stomped out, leaving him alone with the paladin.

Raven was never particularly strong, but he was resilient. He'd always been resilient, and he'd always prided himself on that. Every time he fell, he would dust himself off and get back up again. He was the eldest brother. When he fell and scraped his knee, he didn't cry. He had to help his little brother who had a splinter in his finger. Meliodas had courage, Bedivere had talent, and Elyan had wisdom. Raven *had* to be resilient. He had to take the beatings from their father so the other boys didn't have to. He'd only felt so hopeless three times in his life. Those times were entirely devoid of light or optimism. First, when his baby brother Claudin had died in infancy. Second, when his mother drowned herself in booze following the death of her baby. And third, when his father got sick and didn't get better. Now would be the fourth time. With his jaw shattered, choking on his own blood in a cave in the middle of the most miserable place in Aethel. He was so sure he was going to die there.

The paladin laughed, actually *laughed*, at the tears that shook Raven's entire body, which only increased his agony tenfold. Raven wanted to scream at him, he wanted to spit on him, but all he could do was cry uncontrollably. He started to feel lightheaded. Was it just the pain? Or was he losing too much blood? The world spun even more, and he felt nauseous. The sobs subsided slightly, and he whimpered.

The paladin removed his helmet, revealing a head of slick black hair. His eyes were deep-set in his head, and angry red veins were spread all over it. He looked very ill. He grinned and took a pair of pliers from the side table.

"Now that he's gone, we can have some fun." He chuckled darkly.

Raven struggled against his restraints, all of his remaining strength slowly draining from him. The tears rolled down his face and mixed with the blood that dribbled from his chin. He glanced over to the blade, silently begging it to somehow save him. It didn't budge, obviously, but the hum got louder.

Maybe it's trying to make it easier to stand the pain? he thought, only half-jokingly.

The paladin said something, but Raven had his eyes trained on the blade and his ears focused on the music. His eyes twitched toward the voice, though, and he realized that the paladin wasn't talking to him. He wasn't even looking at him. He was facing away from him, his blade pointed at something in the dark he couldn't make out.

Raven thought he heard another voice, but the blade was deafening now. He couldn't hear anything except the music, which he was now able to tell was less of a hum and more of a chorus. Voices—maybe dozens, maybe hundreds—were singing what almost sounded like an operatic dirge. It was soothing, but at the same time, it made him feel like his ears were bleeding. Maybe they were. All the pain from his body had somewhat blended into a monotone buzzing.

That blade had been a whole lot of trouble, but at least it played nice music.

Raven felt something hot splatter across his face, and he passively looked back at where the paladin was. He wasn't there. Raven frowned. Then he looked down.

"Oh, there you are," he said weakly. But given the state of his jaw, it likely didn't sound as coherent as that.

The paladin was dead; of that much he was sure. He'd seen enough death in the last few weeks to last a lifetime, most of which he inflicted himself. Perhaps it was improper, but he was honestly getting used to it. A pair of shoes stepped into his field of vision, just by the dead paladin's open chest. They were silver but stained with something he couldn't quite make out in the slowly dying firelight. They were pretty.

Raven made a note to ask the owner where they got them and if he could get a pair as well. The boots stepped over the body, splashing in the pool of blood slightly. It probably had some of his too. He would've giggled if it didn't hurt so much to breathe.

The stranger crouched down to meet his eyes. He was older than Raven expected, with heavy bags under his eyes and worry lines on his forehead. His eyes were blue and stormy, filled with something Raven couldn't quite pinpoint. His skin was pale, almost abnormally so, and his hair was dark with streaks of grey.

The man furrowed his brow. "Gods, you look awful." His voice was barely audible over the singing.

Raven shrugged, and as the pain became too much, he whimpered. Then his eyes rolled back into his head.

Chapter Eight

Ashleigh Umber paced the smuggler's den he'd cleared out.

This was *not* the plan. The plan was to travel to the Mirewoods and meet with an ally of Lady Suncrest, a man called Petyr Haken, who would make an introduction between the two. Petyr was thirteenth in line for the crown of Darkwater and had been part of the Darkwater Arcane College and had firsthand experience with Lord Chaplain Helaena's abuse of power. He also had family in the Dragonguard, and Ashleigh hoped he'd be able to offer some insight into the madness that seemed to have gripped the organization.

Dragonguards all over Valmera and Aethel had been going dark, and the few that had been found had been . . . wrong somehow. They were committing random acts of violence, infecting random citizens with the Draugar corruption, and worse. There had been rumors that the High Dragonguard of Valmera had allied herself with some strange new ally, and all of Ashleigh's instincts told him that the emergence of this Harbinger character around the same time was no coincidence. Investigate that. *That* was the plan.

The plan was most certainly *not* to catch news of rogue paladins in the area, news that they'd acquired a powerful Draug artifact. The plan was *not* to get distracted tracking it down to make sure the so-called Harbinger couldn't use its power. The plan was *not* to find that the paladin's camp also included multiple Dragonguards and that he had to kill them. That was *not* the plan. And *the boy* was certainly not part of the plan.

The boy, a complete mystery to the Dragonguard, was lying in his bed. He was unconscious, and his face was covered in a healing salve. His hair and face were both covered in dirt and mud, but even under that, Ashleigh could see that he was rather beautiful. His nose was sharp and defined and came to a point that gave his face an angular look. His chin, too, was sharp. Everything about him seemed sharp, like he'd cut you if you got too close. Judging by his blade, that might just be the case. It was a Draug blade—that much would be obvious to anyone—but it was more unique than that. According to Ashleigh's research, it was a blade from the First Cataclysm, supposedly forged by one of the first Dragon Lords, high-ranking Draugar who took the form of dragons and had the ability to control the horde with psychic abilities.

A year ago, Ashleigh would've written that off as simply myth, that the blade was likely just wielded by a powerful Draug. Now, though, he wasn't so sure. The thing was deeply corrupted. The song of the Draugar seemed to leak from every porous seam and aged fracture in the metal. It was a miracle that the boy was even alive, if barely. There was something else about the blade, too, something Ashleigh hadn't encountered before the conference but now seemed to be everywhere.

It was cursed demon obsidian, crystals from the heart of Phantasma said to hold within them the darkest impulses of mankind. Could this boy *possibly* have chosen a worse blade? It seemed unlikely. How he even got his hands on it was a mystery, but as it stood, he wasn't in a position to be answering any questions.

Ashleigh didn't want to head into the village. Gods only knew if there were Dragonguards hunting him there, but he also knew that without proper healing herbs, the boy would likely die from infection, if the blood loss didn't get him first. The town's healer was a very kind young elven woman. She was not a Covenant sister like he expected (though Caer Deaglan did have those too) but an alchemist. She seemed more than happy to help Ashleigh and even offered to come with him to look after the boy. Ashleigh informed her it was not necessary, and then he paid her a hefty sum for her services and her silence, which she informed him was equally unnecessary.

When Ashleigh returned to the den, the boy was turning in his sleep, muttering to himself and sweating heavily. Ashleigh could sympathize, of course. All Dragonguards knew the horrors of night terrors—the bargain struck to defeat the Draugar carried a heavy price after all—but he couldn't bring himself to pity the boy. He still had no idea who he was. For all he knew, the boy deserved what the paladins did to him. Still, Ashleigh struggled to think of what someone could do to deserve *that*.

Ashleigh put a cold rag on the boy's forehead and got back to work, poring over his maps of the Red Wastes, a region of desolate desert in eastern Valmera, and tried to ignore the black veins that crept up the boy's neck.

Chapter Nine

The Temple hummed with activity as Percival weaved his way through the crowd. His waistcoat and corset were far too tight, and he felt like it was crushing his ribs. At some point, he'd managed to lose Andrea, pawning her off on some pretty young Valmeran thing. It was hard to think with all the noise, but Percy was laser-focused on a banquet table at the end of the hall—specifically, the drinks. He poured himself a tall glass of wine, or something the color of wine at least, and downed it in one gulp. As it went down, it burned more than wine should, but Percy didn't care.

It wasn't appropriate for a noble, let alone a prince, but everyone was too enraptured in their own vapid conversations to care. He hated these things. He'd never been invited to anything like this before, but he already knew that he hated them. He scarfed down a fruity pastry and then grabbed the "wine" bottle by the neck. He snorted as he thought of what his mother would say.

"Percival Alarch Drake!"

Probably something like that. He turned on his heels to see a red-faced Janus fuming while striding toward him.

"Oh, there you are! You know, I was just looking for you." Percy smiled sweetly, twirling the bottle in his hand.

Janus yanked it from him. "By the Gods, boy, pull yourself together!"

"Why should I?" Percy spat, sounding rather childish. "It's not like I'll actually be asked to speak at the conference. I don't even know why the High Cleric even invited us. This whole thing is just a fucking joke anyhow." He swiped for the bottle, but Janus held it out of his grasp.

"This is unbecoming of you, Your Highness. What will people say of Edelheim if they see our future king behaving in such a manner?"

"Same thing they always say—'Where's that?'" Percy laughed bitterly.

"Your Highness!" Janus protested.

But Percy waved his hand and cut him off. "I need some air. Save my place at the table, if I even have one. Come get me when they start serving food."

Janus looked like he was about to say something, but Percy was out of earshot within a few seconds. He wasn't worried about being unprotected. No one would be interested in attacking the inconsequential Percival Drake anyways.

He reached into his pocket and took out a small pipe along with a pouch of herbs. He emptied a pinch into the pipe and lit it with a match, also from the pocket. The herbal smoky scent soothed him, though it didn't do much to fight off the cold. Gods, he'd forgotten how cold the Bulwark Mountains really were. He considered heading back inside, into the warmth, but the thought of being surrounded by all those people, by all that *noise*, it made him feel sick.

He breathed in another puff from his pipe, gazing out at the mountains. Percy often fantasized about running away—from his home, from his life, from his responsibilities. He even almost did when he was sixteen. He had his bags packed and everything. Then his youngest brother, Elyan, found him. He was only six at the time, and he'd had a night terror. Percy told him he was just playing a game and unpacked everything. He'd never tried again. He wondered how many other young men in his position had had the same thoughts. He wondered how many actually went through with it, probably not many.

His frayed nerves seemed to dull, the herbs doing their job. Percy let out a breath. It was less shaky than he expected. He shook his head, straightened up, and brushed his hair out of his eyes.

Right. Back to it, he thought, turning back to the Temple.

Then something connected with the back of his head, and everything went dark.

He was in some sort of room. That was just about all he could surmise when he woke up. His hands were bound, his mouth was gagged, and he was on his back, looking up at the ceiling. It was a nice ceiling, some sort of stone or marble. There were faded colors and shapes, and Percy wondered if it was painted at some point.

It's rather pretty, actually. Percy considered that he probably had a concussion again. *No, not again.* He hadn't had a concussion recently, had he? *Where is this* deja vu *coming from?* he wondered. Then he thought about something else.

Someone in the room was moving, getting closer to him. He tried to struggle against his gag, tried to say something. He wasn't sure if he wanted to call for help or bite whoever's getting closer to him. Biting seemed rather out of character for him. He wasn't quite sure why he thought of it. The footsteps grew closer, and someone was now standing over him.

Percy felt relief fill his body. It was a Dragonguard, so everything was going to be all right. The Dragonguard gazed down at him but made no move to untie him. There was something about his eyes, an emptiness that made Percy's stomach churn. He tried to call out to him, tried to lift his head to gesture to his bound hands. Instead, he was met with a boot to the teeth. He whimpered and stopped struggling. The gag was getting wetter, but whether it was from his saliva or blood was impossible to tell.

The Dragonguard didn't say anything. He just walked away. Percy's jaw ached, but he knew that he had to see more. He had to know what was going on and why the Dragonguards, of all people, were involved. Percy arched his back slightly and twisted his shoulders, allowing his body to lean on its side with his hands supporting him so that he wouldn't fall on his chest.

He had been right on one account. He was, in fact, in a room, and he wasn't alone. There were at least a dozen Dragonguards spread out around the room. They looked like they were setting up some sort of ritual, but it was hard to say. A blonde woman, her hair pulled into two braids behind her head, stood to the side, watching the proceedings. She had a sly smile on her face, and when she glanced at Percy, her eyes were cold and blue. She held a thin finger to her lips and winked.

Percy glanced across the room, and his eyes widened at what he saw.

Janus had been a Dragonguard in his younger days, but that was before Percy met him, before he was even born. Janus never liked talking about that period in his life, said it was a darkness he'd rather leave behind him. He'd entertain the young prince with stories of the Dragonguard if he really begged, but Janus never told his own stories. He'd talk about comrades he'd had or historical Dragonguard heroes. He claimed to have met Sir Horace, the mentor of King Harold himself, when he was a younger man, but Percy never really believed that one. Being part of the Dragonguard had changed him, he said, and it was a life he never wished to return to. So it was baffling to see Janus wearing the Dragonguard regalia now.

"Janus!" he cried through the gag, trying to get his attention.

Janus didn't even flinch. Granted, it was possible he hadn't heard him, but the way he was moving was unnatural, almost mechanical in nature. Then Janus's head turned slightly, almost imperceptibly, but it was enough for Percy to see his face. There was something about Janus's eyes. There was something *wrong* with them. His eyelid twitched and stretched, and a thick black substance oozed from behind his eye.

Percy screamed.

He felt Andrea's hand on his. He hadn't seen her inside, but she was pulling him up and speaking quickly. He couldn't make out any words except "go" and "now." And then he felt metal on the inside of his wrists, and the binding came loose. He felt her hands on his back, pushing him, and when he looked back, he saw her—his friend looking at him with wide eyes. A small trickle of blood ran down the side of her mouth, and she looked down at the long silver blade jutting out from the space just below her sternum.

"Percy, run!"

He was running through the woods, bare feet sinking into the snow and sending sharp spikes of pain up his leg.

When did I lose my shoes? He couldn't remember.

He didn't stop running. His breath was ragged, his movements clumsy. He didn't know where he was going. He just knew he couldn't stop. He *had* to get away. From what, he couldn't remember. Everything past seeing Janus was a blur. There was someone else there—he was certain of that much—but everything about it was a hazy dream.

It?

It was a strange thought to have, but he was almost certain that whatever he saw there wasn't human. At least, it wasn't human any longer. There was also a woman—no, two women. One of the women was young with sharp blue eyes. The other was older. A Covenant sister? Wasn't she wearing Covenant regalia? No, it couldn't be. Was that the High Cleric?

Percy kept running. Then his foot connected with a root buried under the snow, and he felt himself falling. He tried to catch himself, but his hands were still bound. They flailed out in front of him ineffectually, and he landed hard in the snow. He thought he'd hit his head, and based on the blossoming warmth on his forehead, he suspected he was bleeding. He was face down in the snow, but he didn't have the strength to lift himself up.

He craned his neck slightly, looking back at the Temple behind him. Suddenly, it erupted into light. A great plume of iridescent energy shot up from the center of the complex. The whole valley seemed to shudder from the force of the blast, and then a great shockwave washed over it, knocking down every tree within a three-mile radius. Percy tried to shield his eyes, but the force of the blast sent him farther back, and the world swam around him like the inky black sea.

And then he was lost.

CHAPTER TEN

The boy hadn't stirred for the last four hours. The skin around his eyes was dark and sunken, and his lips were pale and chalky. Ashleigh didn't like looking at him. He didn't like the guilt he felt. He hated knowing the sword's corruption was consuming this poor man, that he could save him but wouldn't. He had seen firsthand what being a Dragonguard did to people, how it ate away at you until there was nothing left of you but the mission. No Dragonguard grew old. No Dragonguard had a family. You died fighting the Draugar, or you killed yourself trying to avoid that fate. Only one person had ever successfully escaped, and there was no one who ever lived quite like Lyanna Gael.

Lyanna Gael was a fair-folk elf conscripted into the Dragonguard by Sir Horace shortly before the Tenth Cataclysm. King Marcus had been dead for nearly twenty years at that point, and he was succeeded by his son, Harold. Harold was too young. He had only lived and known peace. He wasn't ready when the dead rose from the depth of the Sea of Shadows, when crops withered and died, when fishwives had their babes ripped from their breasts and dashed against the shore. King Harold wasn't *ready* for the Tenth Cataclysm. In a time of prosperity, Harold would've been a good king, a great king even. But those times were not times of prosperity, and Ashleigh had little faith in the boy who would be king. So he made a choice, and he paid dearly for it.

Sir Horace, King Harold, and the recently promoted Dragonguard Gael had convened at the fortress of Damon's Run to discuss what would be done about the growing unrest in Aethel. Some thought revolution was coming, and the Dragonguard knew that the Cataclysm had to be stopped before all-out famine began. There, deep in the Greenwood, three of the most powerful and tactically minded people met in complete secrecy—*almost* complete secrecy.

Ashleigh was a confidant of the king and of the king's wife, Queen Elspeth Umber. He brought only his most trusted men, men he knew would not hesitate to kill if ordered, and launched an attack. What remained of the fortress was razed, and Gael and King Harold only barely managed to escape with their lives, though heavily injured. Sir Horace was killed in the attack, sacrificing his life to save the king.

Lyanna was a force of nature, and that Cataclysm was the shortest it had been in millennia. By year's end, King Harold had managed to rally his forces and depose Ashleigh's rule. He was set to be executed for his treason, but Lyanna, now High Dragonguard of Aethel, the first elf to achieve the status in history, took pity on Ashleigh. He was conscripted into the Dragonguard instead and ordered to live out the rest of his days paying off his debt to Nymor.

That was ten years earlier, but not a day went by that Ashleigh didn't think about it, about what a fool he'd been, about all the things he could've done differently. Lyanna disappeared not long after, taking with her a small group of Dragonguards into the Unsettled Wilds territory in search of a way to stop the Cataclysms permanently.

Ashleigh knew the risks of being a Dragonguard, the sacrifices it took. He thought it would be cruel to bring the boy into the fold, especially without letting him know the full extent of what he was getting into. But was it not more cruel to leave him like this when Ashleigh knew that the only cure to the Draugar's corruption was to devote your life to their destruction, to leave him rotting in his own skin until he was nothing but a mindless husk?

Perhaps it would be more merciful to give the boy a quick death. But despite his reputation, Ashleigh was no murderer. The years had shown him that acting rashly would lead only to destruction. It nearly led to the death of his son-in-law, the son of his oldest friend. That was a sin he could never atone for, however sure he was of his actions at the time. Lyanna Gael had seen fit to show him mercy. It was more than he could've hoped for. She was a kind woman, kinder than what a man like him deserved. She had given him a choice, and he realized he owed the strange boy that much at least.

~~~

Raven's eyes opened and saw the interior of a cave.

Shit.

Was he still with the paladin? No, he was dead. He *saw* him die. Raven groaned and tried to roll over, but his entire body ached, and he hissed when he twisted his arm wrong.

"Don't move."

It was a man's voice. Raven's memory slowly started to return. It was the man from the cave, the man who seemed to have rescued him. He also insulted him, didn't he?

"Fucking shit buckets," Raven mumbled, clenching his eyes shut. The light of the torch was almost too much to bear, like a burning sun in the center of the cave.

The man chuckled roughly. "Pleased to meet you too. How's your jaw?"

Raven clenched it, then moved it around a bit. It was sore, but it didn't feel like it'd been completely pulverized. Was this man a sorcerer? Raven didn't move his head, worrying his neck might snap from the effort, but he glanced at the man out of the corner of his eye.

"Fine, actually," he muttered curtly.

He had no idea who this man was. For all he knew, the man could be working with them, trying to get him to let his guard down so he'd reveal where he got his blade—*his blade.*

Wait. Shit! My blade!

Raven couldn't hear the song. What had this man done to it? He knew he shouldn't move, but even so, he pushed himself off the bed.

"Where is it? Where's my sword?" His voice was shrill and pitiful, like a young child whining to his mother that he'd lost his favorite toy.

The man shook his head. He placed his hands on Raven's shoulders and gently pushed him back down into the bed.

"I'll explain everything, but I need you to calm down."

Raven's throat felt dry and sticky, like there was a piece of cotton lodged in there he couldn't quite cough up. But he nodded. He was in no position to argue. Looking down at his arms, he could see his skin was white as chalk and that his bones were pressing through the thin flesh. He felt like he was dying.
~~~

"Am I dying?" he asked, his voice barely above a whisper. But the man heard it, and his eyes softened just a fraction.

Ashleigh sighed. "Yes, but there may be a way for me to help you."

"Then why haven't you done it?" Raven demanded, heat bubbling in his core. Anger felt good; he could work with anger. It was better than hopeless. It was better than grief.

"It is more complicated than that. The process is dangerous and painful. It could end up only accelerating your demise."

Raven looked at him angrily. "How could anything be worse than *this*?"

Ashleigh didn't know how to answer that, so he remained silent.

"Who are you anyway? Where am I?" Raven turned his head, looking around the small cavern.

Despite the lack of illumination, he was able to see it quite clearly. There was a large pillar of what looked like limestone in the center of the room with one torch sconce on the side. It was surrounded by tables that were covered in dusty-looking tomes and maps, some of which had daggers stabbed into them. On the edges of the room were large wooden crates. It was impossible to tell what they held, but a few small sacks near them had fallen over and spilled their contents onto the cave floor. It looked like some sort of spice, maybe Dejari pepper. There were symbols painted on the walls, including a black skull with a white blindfold.

Smugglers.

The man noticed Raven's wide-eyed stare at the graffiti, and he shook his head, answering the young man's unspoken accusation, "No, I'm not a smuggler. My name is Ashleigh. I cleared out this smuggler's den to be used as my base of operation. Might I know your name?"

"Raven." He nodded. "It's . . . I'm Raven."

Ashleigh tilted his head slightly, as if he didn't quite believe him. But if anyone could understand the desire to conceal one's identity, it was him.

"Please," Raven weakly grabbed Ashleigh's hand, trying to put on his most convincingly helpless look, "tell me how to save my life."

CHAPTER ELEVEN

Raven was resilient, much more so than Ashleigh had anticipated.

To perform the initiation ritual, Ashleigh would need a number of gruesome and grotesque ingredients. He already had the Draug bone meal on him, but he'd have to go out to get the rest of the supplies. For that, he'd have to leave Raven on his own for a while. Ashleigh still wasn't sure if Raven could be trusted. The young man had been cagey about his past, deflecting whenever Ashleigh asked him where he'd come from or how he'd learned to fight. But then, Ashleigh himself was equally evasive, so he supposed it was fair.

Raven seemed to know little of Aethel's history or politics, so Ashleigh could only assume he must be from the Free Isles. The young man didn't have the accent or the attitude to be Valmeran—or the smell. All the Valmerans he'd met always wore far too much fragrance. Raven also didn't have the dark skin and light eyes of a Dejari. So . . . a Freeman then.

Besides that, Raven was impossible to read. He spoke like a noble but carried himself like a soldier and swore like a sailor. He was a skilled swordsman but fought with a style that was impossible to pinpoint. Some of it reminded Ashleigh of paladins, some of the scrappy rebels he'd fought with as a young man, some of historical stances and attacks he'd only seen in tactical scrolls from the Twilight Age.

The other thing that gave Ashleigh pause in leaving Raven alone was the young man's reaction to the loss of his blade. Ashleigh had already explained the severity of the blade's corruption, but even still, Raven begged to be allowed to hold it. It reminded Ashleigh of addicts cut off from their fix—the cravings and the shakes. Raven had this almost hungry look in his eyes whenever the topic of conversation veered too close to the blade. Ashleigh could see how it tormented Raven. It wasn't hard to notice the angry red marks he'd scratched up the length of his arm.

Ashleigh had considered asking the healer from the village to watch over Raven, but the young man insisted he didn't trust himself alone with someone who couldn't defend themselves. Ashleigh felt that perhaps he was being overly cautious, paranoid even, but in the end, he respected Raven's wishes. So before heading out every day, Ashleigh locked up anything Raven could possibly use to hurt himself and made sure some of his less important books were left outside so that Raven could read them if he wished. They were mostly historical tomes, some on magic rituals. Given that Raven didn't seem to be a sorcerer, Ashleigh wasn't too worried about those books.

<div style="text-align:center">~~~</div>

Raven didn't sleep. He couldn't even if he wanted to. Every time he felt his eyelids growing heavy, all he could hear was *that song*. It wasn't like the blade's. It was darker, more organic, more guttural. It was wet and deep and rotten—and *hateful*. He'd tried a few times to claw his ears off before Ashleigh had stopped him and talked him down. Ashleigh promised it would be over soon. Raven never stop hearing it, but it would fade into the background until he'd learned to ignore it entirely. He wasn't sure if he believed Ashleigh, but the hope was enough to stay his sharp fingers.

Ashleigh had left him alone in the cave again, and he was bored *again*. He was sitting on the floor beside his cot, picking at his nails. They were brittle and starting to peel, but it was almost therapeutic to chip away at the tender flesh. The blood that blossomed from the sores was dark and thick, and he shivered when it dripped onto the dirt of the cave floor. Despite his host's attempts to make him comfortable, Raven always felt cold. No matter how close he sat to a fire, he felt as if his bones were frozen with winter's breath. He felt like the grave.

Then something snapped. He froze his movements, straining his ears to discover the source. Despite his infirmity, his senses were still sharp, perhaps sharper than they had been. The air in the cave shifted slightly.

Someone had opened the gate at the front of the cave.

Raven stumbled to his feet, fighting the urge to cry out from the sudden pressure on his brittle, atrophied legs. He limped toward the table, cursing Ashleigh for leaving him defenseless. He looked around for anything that could be a weapon. There, on the ground, was a long stick.

Ashleigh had intended for him to use it as a crutch, but it would have to work as a weapon now. He braced himself on the table and leaned over, grasping for the stick.

Footsteps were coming closer. Raven strained his fingers, begging to the Gods that they'd let him reach it in time. Something in his shoulder cracked, and he ignored the pain as he was finally able to reach the stick just in time. He stood to his feet, shaking as he pointed the stick at the door. It opened, and Raven almost screamed.

Ashleigh stumbled back, his eyes wide at the wild-looking man waving a stick at him.

"Shit, Ashleigh!" Raven yelled, throwing the twig to the side weakly. "You weren't supposed to be back for hours. I thought you were an intruder!"

Ashleigh lowered his arms, staring at him with bewilderment. "I finished my business quickly. Gods, what did you do to your hands?"

He rushed forward upon seeing Raven's condition. Raven's knees finally failed him, and he collapsed into Ashleigh's chest, his eyes clenched shut.

"*Fuck*, Ashleigh. I can't keep doing this."

Ashleigh led him to the bed and helped him to sit down. "We can do the ritual soon. Tonight," he promised. He just hoped it'd be soon enough.

The final component in the initiation ritual was a mineral known as lepidolite. It was heavily associated with Phantasma and used in only the most powerful of magical rituals. It could only be mined by the dwarves, as it was a volatile substance known to combust if handled incorrectly. It had been difficult to come across but not as much as Ashleigh had anticipated. There had been a group of dwarven "merchants" traveling through Caer Deaglan when he stopped there to speak to Hesperia about his new initiate's condition.

Of course, when confronted, the dwarves quickly confessed to being smugglers. Ashleigh didn't care, of course. Dwarven criminals were a dwarven problem, but it did give him an opportunity. He didn't have much coin left, but he offered to clear the corpses on the road out of the Mirewoods in exchange for a small bit of lepidolite. The dwarves, who weren't very good fighters themselves, gladly accepted his terms, and he returned to his initiate with everything he needed.

Raven had gotten worse, much worse. The man was little more than skin and bones, and he couldn't even stand without assistance. Even if the initiation was successful, Ashleigh didn't know if it'd be enough to save Raven's life. But Raven had survived thus far, so who was to say he wouldn't do so again?

The chalice Ashleigh poured the mixture into was far from the one traditionally used in the ritual. It was barely even a chalice, really, just a roughly hammered piece of silver metal. The fancy goblet Dragonguards usually used was purely ceremonial, an example of one of the things Ashleigh disliked about the Order—their obsession with aesthetics. It reminded him of Valmera and left a bad taste in his mouth.

Raven was shivering, and when he grabbed his shoulder to steady him, he was like ice to the touch, as cold as death.

"Are you prepared to do this? Being a Dragonguard is not like they say in the tales. You will hold no title. You will have no family and gain no fame. You will suffer, and eventually, you will die."

Raven chuckled. "Everyone dies, Ashleigh."

A small smile played on Ashleigh's lips. It was somewhat comforting to hear Raven joking at a time like this.

"Some Dragonguards serve to atone for their sins, right? They die for the greater good to make it up to the people they've hurt. I'd like to do that," Raven said thoughtfully.

Ashleigh nodded and held the chalice up to Raven's lips, knowing the young man's arms were too weak to do it. He remembered his initiation—how painful it had been and the night terrors that followed. Worse than the ones after the occupation, after the rebellion. He hoped Raven's dreams were more pleasant, but he knew they'd be worse. He was barely alive at that point, more corruption than man. It was a miracle the Draugar's song hadn't taken him already.

Raven gulped the concoction down greedily, lapping up every last drop. It was putrid, as one might expect of something made from Draug bits, and it had the consistency of curdled milk. It burned like shitty liquor without the pleasant buzz, leaving only an aching lump in his stomach. He shuddered as he emptied the last of it into his mouth, and Ashleigh pulled the cup away. At first, Raven didn't feel anything aside from the sticky coating on the inside of his throat.

Ashleigh arched a brow and looked like he was about to say something, but that was when everything hit Raven.

The agony that came was worse than anything he'd ever experienced before. He thought getting his jaw shattered hurt. He thought dying from the corruption hurt, but he was *wrong*. Searing heat spread across every inch of his body, inside and out. Ashleigh had said he could die from the ritual, and he was certain that was what was happening. Images flashed in Raven's mind—black dust in the wind, smoke and mold enveloping cities in a second. And the music, Gods save him, the *music*—it was like a choir of a hundred laughing skulls, cracking open his mind so their discordant song could penetrate even deeper into his psyche.

Everything around him faded into the pain, into the burning, into the Cataclysm. Raven felt like he was falling, plummeting to his death in an endless dark abyss. He was wrong. Nothing would ever be enough to atone for the murders he'd committed. The Gods were punishing him for his sins, and he was going to die. He cried out, then felt something separate from the pain. A hand, calloused and rough, rested on top of his clenched fist. A voice cut through the music, like a paladin's blade infused with Astraea's light.

"Raven."

It was just his name, but it was enough. Ashleigh's voice came as a lifeline, tethering him to a world he felt was slipping out of his hands. The burning began to subside, and the fire in his stomach burned a little dimer. He let out a shaky breath. He was breathing. He wasn't dead. His eyes opened slowly, and the cave around him came into sharp focus. Ashleigh was kneeling in front of him, hand clasping his with a concerned look on his face.

"Don't look so disappointed, old man," Raven teased.

Ashleigh smiled slightly and let out a shaky sigh of relief. "You had me scared for a bit there. I've never seen an initiation so . . . violent."

Raven shrugged. "What can I say? I aim to impress."

He laughed, genuinely laughed. It filled his chest with a comforting warmth, but he ignored it. He'd climbed that hill before, and he wasn't willing to fall for a second time.

Chapter Twelve

The next few weeks went by at a snail's pace. Raven slowly regained his strength through tedious exercise. He understood the purpose of it, of course, but that didn't mean he had to like it. The craving for the feel of his blade had lessened slightly, but Ashleigh had still refused to reveal where he had hidden it. Raven couldn't decide if he was grateful or resentful about that. He settled on resentment; it was easier.

"Initiate!" Ashleigh snapped, snatching him from his reverie. "Are you even listening to me?"

Raven shrugged. "Not really, no."

Ashleigh pinched his brow. "By the Gods."

Raven hopped off the bed and crossed his arms. "I feel fine, Ashleigh. Great, even. Let me go out. I can help with the undead!"

"You're not ready. You still look like death, Initiate." Ashleigh shook his head.

"I looked like death long before I got sick. That's not going away anytime soon."

"Fine, but I'm coming with you. I won't have you running into fights we both know you can't win."

Raven rolled his eyes. "Fine, fine. Have it your way"

Ashleigh sighed. Then he stood up straighter and grabbed a thin steel longsword from the table. He tossed it to Raven, who caught it nimbly, earning an impressed eyebrow raise from the older man.

Raven held the sword in his hand, testing the balance. It wasn't nearly as good as *his* blade; in fact, it felt as if its center was focused far more at the hilt than it should've been. He made a mental note to stop by the smith in Caer Deaglan. Even if he couldn't get a new blade, it would be nice to at least try to get this one fixed somewhat. He smiled and sheathed the blade.

Raven wondered if he should've listened to Ashleigh. The two Dragonguards were positioned outside Caer Deaglan's gates, fending off yet another wave of walking corpses. Despite the downpour, Raven felt hot, and his face was coated in sweat. He only knew it was sweat because of the salty drops that occasionally landed on his tongue in the heat of battle. He couldn't count on two hands the number of undead he'd already slain, and it seemed Ashleigh had slain twice that amount. Despite their efforts, the enemies seemed to be never-ending.

"How do they just keep coming? Surely there can't be *this* many dead people in the Mirewoods."

Ashleigh pulled his blade from the corpse it was buried hilt-deep in and grunted. "They're Nightmares from Phantasma. No matter how many we slay, as long as that portal in the lake stays open, more will pour out and re-inhabit the corpses."

"Well, that just isn't fair," Raven huffed.

Ashleigh rolled his eyes, and Raven's hand flashed, burying a thrown dagger in the skull of a corpse that had risen behind the older man. Ashleigh turned to the corpse and then back to Raven, who grinned back.

Then Raven took off into the bulk of the horde. His sword slashed through the air, cleaving into the nearest undead creature. As thick black blood splattered across his leather armor, he wrinkled his nose at the smell. The thick rotted blood caught onto his armor like curdled milk. But he didn't have any time to react further as another ran toward him from behind, waving its flimsy iron sword wildly in the air. It brought the blade down in an arch, and Raven only barely had time to block it with his own.

I should ask Ashleigh for a shield, he thought miserably as his torso twisted uncomfortably toward the corpse. He drew another dagger and plunged it into the corpse's stomach, causing it to stumble back so he could adjust his footing. He lunged for it and took its head cleanly off its shoulders.

"Duck!"

Raven did immediately, and an arrow whizzed over his head, shooting directly into the eye of the undead who had almost caught him by surprise. He shot Ashleigh an appreciative grin, and the older man nodded, then nocked another arrow and let it fly. Raven looked back toward the horde. It seemed they were thinning, at least a bit. They'd be back, of course, but as he cut down the last of this wave, it seemed Caer Deaglan would be safe for the moment.

Ashleigh wiped his brow and smiled at him. "You did well, Initiate."

"Nice to hear my efforts being appreciated for once," Raven said jokingly, hoping the poor lighting would hide the rosy color blooming on his cheeks at the compliment.

Ashleigh rolled his eyes. Sheathing his blade, he turned his attention to the thin man approaching them from Caer Deaglan's now-open gate, a man Raven was only vaguely familiar with. From Ashleigh's explanation, this man was the mayor of Caer Deaglan. He was a squat man with a pudgy round nose and large eyes that made it look as though the poor man was perpetually on the verge of tears.

"Goddess preserve us!" the mayor exclaimed, dabbing at his brow with a handkerchief. "You drove them off!"

Ashleigh shook his head. "For now. They will return, however. It would do you well to establish some patrols around the gates."

The mayor frowned. "But we don't have the men for such an endeavor!"

"Try mercenaries," Ashleigh grunted. Then he turned on his heel and started walking away, leaving the mayor dumbstruck on Caer Deaglan's proverbial doorstep.

Raven shot the mayor an apologetic shrug and then followed after. Ashleigh was frustrated—anyone could see that—but it wasn't with the mayor. It was with a number of things: the Gods, himself, and even Raven, a bit. Raven didn't blame Ashleigh; he couldn't. Despite his separation from his blade, he still felt that boiling rage, that bloodlust. He supposed that was due to the twenty-five years of emotional repression.

"You needn't have been so unkind to him, you know. He's only trying to protect his people." Raven fiddled with the straps on his cuirass while they walked, feeling that same childlike embarrassment he felt when he pointed out something his father had done wrong.

Ashleigh sighed. "You're right, but he should be doing better."

"We can't all be Dragonguards, Ashleigh."

Ashleigh crossed his arms and walked a little faster. He wanted to say more—Raven could feel it—but for some reason, Ashleigh decided to stay his tongue. That wasn't like him. As badly as Raven wanted to press the issue, the fight had taken a lot out of him, and he couldn't wait to get home to a hot meal.

Home.

That was odd. He'd only been in that cave for a few weeks, yet he already considered it a home. Was it just the cave itself or the things held within? It made his heart race and his stomach rise. He thought about something else.

Gods save him, Raven was fucking *infuriating*. He challenged Ashleigh on every decision and teased him relentlessly. In other words, he made his life a living nightmare. Then why couldn't he stop thinking about Raven? The way he invaded his every waking thought was the other thing that drove the heat in his chest. He decided to say it was anger; anger was the easiest to contend with.

Raven was sitting on his cot, tongue between his teeth, whittling away at a block of wood. It was impossible to say what it was. His movements were unskilled and jerky. He'd never carved before—that much was obvious to Ashleigh—but he was clearly trying. He had this arrogance where he believed he could do anything—or at least he pretended he could. Ashleigh would've found it irritating, but frankly, it was charming. It reminded him of the young rebel king he once knew.

The fact that Raven reminded him so much of Marcus made Ashleigh uncomfortable. After they had won the rebellion and ousted the Valmeran despots, Marcus had made Ashleigh baron, and no one in court questioned him. No one challenged him. Ashleigh was the Hero of Aegisfjord, the tactician who won the Battle of Crossed Swords and saved King Marcus and Queen Roweena from overwhelming odds. Surely his decisions must be wise and just.

After Damon's Run, when he betrayed Marcus's son, his own *son-in-law* and the king of Aethel, their admiration turned to fear.

And then he was conscripted into the Dragonguard to atone for his betrayal, and he was belittled and scorned but never truly challenged. Anything he said would be disputed, no matter the validity. Only Marcus had held him accountable, both in his reckless youth and his tired age.

Raven cursed and stuck his bleeding thumb in his mouth.

Ashleigh rolled his eyes. "Gods, if you're not going to be careful, I'm going to take that knife away from you."

Raven stuck his tongue out at him and wiped his thumb on his tunic. Then he went back to his work, his hair dangling over his face.

Ashleigh stood up from where he'd been hunched over a pile of indecipherable maps and walked over to him. "You're going to hurt yourself."

Raven rolled his eyes. "I'm fine, Ashleigh."

"You're going to get your hair caught on your blade, for pity's sake. Can't you at least braid it out of the way?"

Raven's face went red, and he ignored Ashleigh's question.

"Raven?"

"I never learned."

"Pardon?"

"I never learned to braid my hair, all right! I always had someone else to do it for me."

Ashleigh sat on the bed behind him. Then he rolled up the sleeves of his cotton shirt. "May I?"

Raven sucked in a shuddering breath, then nodded. Ashleigh began by parting Raven's hair into three segments, carefully running his calloused fingers through the hair to make sure they were even. He didn't know how to do complicated braids, granted, but the simplistic kind he'd worn as a younger man would be more than serviceable. Raven's hair was thin and dry, and as Ashleigh made his way up the younger man's scalp, he could see the flaxen hair becoming ashen.

"Where'd you learn to braid hair?" Raven asked quietly.

Ashleigh smiled softly. "My mother. My hair was longer when I was young, and she wanted it out of my face."

"She sounds like a good woman."

Ashleigh folded one segment of hair over another. "She was."

"My mother was always busy—with her work, with my siblings, with her liquor cabinet." Raven laughed bitterly.

"You have siblings?"

Raven nodded. "Three brothers, all younger."

"Do you hope to see them again?"

Raven looked down at his hands, which were clasped in his lap. "No."

It was clearly a sore subject for him.

Ashleigh reached the end of the braid and tied it with a length of twine. "There. That should keep it out of your face."

Raven craned his head to look back at him and was suddenly very aware of how close their faces were to each other. He slid away slightly, giving Ashleigh space to catch the breath that had so rudely vacated his lungs.

"Um, thank you, Ashleigh."

Ashleigh nodded and stood up, immediately turning away from him. *Gods, am I blushing? What the fuck is wrong with me? A pretty young lad looks at me, and I'm blushing like a schoolboy? I'm a Dragonguard and a distinguished general. I should act like it.*

He made his way back over to the maps, not noticing how softly Raven stroked his new braid, not noticing the admiration with which he looked at him.

~~~

Lady Suncrest would arrive soon, and Raven's world would come crashing down around him. Nearly two months had passed, and he had gotten used to the steady rhythm he and Ashleigh had fallen into. He'd grown more comfortable around him, even bouncing ideas off him when he hit a roadblock in his investigation into the other Dragonguard and this mysterious Harbinger character.

Raven felt alive for the first time in decades, and he didn't want to lose that. He didn't want to lose this life. He didn't want to lose *him*. He'd have to leave. He'd have to run away *again*. Only this time, he didn't want to go. This time, he wanted nothing more in the world than to stay.

It was midnight, and Raven was pacing. He did that a lot lately—paced up and down the tunnel leading up to the main chamber of the cave. It didn't help, not really, but it gave him an excuse to get away
~~~

from Ashleigh. It gave him time to think, time for his mind to spin wild hypotheticals of his doomed future, and time to feel sorry for himself for the rotten hand he'd been dealt.

He couldn't blame it all on the world, of course. He had his own share of the blame in his ordeal, but if he started down that path, he knew how hard it would be for him to come back. He'd watched his mother drink herself to death over guilt like that after they lost Claudin. Raven refused to be anything like his mother. He wouldn't fall upon his blade out of pity for a past he could do nothing to change. He wasn't a martyr, and he wasn't a hero.

He paused that train of thought.

But he *could* be. He was a Dragonguard now. He had the chance to actually help people and do something with the life he had done so little to deserve. But he couldn't do that if he ran away, if he didn't see this through with Ashleigh, if he didn't help the legion. He couldn't do that without Tessia. So he'd stay. He'd stay and hope that whatever justice Lady Suncrest saw fit to execute wouldn't end in his demise, that Ashleigh wouldn't hate him for what he'd done, and that he could find redemption in stopping the Harbinger and repairing whatever damage had been done to the Dragonguard, whatever the cost.

Chapter Thirteen

Caer Deaglan was a miserable place. That was Tessia's first impression. Everyone seemed to have a perpetually dour expression. Even the houses looked sad, drooping dejectedly from the weight of the constant downpour.

The elven sorcerer Hawthorn had a perturbed scowl on his face that never seemed to leave. But then he seemed vaguely irritated no matter where she took him, so she didn't give that much weight. Minthe and the orcish paladin Dame Nestra seemed relatively unbothered, given the circumstances. Minthe was mortified by the undead, of course. Tessia had picked up on her dislike of anything even remotely magical (except herself), so she tried to give Minthe's hand a comforting squeeze whenever it seemed too much for her.

For her part, Minthe was unused to having such public displays of affection. Sure, it was just holding hands and an occasional peck on the cheek whenever they rested at camp, but compared to her past dalliances, it was . . . a lot. The girls she'd been with before mostly consisted of scullery maids having a quickie in a broom closet or a castle runner who was only interested in the exoticism of being with an elf.

Tessia was different. She was soft and sweet, and Minthe worried that if she pressed too hard, she could break. Tessia's magic scared Minthe, especially in the heat of battle when shards of ice swirled around her graceful form. But then it was over, and if Tessia exerted herself too much, she might fall over. Minthe would always catch her despite her fear—or maybe because of it.

Petyr had been vague with his description of his Dragonguard friend's location, to say the very least—southeast of the village of

Caer Deaglan and just east of Fort Locke. There was no road to follow, not a landmark to look for. There was a hidden smuggler's den southeast of Caer Deaglan. Understandably, they got a bit distracted.

The mayor of Caer Deaglan begged them to help with the undead, and everyone had agreed it was the more immediate issue to deal with. After all, how could they refuse those large sad eyes of his? Strangely enough, though, when asked, the mayor said there were *two* Dragonguards who'd been helping defend the village. Maybe Petyr had been helping, and the mayor had been mistaken? That was what the others seemed to think, but Tessia wasn't so sure.

The networks of caverns under the lake were massive and labyrinthian, and the group was forced to fight through wave after wave of possessed undead to reach the portal at the center of the maze. Netsra's training, in particular, came in handy. Her specific experience hunting runaway sorcerers and using her martial training to neutralize magic virtually nullified a large amount of the threat. Finally, after what felt like hours of non-stop fighting, they reached the center.

The portal was massive, bigger than any other Tessia had ever seen. It pulsed like a massive beating heart, feeding off the cycle of death and destruction it fueled as it funneled spirits into the waking world to possess the dead of the Mirewoods. Minthe held up her hand to shield her eyes, and even Dame Nestra, who had more experience fighting magical threats than any of them, shrunk back under its light. The only one who didn't seem bothered was Hawthorn, who seemed to almost bask in the headache-inducing iridescent glow.

"How . . . how do we even close that?" Tessia swallowed, not taking her eyes off it.

"The same way you close the smaller ones, I would imagine." Hawthorn shrugged, taking his staff from its sheath on his back. "We hit it until the Nightmares stop coming."

Tessia nodded. "Right." Her fingers crackled with blue-violet electricity. "Let's do it."

After the portal under the lake was dealt with, the sky itself seemed to feel the relief. Tessia wondered if it was just a coincidence. She'd never heard of Phantasma impacting the weather of the waking world, and she hadn't seen any similar effects from other portals.

Hawthorn said something vague about the "flow of interconnectivity" or something along those lines. Tessia was no fool when it came to magical theory, but Gods, she could hardly keep up with him most of the time. He didn't seem to mind. She thought he might just like the sound of his own voice.

Eventually, they were approached by one of Isadora's couriers while resupplying in Fort Locke. "A missive from Lord Haken, Your Eminence." The runner bowed her head slightly, handing over the rolled-up piece of parchment.

Tessia flushed slightly before taking the document. She hated the pageantry, the reverence everyone treated her with. She was glad Tyr's aspect had saved her from the Harbinger's explosion, even though she didn't understand why, but she just wished people would treat her as she was—a confused woman just trying to stay afloat in these tumultuous waters.

The missive requested her presence at the smuggler's den as soon as possible. Apparently, Petyr's unnamed Dragonguard friend had made a breakthrough, and there wasn't a moment to spare. Tessia exchanged a look with Minthe, who had been unsubtly reading the letter over her shoulder.

"Well, I suppose there's no point in delaying any longer." Tessia shrugged, rolling up the missive and slipping it into her satchel.

"Good." Hawthorn nodded. "We've dallied long enough."

He was right, of course, but did he have to be so patronizing about it? Of course, he did. That was his default setting after all. Tessia finished up making preparations, and the four of them set off from Fort Locke. The Gods only knew what awaited them, and not even they could've prepared Lady Suncrest for what did.

Chapter Fourteen

"Her Eminence should be here within the hour." Petyr crossed his arms, looking incredulously at Ashleigh.

He had nothing against Ashleigh *personally*. But the man's reputation preceded him, and Petyr's family had been personally affected by the chaos following the betrayal at Damon's Run and the power vacuum left behind after the presumed death of King Harold. It didn't help that Ashleigh had been especially dodgy since Petyr arrived, insisting he wait outside the cave for Lady Suncrest.

Ashleigh seemed paranoid, but about what? The rest of the Dragonguard couldn't know he was here. Anyone who got close had been scared off by the paladin patrols, wild animals, or up until recently, the roving undead. So it had to be something else.

"About damn time," the older man grumbled, shifting impatiently on his feet.

"She has other things to do, you know," Petyr pointed out. "I'm sure it hasn't escaped your notice that the sky's cleared and the undead have stopped coming in such numbers?"

"The Dragonguard's madness and the Harbinger should be her *primary* priority."

Petyr sighed. "Still the same old Lord Umber, I see—more focused on the 'greater good' than the people actually affected."

Ashleigh cringed at the use of his proper title, and he opened his mouth to protest but quickly closed it. Suddenly, he was distracted by something, freezing up and straining his ears.

"Stay here," he ordered, turning back to the cave.

"You know you're not *actually* in charge of me, right?" Petyr called after him, but Ashleigh was long out of earshot.

By Astraea, thought Petyr, *this can't end well.*

~~~

Raven was pacing and muttering to himself. His whole body shook, and he did his best to get the energy out. But it seemed a fruitless endeavor. Every time he felt his pulse and breath slowing, some other horrible scenario would pop into his head.

What if Tessia attacked on sight? Could he even defend against her magic? What if she got to Ashleigh first? What if she convinced him to strike him down? Could Raven even bring himself to raise a blade against the only man who'd shown him such unconditional kindness?

Suddenly, Raven felt a hand on his shoulders, and he jumped.

"Calm down." Ashleigh shushed, his voice low and rough. "It's only me. What's wrong? Talk to me, Raven."

Raven bit his lip. Better it come from the horse's mouth, right? At least he'd have more time to run if Ashleigh reacted poorly.

No, Raven reminded himself. *No more running.*

Whatever happened, he'd face it. Pulling away from Ashleigh, Raven turned and sat down on his bed. His hands were folded in his lap, and he wasn't looking at Ashleigh. He knew he should. He knew he should face Ashleigh when he revealed how little he actually deserved the man's kindness. But he couldn't, not yet anyway.

"I . . ." Raven took in a shuddering breath. "I've met Tessia—Lady Suncrest, I mean." He paused for a moment but not long enough for Ashleigh to interject. He wanted Ashleigh to hear everything first. "I was at the Temple of Last Rest . . . Gods save me, Raven isn't even my real name. It's Percival Drake!" He laughed, but it was less of a laugh than a shuddering sob. "They thought I was involved with the explosion. I didn't have Tyr's blessing. They just found me unconscious a mile or two from the blast. My family crest was near the epicenter. That was enough proof for them, I suppose." He held his face in his hands. "I escaped . . . Ashleigh, I *killed* people—innocent people, people who *helped* me. I cut them down. I *murdered* them. And it felt *good* to hurt them. It felt *so* good, Ashleigh." He sobbed. "I don't deserve your sympathy. I don't deserve to be a Dragonguard."
~~~

Ashleigh took a step forward and lay a hand on Raven's shoulder. "Raven, the blade—"

"Isn't an excuse!" Raven shouted, finally looking up at Ashleigh.

He expected to see anger, disgust, and hatred. Instead, he saw pity and compassion.

"Ashleigh." He took a deep breath. "If Lady Suncrest tries to arrest me, if she tries to hurt me or kill me, I want you to let her. I deserve whatever justice she deems appropriate."

He shook his head. "No." "Ashleigh—"

"No, Raven. This is not about any *sentiment* I might hold toward you. This is about precedent. When you join the Dragonguard, your past, however heinous, is washed clean." Ashleigh knelt down to Raven's level, placing his leather-gloved hands on his shoulders. "You are no longer the man who killed those people. You are no longer Percival Drake." His eyes were soft, the usual stormy blue seeming to clear into a bluebird day. "You are Raven. You are a *Dragonguard*. And I will not allow anyone to take that from you."

Raven smiled softly and nodded, feeling a renewed sense of purpose.

Raven had a sword to his throat again. Gods, what was that? The fourth time in twice as many months? Surely the average person had to deal with that far less.

"Eminence, is this he? The man you spoke of?" The orcish warrior growled, her blade nicking Raven's skin and causing a small trickle of blood.

Tessia's eyes were wide, and she was shaking. Then another blade was drawn, this one pointed at the paladin's head.

"Your Eminence, I would advise you to tell your woman to stand down." Ashleigh didn't look at the paladin, simply glowering at Tessia.

Petyr, ever the peacemaker, stepped between the two. "How about we *all* put away our weapons and talk like civilized folk?"

"This man is a murderer! He—"

"This man is a *Dragonguard*, and I will not allow you to threaten him."

Dame Nestra grunted but made no move to sheathe her blade.

Finally, Tessia seemed to find her voice. "Nestra, it's all right. You can stand down."

Dame Nestra looked like she wanted to protest, but she obeyed the command.

Tessia almost didn't recognize Percival. His hair was darker, and his eyes were clearer, aside from the ring of reddened skin around them. He looked less troubled, less confused—not to mention he was dressed in a simplistic steel cuirass that held the Dragonguard emblem, the disembodied head of a Great Wyrm, its eyes empty and lifeless. He looked a bit ill, though, with heavy dark bags under his eyes that matched his companion—Ashleigh Umber.

Of all the people Tessia expected to meet in this cave, these two were perhaps the most unlikely, aside from King Harold or Empress Élisabette themselves perhaps. She watched as Ashleigh made his way over to Percival, gently placed a hand on his shoulder, and brushed a stray hair from his face with the other.

"Are you all right, Raven?"

Ashleigh inspected Raven's throat carefully, noting the nick in his skin. There was a bead of blood forming from the small cut, but it didn't look to be more than a flesh wound. He instinctively licked his glove then and wiped it across Raven's neck. Raven shuddered slightly but had gotten quite proficient at stopping the blush that plagued him whenever Ashleigh got too close.

He cleared his throat. "Yes, I'm fine."

Raven stepped back, his hand shooting up to his throat. Was the warmth he found from Ashleigh's hand or his own treacherous body? *Another one of the Gods' baffling little mysteries.*

"Raven?" Tessia interjected, her brows furrowed.

He looked back toward Lady Suncrest. "Yes, that's . . . That's what I've been calling myself."

Ashleigh nodded. "As a Dragonguard, it is within his rights to abandon his previous identity."

Raven shrugged. "My family has disowned me. I didn't see any point in keeping their name, aside from drawing unnecessary attention."

Tessia bit her lip. She didn't like this, not one bit. It was hard to say if Percival—*Raven*—was remorseful. She'd only known the man for a short time, but she could never quite get a bead on him. He held a lot of anger—that much was obvious—but all that anger couldn't exist in a vacuum. Tessia knew there had to be more underneath it all. He was different now, though. The anger was still there—she could see it in his red-rimmed eyes—but whatever was buried underneath had ridden to the surface. But what that internal truth was, Tessia couldn't guess" Per—*Raven*, you have to understand, even if you are a Dragonguard . . . you *killed* two people. Surely you can't expect to just . . . to just get away with that?"

Raven shook his head. "I don't. I will spend every day of my life atoning for what I did. I don't think it'll be enough, but if the Dragonguard is giving me a second chance, a chance to be better, I'm going to take that chance, Tessia."

A small smile played on Lady Suncrest's lips. She was relieved. She hadn't misjudged him. Raven's crimes were unforgivable, but that didn't mean he couldn't try atoning for them.

"All right, if Petyr trusts Ashleigh and Ashleigh trusts you, then so will I."

"But Tessia—"

"Your Eminence, you can't be seriously considering—"

"What? My lady—"

Her companions simultaneously voiced their objections, but they went largely unheeded. They put her in this position, a position where she'd have to make the hard decisions. It wasn't her fault if they weren't the ones they liked.

"Thank you, my lady. You won't regret it." Raven bowed his head slightly.

"Make sure I don't."

He swallowed and nodded. Then he turned away to give Tessia, Ashleigh, and Petyr space to discuss what they'd found. Ashleigh hadn't told her much, just that he'd discovered evidence of some sort of ritual being performed in the Red Wastes. Raven suspected that was all Ashleigh even knew. Whatever the details, it had something to do with drawing forth an immense amount of energy from Phantasma. That meant Nightmares, in the hundreds at least. Which meant bad things for Valmera. Even Ashleigh couldn't get behind that.

Raven didn't have anything to add to the conversation, so he wandered over to an unoccupied corner of the cave to wait to be needed. That was when he heard it—a soft hum, melodic and soothing. His whole body stiffened, his system suddenly flush with adrenaline.

Had it been here the whole time? How had it escaped his notice? He felt his mouth water, hungry for the ecstasy he knew the *blade* would give him. His chest ached for it; the song alone sent spikes of energy rushing through his veins. Raven clenched his fist, digging his brittle jagged nails into his palm. He focused on the pain, anything to ignore the coppery sweet smell that was quickly overwhelming his senses.

"You look ill." A voice snapped him from his stupor.

Raven looked up at the source of the voice. It was a man, a tall pale-skinned elf with thin white hair who stood with his arms crossed and his back just a bit too straight for Raven's liking.

"Why does everyone insult me when they meet me? Doesn't anyone ever just say 'hello' anymore?"

The elf scoffed, "Just pointing out the obvious."

Raven snorted. "Well, you're no rose yourself." He gestured to his attire.

The elf was dressed rather like exactly the kind of wild elves Raven's father used to tell stories about who wandered the woods outside the city. His clothes hung off him oddly, like he'd stolen them from a clothesline and never bothered to find anything that fit better.

At Raven's words, the elf looked mildly offended, curling his upper lip slightly. "We have actually met before, you know."

Raven raised an eyebrow, disbelieving.

"At the Temple, when Lady Suncrest defeated the Nightmare, although I suppose 'met' would be generous. I didn't so much as share a word with you."

Raven nodded, the memories slowly returning to him. "Right. Hawthorn, wasn't it?"

"You know my name?"

"You're an elven sorcerer working closely with the leader of a massive Covenant-backed religious movement. People talked about you."

"Before you escaped and killed a man to do so."

"Correct." Then Raven's more spiteful nature got the better of him. "You really are as smart as they say, aren't you?"

Hawthorn's garnet-colored eyes darkened, and he growled, an almost wolf-like snarl. "Your glibness does you no credit, Dragonguard."

Despite the cool tone of his voice, there was a veiled heat behind those words. For some reason, it scared Raven more than Tessia's magic had. He folded his arms over his chest and looked away, struggling both to ignore Hawthorn's presence and fight the gradually mounting song emanating from the crate next to them.

"Is there something you needed, or did you just come over here to bother me?" Raven clenched his teeth, his hands balling into fists over his knees.

"Despite what Suncrest might think, *I* still don't trust you. A wolf cannot change its nature. It cannot quell its thirst for bloodshed."

Raven turned back away from him. His fingers itched, and Hawthorn was not making it easy to resist the urge to take his head off. Maybe he wouldn't even need the blade. He could just choke the life out of him with his bare hands. The thought filled him with more satisfaction than he would ever admit. He glanced over to the three tacticians—Petyr, Lady Suncrest, and Ashleigh. The pit in his stomach deepened, and he unclenched his fists.

He laid his palms flat on the bench, focusing on his breathing, the steady flow of air entering and leaving his lungs. He did his best to breathe out the rage that seemed to vibrate in his every cell. He thought maybe the sorcerer said something, but he wasn't listening. The song quieted slightly, but it didn't vanish completely. He stood up and started toward Ashleigh. He felt like a child asking his governess to visit the market with the other boys, but he swallowed his pride and tapped him on the shoulder.

Ashleigh turned to him. "Yes? What is it, Raven?"

"Might I take a walk? One of Lady Suncrest's people can accompany me. I just—" His eyes darted back toward the direction of the blade, and Ashleigh's eyes widened.

"Are you sure you're all right? I can come with you if you need."

Raven shook his head. "No, I'm all right. You're needed here. I just need some air."

Ashleigh's hand went to his arm, running down it until he was holding his hand. He gave it a comforting squeeze and smiled softly.

Gods, I want to kiss him. Wait, no! No, I don't.

Now, Raven really needed some air. He hoped Ashleigh didn't notice his pulse racing with the blood that rushed to his face. Hopefully, he assumed Raven was just anxious about the blade.

"I will accompany him."

Raven squeaked and jumped, and he spun around to find Hawthorn standing directly behind him. The elf raised a brow, clearly amused by his reaction.

Tessia looked at them now, brows furrowed in concern. "Are you sure, Hawthorn? I've seen him fight. If he tries to escape—"

"I am quite certain I can handle him, Your Eminence."

"Just scream really loud if you need anything," Petyr interjected, a lopsided grin on his face. Hawthorn rolled his eyes, but Raven saw just a hint of hesitation in his movements.

Raven's legs dangled over the side of the dock, kicking up water and watching as the fish scattered with the disturbance. It was peaceful out here—pretty, even. He ignored how much it reminded him of the dock at Sanctuary. Gods, a lot had really happened in the last few months. He'd gone from being a Freeman noble to a suspected terrorist, to a murderer, and then to a Dragonguard. It was almost too much to keep track of.

The legion had grown in influence in the intervening months as well. They'd gained allies and enemies and had been forced to relocate to a fortress in the center of the Bulwark Mountains that made up the border between Aethel and Valmera. The Harbinger's forces had grown in power as well, and the first casualties of the inevitable war had already fallen.

The continent was on the brink of chaos, and it seemed Tessia Suncrest and the legion's faith were the only thing holding it together. It was a lot to think about.

"You're really not going to try and run, are you?"

Raven flinched slightly. He'd almost managed to forget Hawthorn had accompanied him at all and was standing over his shoulder. He didn't respond, just shrugging and lobbing another stone. He heard the sound of fabric rustling, and then the rotted wood of the dock creaked slightly. He looked down at his boots to see another pair of feet dangling next to them.

"Why did you do it?"

Raven's shoulders tensed. "You're going to have to be more specific."

"Why did you run? Why did you kill the guard? Why did you murder that woman in the woods?"

Raven's head lolled back until he was looking at the sky, clear and sunny. "I was tired of being a prisoner. He tried to stop me from leaving. The sword I stole both had Draug magic and demon obsidian, which fucked with my head and made me think she was a Nightmare." He tilted his head to the side, glaring at Hawthorn with half-lidded eyes. "Anything else you're wondering about?"

Hawthorn opened his mouth, then closed it again, and then opened it again. "The sword? The one from the First Cataclysm? It had *demon obsidian*?"

Raven shrugged and looked back over the lake. "That's what Ashleigh said. He seems to know more about this shit than I do."

"He is an—" Hawthorn hesitated—"interesting man."

"I suppose."

"How have you found him?"

Raven looked back at the elf, the first time he'd properly done so since they left the cave. He frowned, his brows furrowed. "What do you mean?"

"I mean it must be odd, spending time with a man with a reputation like his."

"By Astraea, can you sorcerers ever speak plainly?"

Hawthorn's eyes widened. "You really don't know?"

Raven glowered.

"He's Ashleigh Umber."

"It rings a bell . . ." Raven frowned, thinking back to his studies in Aethic military history. He rarely paid attention in his classes, especially concerning the recent history of the continent, but the name Umber did seem vaguely familiar. "He was some sort of general, wasn't he? Was he very important?"

Hawthorn chuckled, which only made Raven more frustrated. He was very tempted to push the elf into the lake but figured that would do nothing to endear himself to Tessia.

"Ashleigh Umber," Hawthorn explained, "the usurper of the Aethic throne, and father to Queen Elspeth. He almost started a civil war after he attempted to assassinate King Harold but was spared from the executioner's block by High Dragonguard Lyanna."

The first two sounded *vaguely* familiar, but even someone like Raven, who had no interest in Aethic politics, knew of Queen Elspeth and King Harold. And everyone from Orcanum to Dejar knew of Lyanna Gael, the first Dragonguard in the history of the Cataclysms to slay a Dragon Lord and live to tell the tale.

"Wow, that's . . . Wow. He has a daughter?"

Hawthorn raised an eyebrow. "Yes, and his actions also indirectly led to the death of nearly every Dragonguard in Aethel."

"What about his wife?"

Hawthorn looked at him like he'd lost his mind, and Raven honestly wasn't sure he could correct him on that.

"As far as I know, Lady Umber passed shortly before the Tenth Cataclysm. Do you not care about the rest?"

Raven shrugged. "Nobody's perfect. Besides, the Cataclysm was ten years ago, and he's a Dragonguard now. Surely you can't expect me to believe *you* are the same person you were ten years ago?"

Hawthorn didn't say anything, which Raven read as confirming his point.

"He didn't judge me when I told him what I'd done, and that was only a few months ago. What right do I have to judge his past actions?"

Once again, the elven sorcerer was silent. Raven liked him better like that. Truly, it didn't bother him that Ashleigh had a past, that he'd been a traitor to Aethel, which was likely because he didn't know much about the Tenth Cataclysm as it never reached the Free Isles. The only thing that bothered him was that he'd hid it from him. But why hadn't Ashleigh told him that he had a daughter? What was he worried about? And surely after Raven revealed himself, Ashleigh could've done the same.

Raven didn't understand why Ashleigh would hide those parts of his past. He tried to tell himself that he wasn't hurt, but he knew that was nothing but a bold-faced lie. The more he thought about it, the more it hurt. He didn't like hurting. He didn't like feeling weak. He didn't like that Ashleigh had that power over him. He didn't like that he *let* Ashleigh have that power over him. He thought about something else.

~~~

Petyr and Lady Suncrest were talking about something, but Ashleigh wasn't really listening. He was just worried about Raven and what he'd do with the blade now that he'd found it. Ashleigh couldn't keep it there, of course. Even though Raven had proven his strength in resisting it once, there was no way to tell if he'd be able to continue doing so. He trusted Raven implicitly. What he didn't trust was that blasted sword.

Ashleigh crossed his arms, pretending to pay attention to the conversation, but secretly, he was straining his ears for the music Raven had described. He had said it was similar to the Draugar's song, only more refined. Ashleigh had taken the blade out multiple times before while Raven slept or was out gathering firewood or supplies. Ashleigh had held it in his hand, but he never heard any sort of song. He could *feel* the corruption coming off it, bleeding out like a festering wound, but the blade remained silent for him. Maybe it needed to taste blood to speak with the wielder, or maybe it had bonded with Raven in some way. Both options were equally unappealing.

A draught moved through the cave, and it seemed Raven had returned. Ashleigh straightened up and stopped wringing his hands, though he wasn't sure when he'd started doing that. Raven looked better, refreshed. He still looked worried, though it didn't seem like it was from the blade. His chaperone, the elf, was with him. The elf's garnet-colored eyes had softened somewhat, and it seemed to Ashleigh that the two had come to some sort of understanding, if an uneasy one.

Raven smiled weakly when he saw Ashleigh. "Can we talk when you've finished?"
~~~

Ashleigh frowned but nodded. Before he was able to ask for more information, Raven made his way over to another corner of the cave, this one as far away from the crate with the blade as he could manage. Ashleigh turned his attention back to the other two. It was time to be a general again.

~~~

Ashleigh's fingers worked nimbly through Raven's hair, pulling it apart and combing through it. "You know, you're going to have to learn to do this yourself eventually," he said lightly.

"Why didn't you tell me you had a daughter?"

Ashleigh's fingers froze, and he swallowed heavily.

"I'm not angry," Raven said. "I just . . . Why didn't you tell me?"

"How did you find out?"

"Hawthorn, the elven sorcerer . . . he told me, among other things."

"And?"

Raven turned back to him, eyes pleading. "And I don't *care*, Ashleigh! By Astraea, do you truly think so little of me that I would . . . What? *Judge you*? Do you think me such a hypocrite?"

Ashleigh pulled his hands away and shook his head. "No, no, of course not. Raven, you're the most brilliant man I've ever met. I just . . ." He sighed. "I *liked* not being that man. Everyone I meet sees me as a traitor or a *monster*. I just liked being a man for once."

Raven nodded. "I understand. It's just . . . Can we agree to no more secrets?"

Ashleigh smiled softly and lifted a hand to brush a hair from Raven's face. "No more secrets."

Almost without his permission, Raven felt his body leaning closer, an instinctive need to feel nearer to Ashleigh. His breath caught in his throat. They were almost close enough that their lips might brush up against each other if one of them were to move ever by a hair. He was looking at Ashleigh's eyes, which were beautiful and stormy. And *Gods*, had they always been that blue? Ashleigh, however, was looking squarely at his lips.

Crack!

A sound like thunder echoed from outside the cave, causing the two of them to jump apart. Another *crack*, louder this time. The two
~~~

of them traded a look, the previous exchange quickly forgotten. Or at least they both pretended it was. Another *crack*, yet louder, and this time accompanied by an unmistakable flash of iridescence.

"A portal?" Raven suggested breathlessly, eyes wide as they remained fixed on the doorway.

Ashleigh nodded.

Suddenly, there was a loud *bang* on the flimsy wooden door. Something was trying to get in.

"Nightmares," they both said in unison.

Ashleigh and Raven leapt from the bed. They were not dressed for battle, and were both in linen tunics and trousers. Raven wore a small rabbit's fur shawl, but that was solely for warmth and would offer little in terms of protection from a Nightmares' assault. The door splintered with the force of a second attack, and it was very apparent that time was running out.

Ashleigh grabbed his blade, fine sharp silver, perfect for cutting down Nightmares and Draugar alike. Raven cursed as he reached for his. In all the chaos leading up to Tessia's arrival, he hadn't managed to visit Caer Deaglan to get a new blade. This one seemed to grow more brittle with every strike, and he was beginning to notice hairline fractures along the edge and fuller. He just hoped it would carry him through this fight. Then he could get a new one before they travelled to the Red Wastes. He did his best to ignore the perfectly good—the perfectly *sublime*—blade in a crate no more than ten feet from him.

The wooden door split down the middle, revealing a creature cloaked in shadows that moved like silk with large spiked pauldrons and a jagged metal helmet.

Raven surged forward, not bothering to check if Ashleigh was following. The Nightmare swiped a clawed hand at him, but he ducked, going after its "legs," if they could even be called that. He must've hit something important because the Nightmare cried out, swiping wildly at him. Raven grinned, but it seemed that he had gotten too cocky.

He felt a burst of hot white pain in his shoulder and hissed, dropping his sword. He rolled out of the way of the shade's claws. Hissing, he glanced toward the source of the pain. His shoulder was completely scorched, and the skin was burnt and bubbling, glowing with a faint purple light. He tried to lift his arm, but evidently, it was out of commission for the time being. He internally cursed himself for not seriously considering it when Janus suggested he learn how to fight with his non-dominant arm.

He sighed, picked up his discarded blade, and readied himself to rejoin the defense. He glanced over the shade's shoulder to see a pale violet wisp hovering in the doorway. Before he could strike, though, an arrow soared through the air from behind him and struck the creature's incorporeal skull. The wraith crumbled to the ground, an inky pool of ichor forming under it.

Good, Raven thought. *Ashleigh has his bow.* Ashleigh was always better at long range; the blade was where Raven found his footing.

Another arrow penetrated the shade's neck, causing it to stumble back but not fall. It gave Raven the opening he needed. He lunged, stabbing into the center of the creature's chest. It screeched again, flailing its arms toward him like a cornered animal. He withdrew his blade, and the shade collapsed into a pile of rags.

He turned back to Ashleigh, smiling widely. Ashleigh's look of concentration quickly turned to horror, and he shouted. Raven frowned, but before he could turn to see the threat that loomed behind him, he felt a sharp warmth from his lower stomach. He looked down and whimpered. Three long claws, sickly green in color, protruded from the space below his ribs. Bright red blood oozed from the punctures, staining the entire bottom of his tunic sanguine.

Another shirt ruined, he thought irritably, quickly becoming dizzy from the rapid blood loss.

The Nightmare withdrew its claw and tossed him aside. His skull cracked against a crate, making his head spin.

Something's broken, surely. Maybe another concussion?

Raven glanced to his side, to his sword. As if the situation couldn't get any worse, it was completely shattered, leaving only a jagged edge near the hilt. He groaned, clutching his stomach. He was losing blood, and fast. Too fast. He was dying. He put his one remaining functional hand on top of the crate. His blood coated the wood, and he almost slipped on the sticky substance but was able to maintain his balance. He couldn't see Ashleigh. He had no way of knowing if he was even still alive.

His ears rang, making it impossible to make out any noise, except one—the one noise he didn't want to hear but desperately needed to.

His blood dripped through the slits between the wood, pooling onto what was held within. The song grew into a forte, just slightly lessening the buzzing in his head. He glanced back at his broken sword; the shattered pieces were scattered across the cave floor. His left arm hung limply at his side, but still he turned to try to open the crate.

He hadn't come this far just to die in a fucking cave. His fingers dug into the space between the planks, pulling with what little strength he had left. Unfortunately, Ashleigh had affixed the lid tightly—a good idea at the time, perhaps, but one that was quickly making Raven's life infinitely more difficult now. Something in one of his fingers snapped, and he screamed. But he didn't hear it, and he didn't stop. Finally, he was able to gain some purchase. It felt like his wrist was about to be ripped from its socket. Even still, he pulled. The wood splintered slightly at the point above his hand, and it seemed his blood had somehow weakened the timber. It gave him enough encouragement to continue.

He heard two sounds at once, extremely similar in nature. One was the wood snapping open, revealing his dark blade, pulsing brighter than ever. The other was the snap of his wrist bone. He sobbed, staring at his bloodied and limp hand. This was it. He was going to die without ceremony or glory, with nothing but blood and the stone walls of the cave to remember him. Suddenly, the out of the deep onyx blade shot tendrils of red smoke, wrapping around his wounded hand. He screamed. But the music was too loud now, and his voice only added to the deafening dirge. He tried to pull away but was already very weak, and whatever magic was used to forge this blade was ancient and powerful.

The tendrils snaked up his arm until it was entirely bound in sanguineous shadows. It burned his skin, but it was almost a rejuvenating burn, like a blaze scouring the weeds and underbrush from the forest. He felt strong, and he looked back down at his hand. It was entirely enveloped in crimson smoke. He flexed his fingers. They tingled with something—something ancient and powerful.

Raven glanced back at the doorway. It seemed the Nightmares had written him off, left him for dead. He took ahold of his dominant arm, allowing the mist to travel over and envelope it as well. Almost as soon as the blade's magic touched his skin, the sensation returned to his arm. First came the burn, the agony, and then the buzz of potential. He would've cried with relief if his body wasn't so flush with adrenaline that he could think of nothing other than fighting.

The sword was radiant with heat and light, the previously coal black blade now a deep ruby red, matching the obsidian stones on its hilt. He reached in, his hand wrapping around the tightly bound leather of the hilt. Oh, how he missed that warmth. He withdrew the blade from its wooden sarcophagus, marveling as its magic shot for his stomach and stitched the wounds together with precise, painful incisions.

He clenched his teeth, turning back to the Nightmares. His vision itself seemed tinged with blood, a slight red haze over everything. Had the red smoke travelled to his face? He couldn't tell, and he didn't care. His head felt light, but every other part of his body felt strong, stronger than he had felt since . . . ever. He'd never felt this kind of power before.

Is this how sorcerers feel all the time? No, he decided. *This is how* gods *feel.*

He moved like water—no, like blood—through the assembled horde. Every move was through instinct, the centuries of the blade's existence and experience filling him with the knowledge and skill of its previous wielders. He couldn't even keep track of the Nightmares he cut down. Eventually, he was just a flurry of blood and black ichor. It was hard to tell where he ended and the carnage began. Every time he cut one down, its life force ebbed into the blade, filling him with a renewed vigor and a renewed bloodlust.

His blade embedded itself into the chest of another Nightmare, and its fluids sprayed into his face. But this time, he didn't resist the urge to lick his lips. Salty, like sweat, with an earthy aftertaste. Like a mouthful of mud. The Nightmare crumpled to the ground, and Raven prepared himself for the next attack, only to find the chamber entirely empty. He frowned, letting his arms fall to his side.

That was when he finally saw him. Ashleigh was splayed out on the ground, a massive gash lacerating him from shoulder to hip. The fog seemed to clear from Raven's eyes, and he rushed toward Ashleigh, dropping the blade in the process. It clattered loudly and pulsed weakly, seemingly whining, but he wasn't paying any mind to that. All of his focus was solely on Ashleigh, on his weakening breath. Raven knelt down next to him and began trying to stem the bleeding, muttering prayers to every god he'd ever heard of in any book he'd ever read. He pressed his hands over the wound, clenching his eyes shut and praying quietly.

"Please, Gods, not him, not *yet*. I can't lose him yet."

Ashleigh's eyes fluttered open weakly, and he almost didn't recognize the man kneeling over him. His face was framed by his hair, drenched in a combination of dark red blood and black-brown ichor, coloring it a dark color. His eyes were wide and bloodshot, the whites completely invisible behind the film that covered them. His whole body seemed to glow with an unearthly red light, but the longer he stood over him, the dimmer it got.

"Raven?" Ashleigh grunted.

Raven let out a sigh of relief. "Gods, I thought you . . . I thought I'd . . . *Fuck!* I'm glad you're all right."

Ashleigh tried to push himself up from the ground but cried out and fell back. "Perhaps 'all right' is a bit of an exaggeration."

Raven cursed. "Do you have any healing potions?"

Ashleigh nodded, groaning as he pointed to a small chest next to his bed. Raven scrambled over to it, grabbed the largest potion he could find, and brought it back to him. Ashleigh was still unable to lift himself up, so Raven gently placed his hand under Ashleigh's head and lifted the potion to his lips. He was careful to not pour it too quickly so that Ashleigh wouldn't choke. Raven knew what to do from giving his father his medicine early in his illness, before the doctors decided it'd be safest for him not to see his father.

"There." Raven poured the last of the potion into his mouth. "Feel any better?"

Ashleigh grunted, straining to look down at his chest. The gash hadn't scabbed over yet. But the bleeding had stopped, and it looked like it was starting to clot. He smiled weakly and nodded.

"All right. Do you think you can stand? We need to move you onto your bed."

Ashleigh clenched his teeth and nodded. Raven didn't entirely believe him, but he helped him to sit up. Raven wrapped his arm under Ashleigh's shoulders and pulled him to his feet. Ashleigh's fists were balled and white; he was clearly in pain but was too bull-headed to say anything.

Raven sighed and rolled his eyes. "Stubborn old man."

Raven's bed was closer so he moved in that direction . Ashleigh protested because, of course, he did, but Raven would have none of it. He laid Ashleigh down onto the bed, resting his head on his nice goose-down pillows, one of the few things he'd insisted on getting from Caer Deaglan.

"There. Now you need to rest. We'll leave for the Red Wastes as soon as you've regained your strength."

"But Lady Suncrest—"

"Her Eminence will have to wait for you to be well, Ashleigh. You wouldn't let me out of the cave for ages after my initiation. Now, I get to return the favor."

Raven smiled mischievously, but it wasn't hard to see the very real concern behind his eyes. The red film had mostly vanished, except for around the center of his iris. It seemed whatever magic had caused it had left a stain on him. Ashleigh didn't have time to ask, but Raven seemed to read his intention.

"I used the blade," Raven said.

Ashleigh's eyes widened.

"My sword had shattered. I would've died. You have to believe me—I had no choice!"

Ashleigh nodded. "I do."

Raven had planned on rebuking whatever criticism Ashleigh might've leveled against him, so he was caught off guard by his acceptance. "I'm going to get rid of it, Ashleigh. I'm going to put it somewhere it'll never hurt anyone ever again."

"Where?"

"I could tell you, but then I'd have to kill you," Raven said jokingly. "It's better if you don't know."

Only a few weeks ago, Ashleigh would've tried to stop him. He would've demanded he tell him his plan. But now? Now, Ashleigh trusted Raven more than he'd trusted anyone for a very, very long time.

Raven leaned close and placed a chaste kiss on his forehead, smiling slightly as he pulled away. "Don't move, all right? I'll be back in a little bit."

Ashleigh nodded, too caught off guard by the affection to say anything.

Raven stood up and walked to the blade's place on the ground. He leaned over to pick it up, only hesitating slightly when weak red tendrils reached up to meet him. He took a deep breath and wrapped his fist around it. The warmth wasn't comforting this time. It was a reminder of the people he'd hurt, of the lives he'd ended before their time.

Karya.

He was doing this for Karya. He pushed open the door to the tunnel and was blinded by the light of a gently pulsing portal.

CHAPTER FIFTEEN

Dinas Fridd was a fortress situated in the heart of the Red Wastes. In the past, it had been home to the Dragonguard of Valmera, but now the Harbinger's forces had gathered there. To say that Dinas Fridd was big would be a disservice, not only to the structure but to the common tongue itself.

It was built in the Twilight Age shortly before the Second Cataclysm with the help of the dwarves. It had repelled countless Draugar assaults. But then, Draugar didn't use siege weaponry. It wouldn't be enough to bring down the walls, but it would damn well rattle the forces within. And it might be enough to draw their attention just long enough for Lady Suncrest and her allies to slip past their defenses.

"This is a foolish plan, my lady. I urge you to reconsider." Ashleigh crossed his arms over his chest. He was decked out in full Dragonguard regalia and looked every bit the general as he did in his prime. Raven thought he looked quite dashing, but he'd never admit it to him.

"And what precisely would you suggest I do, oh, master tactician?" Tessia bit back.

For her part, Tessia was dressed in Valmeran-style fatigues that the diplomat, Lady Alcàntara, had commissioned for her for just this occasion. Despite the Valmerans' usual tendencies toward form over function, the armor was sturdy and flexible and fit like a glove.

"Send your soldiers in ahead of you. Let them clear a path. There's no reason for you to put yourself into danger unnecessarily."

She narrowed her eyes. "Our men are not *disposable*, Ashleigh."

He opened his mouth to protest, but Raven cut him off. "Lady Suncrest won't be alone, Ashleigh. We're bringing a few soldiers along, and she'll have her friends, Petyr, and the two of us." He continued addressing Ashleigh but made eye contact with Tessia. "We will not let her fall."

Tessia smiled slightly.

And that was when they heard the signal. It wasn't hard to miss—fifteen vessels of black powder, positioned at key points around the fortress, going off in perfect unison. Petyr had a contact in Orcanum, one who was happy to pay off a debt she owed him.

Immediately, chaos erupted. Even from their place outside the fortress, the group could hear the chaos unfolding within. There were men shouting, most in the common tongue but some in Valmeran. Tessia thought she could even hear some Dejari curses in there, but it was hard to tell.

Just around the corner, Edric was barking orders to his troops over the clamor of battle. The sound of the battering ram crashing against the gate rang out, and the cracking of wood mixed with the sound of cracking skulls as the Harbinger's Dragonguard and the Nightmares they'd summoned hurled rocks down from the battlements. It was overwhelming, to say the least. No one assembled had ever been a part of anything like this. Even Ashleigh, who had lived a good portion of his life as a celebrated general, had never taken part in a siege of this scale.

Lady Suncrest and the rest moved forward toward the small escape tunnel that Isadora's contacts had discovered, but Ashleigh and Raven hung back for a moment.

"Are you ready?" Raven placed his hand on his blade.

It was a sturdy thing, made of deep green oxidized bronze. It was well-balanced and glowed with a pale light due to a demon-slaying enchantment that the legion's arcanist had made for him.

Ashleigh nodded. "This is not my first time seeing battle. In truth, I worry more for *your* mental state."

"I . . . I'll be fine, I think. I feel more myself than I have in a long time. I trust myself for the first time in a long time."

Ashleigh smiled. "Right. Then let's go kill those bastards."

The sound was ear-piercing as a Nightmare, a great green thing with spindly limbs and a tail spiked like briar, fell to Raven's blade. He wiped the sticky black ichor from his face and smiled at his ally.

Lady Suncrest had ordered them to split up into groups to make way for the forces on the battlements. Tessia, Minthe, and Dame Nestra had been one, Ashleigh and Petyr had been another, and Raven and Hawthorn had formed the third group.

Hawthorn was a strange man, and Raven found himself wondering more than once if he was "all there," so to speak. Nevertheless, he was a formidable sorcerer and seemed to be even more so when Lady Suncrest wasn't present. Raven assumed it was a sorcerer tradition; perhaps if his superior was one as well, he would be expected to act less powerful than them to preserve their ego. It didn't make much sense, granted, but very little about magic made sense to Raven.

"Well done, Dragonguard," Hawthorn said, panting, taking a moment to rest his weight on his staff. "You wield that blade well for one who not so long ago was a nobleman."

Raven laughed. "You haven't seen anything yet, sorcerer."

Hawthorn rolled his eyes, and Raven rushed back into the fray. This blade was different from the onyx blade. Fighting with it felt less natural in a way, and he was aware of the sword as a separate piece to him rather than an extension of his arm. He felt like a newborn deer trying to find its legs for the first time.

Despite his apprehension, the green blade whizzed through the air, cleanly removing a maddened Dragonguard sorcerer's arm from her body. Unnervingly, she didn't scream, she didn't even flinch. She just picked up her staff with her other hand and continued casting. The idea that one could have their mind lost to them so completely that the loss of a limb would be nothing more than an inconvenience was unsettling, to say the least.

Raven recoiled back, narrowly dodging a ball of electric blue energy that the sorcerer launched at his face. He growled and, lowering his body, swiped for her abdomen. The blood that burst forth was black and rancid, smelling acrid and sour like rotting meat. The smell of the corruption was unmistakable, but it shouldn't have been this intense in such a young woman. Whatever the Harbinger had done to them had embedded the rot so deeply into them that the Dragonguard were barely even alive. It seemed that killing them would be a greater mercy than any other Raven was able to offer.

The sorcerer stumbled back and, dropping her staff, reached for her stomach to stop the viscera from spilling out. Despite her efforts, shriveled brown entrails slipped from her grasp and stained her copper and red robes black.

Raven raised his blade to finish her off, but before he had the chance, she was immolated by blue flame. He turned to glare at the sorcerer responsible.

"I *had* her," he growled breathlessly.

Instead of answering him, Hawthorn let another fireball fly, missing Raven by a hair's breadth and causing the blue wraith that hovered behind him to be immediately incinerated.

"Show off," Raven muttered to himself, not quite missing the cocky smirk that appeared on Hawthorn's face.

It seemed like the elf was about to say something, but before he had the chance to do so, a sphere of purplish-blue electricity connected with his chest, sending him flying ten feet back and landing flat on his ass. Raven would have laughed if it didn't look like the massive Nightmare responsible was gearing up to do the same thing to him.

"Fucking Nightmare magical bullshit!" he shouted to no one in particular as he dashed around the beast's legs, trying to find some kind of opening to take it out.

The thing was covered head to toe in plates of jagged black chitin. It just laughed as arrows from soldiers who'd managed to make it over the wall bounced harmlessly off it. Raven tried to think back to what Hawthorn had told him about Nightmares as they crept through the catacombs beneath the fortress.

"Nightmares are humanity's greatest sins and fears made manifest, and every Nightmare has a weakness. You just need to find it and exploit it. Their weaknesses are often apparent in their nature, so start with that."

Their nature, their nature . . . Fuck, what kind of sin was this? Not avarice, not sloth, not lust . . . *What would be so sure of itself as to laugh at its enemies' failings?*

"Pride!" he said aloud. But then, what was he going to do with that?

Exploit it. But how do you exploit pride? Right. By feeding it!

This time, when the Nightmare swung at him, he dodged it but not as swiftly as he could have. He could feel the heat of the attack on his neck, smell the acrid ozone in the air, and taste the static in the back of his throat.

Raven felt the air leave his lungs as he stumbled and hit the ground hard. His hands stung as tiny bits of gravel and debris pierced his flesh and burrowed into his bloody palms. He cringed, clenching his hands into fists, and stumbled to his feet. He turned back to the Nightmare and held out his sword in front of him, his arms trembling slightly.

"That . . . all . . . you got?" he said, panting.

The Nightmare sneered and lunged at him, swiping with one of its claws. Raven's armor protected him from any serious damage, but it didn't stop him from skidding across the battlefield. His back slammed into a large stone turret, but he managed to remain conscious as he fell to one knee. He raised his head, watching keenly as the Nightmare laughed at his humiliation.

Then he smiled and blew a stray hair from his face. He'd have to ask Ashleigh to tighten his braid once they reconvened. The Nightmare raised its hand to attack again, and Raven took a bolt of lightning straight to the chest. Were it not for the magic-dampening enchantments of his cuirass, he would've been cooked where he stood. The Nightmare laughed as Rave fell onto both knees. He was shaking from the white-hot lightning still dancing across the tender skin of his cheeks.

That's going to leave a scar.

As Raven rose to his feet, the Nightmare didn't stop laughing. Its six heather-toned eyes were closed in its rapture, its head slung back, and its chest shaking with every roar. Then it stopped laughing. Instead of deep gravelly hysterics, pitch-black ichor gurgled from its jowls and dripped down onto its chest.

Raven grinned, his sword buried deep into the creature's exposed fleshy throat. The Nightmare blinked in shock and then let out one final pitiful chuckle before it slumped to its knees and keeled over to the side. Raven smiled and turned back to the elf in order to taunt him with his prowess.

Shit, Hawthorn!

The sorcerer was still where the Nightmare had sent him at the start of the fight, lying face up and completely out cold. There was a small puddle of blood beginning to form under his head, and his breaths were slow and labored.

Raven cursed under his breath. "Don't you dare die, you son of a bitch." He reached into his satchel and began fishing around for a healing potion.

Empty.

He discarded the useless bag and started to feel around for where Hawthorn wore his. He momentarily thought how strange this whole thing must look without context, but he quickly banished the thought when his fingers brushed against the distinctively cool glass. He quickly yanked it from where it was fastened at his side and began fiddling with the cap.

"Come on, come on . . ." he muttered, his bloody hands sliding uselessly across the bottle. "Fuck it."

Raven brought the bottle to his mouth and bit down on the stopper at the top. With one swift yank of his neck, the cork came free. He spat it out onto the ground and carefully lifted the sorcerer's head before bringing the potion to his lips. They parted ever so slightly, and he was able to empty the contents into his mouth. Within moments, Hawthorn's eyes opened, and he coughed harshly, spittle and blood flying everywhere, even reaching Raven's face.

"Oh, for—" His hands instinctively shot up to cover his mouth, dropping Hawthorn's head in the process.

Fortunately, Hawthorn was able to stop his skull from cracking against the stone. He glared at Raven. His attitude changed, however, when he saw the slowly disintegrating body of the Nightmare and the various legion soldiers just beginning to make their way onto the battlements.

"Did you—"

"Yes, all by myself. Now, come," Raven insisted, wrapping his arm under Hawthorn's shoulder and pulling him to his feet. "Her Eminence is waiting."

As it turned out, Lady Suncrest was not waiting, at least not in the courtyard with the Dragonguard. Hawthorn and Raven were the first to arrive, followed shortly after by Ashleigh and Petyr, and then finally, Lady Suncrest and the rest. Raven had planned to tease Ashleigh when he saw him next and brag about how he single-handedly took down a Nightmare bigger than a Draug goliath, but when he saw Ashleigh, any thought of that left his mind. Ashleigh was covered in blood, some of which must've been his own, and his shield arm hung uselessly at his side.

Raven couldn't do anything to help him, however, because that was when High Dragonguard Ghiselle Fontaine started talking. She had led the Dragonguard of Valmera for the last fifteen years wisely and fairly, but this time, her eyes were clouded by fear and doubt.

"Dragonguard! We have been betrayed by the very world we swore to protect!"

She was standing at the top of a staircase, joined by a tall creature with skin that shone like black obsidian and inscrutable ruby eyes. It was at least eight feet tall and cloaked in ragged robes that hung off it at odd angles, exposing its rotted and pockmarked skin. On its head, it wore a jagged crown made of corroded red iron with gaping holes that might have once housed precious stones; now they were empty save for the bits of rust that occasionally broke off and drifted down over the creature's expressionless face—the Harbinger.

"This so-called legion has come to stop us, claiming erroneously to have divine purpose! They are nothing but false prophets!"

The High Dragonguard pointed her staff at Tessia, and Minthe's hand tightened on her bow.

"I didn't come here to kill Dragonguards!" Lady Suncrest declared. "You must see that you've gone too far. The Harbinger doesn't care about the Dragonguard. It only wants the return of Wyveria. Look at what's become of your people, Fontaine."

Some of the Dragonguards hesitated, looking at one another.

"Is this what Lyanna would've wanted from the order?" Ashleigh spoke up, a pleading tone in his ragged voice. "The High Dragonguard gave her life to stop the Cataclysms, but not like this. *Please*, Ghiselle."

The other Dragonguards started to murmur among themselves, discontent spreading between them. Fontaine turned to the Harbinger and seemed to converse with it, though its face didn't change and the thin line that made up its mouth didn't move.

What interrupted the growing unease was the ear-piercing scream of a massive black dragon as it landed on the tower across the courtyard. Its scales pulsed with red light, with demon obsidian inlaid into its very flesh to form an extra layer of scales over its body.

Dragons had been thought of as extinct for centuries, the last of the Great Wyrms thought exterminated by the original Dragonguard around the end of the Twilight Age. Growing up, Raven had seen the mounted heads of amphitheres in his father's great hall, legless winged reptiles the size of horses with teeth as large as carving knives. He'd even seen illustrations of dragons in books that fascinated him as a child, but nothing could've prepared him for the sheer scale of this beast. It towered over them, its tail alone large enough to fall an entire battalion of men. Its skull was big enough to swallow a mounted soldier hole, and when it opened its mouth, it was nothing but a black void, lined as far back as he could see with rows and rows of uneven teeth.

For a long moment, Raven found himself frozen, unable to move or even breathe. His vision tunneled, and he could hear nothing but his own heartbeat in his ears. And just for a moment, so quickly anyone else would've missed it or written it off entirely, the dragon turned its head. Raven could feel that it was looking at *him*. He let out a breath and realized that the beast's chest and his were moving in perfect tandem.

Then a hard metal gauntlet latched onto his arm. He jumped and turned to see Petyr's hand.

"We'll have time to admire it *after* it's dead." Petyr nodded and then gestured to where the others were already chasing after Fontaine.

Raven smiled tightly, ignoring the sudden empty feeling that had begun to form in his stomach.

It seemed that with every step, Nightmares erupted from the ground, doing everything in their power to impede the group's progress.

"Why is it always shitting Nightmares?" Minthe whined as one of her arrows landed squarely in one of the big green things' throats.

"You're doing great, lover!" Tessia shouted back, quickly raising a barrier around her to block the incoming attack from a particularly hardy wraith.

Minthe rolled her eyes and jumped backward, letting a barrage of arrows go, which pierced two Nightmares through the top of their heads.

"Petyr, do you have eyes on Fontaine?" Tessia raised her hand and quickly slammed down, bringing a wave of force crushing down on a shade with dark robes.

He launched a fireball into the fray. "No such luck! Last I saw her, she was headed for the bridge!"

Dame Nestra grumbled, slashing a searing blade across the chest of a Nightmare of her own and then quickly downing a healing potion. With the final Nightmare defeated, Tessia grasped her staff tight and weaved Phantasma around her feet, which sent her forward with great speed, hopefully enough to catch up to Fontaine. The rest followed after her, but without the aid of magic, they quickly fell behind.

Lady Suncrest easily reached the bridge first, coming to a stop quickly as Fontaine hurled balls of lightning at the Harbinger. The electricity connected with the creature's chest, searing away the loose fabric, but it showed no reaction, only looking at her with the same impassive eyes.

"You destroyed the Dragonguard!" Fontaine accused, her voice cracking and her hand crackling with vibrant violet energy.

"You did that to yourself." The Harbinger's spoke for the first time, a faint sense of amusement behind every syllable. It's voice was soft and melodic, and held an almost paternal tone to it, if you ignored the venom behind its words. "I only lit the match. You were all too eager to set the blaze."

Fontaine raised her hand to finish it off, eyes burning with righteous fury. Then the jagged teeth of the dragon sank deep into her stomach, and Fontaine was lifted off her feet. She was then flung into the air and smacked bonelessly against the far wall.

Then the dragon dropped down behind the party and began slowly slinking toward them. Once again, Raven could *feel* the dragon looking at him with something between hunger and familiarity. The empty pit in his stomach deepened, which he now recognized as a mutual feeling of *hunger*.

As the dragon stepped over the still form of Fontaine, her body seemed to stir in defiance of the blood quickly escaping the gaping wound where her stomach once was. Her hand raised, once more crackling with energy. The dragon lunged.

"*Va en enfer*, you son of a bitch!" Fontaine let forth a massive bolt of lightning.

It shot through the dragon's chest and sent it stumbling off-kilter. It overshot to where Lady Suncrest and her group stood, tumbling headfirst into the already-crumbling stone bridge and into the deep chasm below.

The dragon disappeared over the edge, but the trouble wasn't over.

The bridge began to crack and crumble. Ashleigh, who was at the back, wasn't quick enough, and his foot slipped off the side. Tessia grabbed his hand, pulled him from the edge, and they continued to run. The edge of the bridge was in sight, just a heartbeat away. Another step, and they'd be home free.

But when Tessia's foot fell, it didn't meet stone. It met air, and she began a free fall. Everything seemed to slow down. Tessia could see those falling around her—everyone except Dame Nestra and Minthe. She felt the air around her pulse, the sharp smell of ozone permeating her every sense. The last thing she saw was a blinding flash of iridescence, and then came darkness.

Chapter Sixteen

Black.
White.
Black.
White.
Blackwhiteblackwhiteblack . . .
Red.

Raven could see the breath in front of his face, but that was just about all he could see. The rain that came down all around him was heavy, and the fog on the ground rose up to his knees to block the path in front of him from view. The smell of death hung heavy in the air, so he could be relatively sure he was in the Mirewoods.

He trudged through the mud toward a small flickering light in the distance. He wasn't sure what he expected to find there, but anything would be better than this miserable weather. The light grew larger and brighter, and suddenly, it seemed less like a structure and more like a lantern gently swaying in the wind and carried by a figure cloaked in shadow.

"Hello?" He jogged toward the figure. "Can you help me, sir? I think I might've lost my way."

Raven reached out to grab the figure's shoulder, but the moment he made contact, it collapsed into a pile of loose fabric. The lantern shattered on the ground and plunged him into darkness. Raven dropped to his knees, frantically feeling for anything to alleviate his blindness. Instead of cold mud, however, his hands hit hard stone. When he looked up it wasn't raining anymore.

He was in a ruin surrounded by blackened bodies and charred stone. Everything as far as he could see was covered in a layer of ash, and all was quiet except for his own labored breaths. He was in the epicenter of a great explosion. He was at the Temple of Last Rest. Raven scrambled to his feet and turned in every direction, desperately searching for any sign of life.

"You killed them all, Percy," a voice in his ear hissed.

Raven quickly drew his blade and turned, only to find the space empty.

"St-stay back!" he shouted into the air.

In response, the voice only laughed.

"I'm n-not afraid of you!"

"Oh, but you *are*, little dragon."

The voice seemed to come from right behind him, so without thinking, he swung his blade. It connected but not with the source of the voice. A young man, no older than himself, stared in dismay as Raven withdrew his sword from his throat. Blood gurgled from the young man's mouth, and his eyes rolled back into his head. Then he collapsed.

"No!" Raven exclaimed, stumbling back from the corpse frantically.

"Killing is what you *do*, little dragon. Embrace it!"

This time, when Raven swung his sword, it whistled through the air. There was shockingly little blood as, this time, an elven woman's head was cleanly removed from her body. Raven screamed and started running.

The voice laughed, and the sound seemed to come from all around him at once. Every time he swung his sword, someone else fell. First, it was strangers, young men and women he was certain he'd seen before but couldn't remember where. Then it was people he knew. His sword sank deep into his mother's belly. It sliced across his brothers' chests. It slashed across his guardsmen's faces. And then the next thing he knew, it was straight through the heart of his dearest and oldest friend. Janus's face was vacant and empty as he fell to his knees, his sword clattering from his hand.

"Stop this, *please*!" Raven screamed, the tears that welled in his eyes clouding his vision.

"You could end this if you wished, but you *do not* wish that, do you?" The voice laughed. "You *like* the power. You *like* the killing!"

Raven's grip tightened on his blade, and he pulled it out of his friend's chest.

"No!" His voice thundered through the clearing, shattering the rocks like glass.

The next moment, he was falling, falling, falling through the air, through the pitch black of the void. He landed on his back, and then someone was on top of him, a gloved hand covering his mouth.

"Shh! Don't worry. It's only me."

As the figure removed his glove from his mouth, Raven gasped. "Ashleigh?"

Ashleigh stepped away and held out a hand to him. Raven gratefully took it and was easily pulled to his feet.

"H-how did you find me?" Raven shuddered, looking around.

He wasn't in the Mirewoods anymore, nor was he in the ruin from before. The air was hot and dry and tasted of sand. Large white pillars rose up around them with intricate carvings all across them. They depicted great battles and great heroes—heroes who wore the Great Wyrm's head on their breastplate.

"Where . . . where *are* we?" He frowned.

Ashleigh's brows furrowed. "I believe this is meant to be the Watchtower, the Dragonguard's headquarters. I've only been there once myself, but it seems my memories were enough with which to construct this . . . illusion."

"What?" Raven turned back to Ashleigh.

"Surely you must've realized this isn't real. This is Phantasma, the birthplace of magic," Ashleigh explained. "We've entered the domain of a Nightmare or something like it . . ."

The more Raven looked at the reliefs on the walls, the less *real* they seemed. The horses had too many legs. The riders had too many fingers. Not to mention the eyes—they seemed to follow him wherever he looked.

"I don't . . . I just don't remember—"

Ashleigh cut him off. "It doesn't matter. We must reach the others."

He was right, of course. Raven didn't remember much, but he remembered that he trusted Ashleigh. If Ashleigh had a plan, Raven would follow him.

Then Ashleigh started moving, not waiting for Raven to follow. The pair weaved their way through the labyrinthian fortress, but Ashleigh's memory seemed solid because he never faltered for a moment. The structure was entirely empty save for the two of them, but they both held their swords in a defensive position as they moved.

Suddenly, Ashleigh turned off into a hallway, and Raven lost sight of him. When he rounded the corner, he found a pitch-dark passageway that seemed to extend forever into nothingness. His throat bobbed, and he considered turning back. But his blade pulsed with pale energy, and he was urged forward.

Once again, he was plunged into darkness. This time, he had the light of his blade to guide him, but he still did not relish stumbling through a dark passageway into the unknown.

"Ashleigh!" he called into the darkness.

"Come on!"

Ashleigh's voice sounded far away, much farther away than he should've been able to get in the time it took for Raven to round the corner after him. Had Ashleigh run ahead? Raven would've heard the clatter of his heavy armor if he had, wouldn't he?

"Ashleigh?" he called back again, but this time, Ashleigh's reply sounded so far away that Raven couldn't make out any of the words.

Then he heard something behind him—quiet at first, then louder, skittering like a hundred tiny footsteps, covering every inch of the stone. And then something else came—laughter. It was getting closer.

Raven didn't think; he just ran. The sound of heavy footfalls against the stone rang in his ears. It was getting wetter. He must be heading deeper underground, but he knew that whatever he did, he *must not slip*. He didn't know what would happen if he did, but he knew he'd never leave that tunnel.

He didn't worry about being heard. That *thing*, whatever it was, already knew where he was and what he'd had done since he got here. This was *its* domain, and Raven was a fly trapped in its web. He couldn't hope to hide from whatever it was. All he could do was *run*.

"I will catch you, you know. I will *always* catch you, little dragon." The voice cackled. "You cannot escape your fear!"

"Fuck you!" Raven screamed back.

And then he did the unimaginable. Raven slipped on the wet stone, and the darkness overtook him.

~~~

Tessia's hands were shaking. She was in Phantasma. That much would be obvious to any sorcerer, but aside from that, it was hard to tell. She remembered falling. She remembered reaching her hand out, and then . . . nothing.

No, she remembered the light, the smell of ozone, the iridescent shimmer in the air. It seemed that, once more, the Gods had interceded on her behalf, and a portal between the waking world and Phantasma, the realm of dreams and spirits, had opened for them. She examined her surroundings, knowing well of the Nightmares that would try to tempt her.

Her surroundings resembled her room at Eastwell College, but it seemed to shimmer like a mirage.

"I will *not* be your plaything," Tessia snarled.

Then she heard a whisper in her ear, but she quickly waved her staff, igniting the cloaked figure that watched her from the corner. The Nightmare screamed and then vanished.

"My mind is my own."

~~~

Ashleigh was covered in blood. It was the blood of the men who had destroyed his farm, raped his mother, and killed his father. He was a young man, no more than fifteen or sixteen, but already he had seen enough atrocities to last a lifetime. Then he stood on a parapet beside Marcus, looking down at the vanquished Valmeran army.

"Ashleigh Umber, the hero of Aegisfjord," a voice whispered sweetly in his ear. Then he was on a battlefield, standing over the mangled body of his best friend's son.

"Baron Umber, the Betrayer," the voice hissed.

Next, he was at Dinas Fridd, watching as Lady Suncrest immolated Dragonguards by the dozens.

"You destroy everything you touch."

Then Raven was on his knees looking up at him, coughing and shaking. Deep black veins spread up his neck, and his eyes were milky white. "Please, kill me," he pleaded, thick black blood gurgling up from his throat.

"You doomed him to a life of service to a world that doesn't care for him and a miserable death in the dark, and for what? Pity?"

Now Ashleigh was the one on his knees, gazing up at the woman who held his life in her hands so many years ago. Lyanna had shown him a kindness he had denied his own men who died at Damon's Run in his misguided grab for power. He felt much older, but she looked just as beautiful as she did the day she deigned to show him mercy, the day she showed him pity. She raised her blade and pointed it at his throat. She spoke to him, her voice filled with venom and rage. It was an elven saying, common among the High Dragonguard's people from what Ashleigh had heard. He did not know the words, but he understood the meaning—she was revoking her forgiveness.

"I'm sorry," he whimpered pathetically.

She raised her blade to strike him down, but she was interrupted when her hand was severed from her arm. Lyanna let out a shriek, and her auburn hair turned to fire as she turned to face her attackers.

"You wear the face of a people not your own, creature," Hawthorn snarled as he lowered his staff, the bladed edge dripping with ichor.

"Dragonguard!" Tessia shouted, summoning a fireball in her hand. "That creature is a Nightmare. Fight it!"

Ashleigh clenched his eyes shut and shook his head. When he opened it again, instead of the young fair-folk woman he remembered, there stood a spirit cloaked in red fire. The rest of the illusion fell away, and he jumped to his feet and drew his blade on the spirit. The Nightmare leapt back but not quick enough, as the Dragonguard's blade sliced a deep gash across its chest. It stumbled, and Tessia let fly the icy sphere she had prepared. And with that, the Nightmare was dead.

"You have my thanks, Your Eminence—and you, sorcerer. I do not know how I could not see the Nightmare's deception." Ashleigh sheathed his blade and bowed his head respectfully to the two sorcerers.

Hawthorn shook his head. "Phantasma changes itself to fit your perceptions. One could not expect anyone not experienced with—"

Tessia rolled her eyes. "Phantasma is bullshit. Sorcerers like us just know how to *deal* with the bullshit."

"Yes, tactfully put, Suncrest."

Ashleigh looked around. "Where are the others? Why aren't they with you?"

"Minthe and Nestra managed to get off the bridge in time, and we haven't seen any sign of Petyr or Raven. You're the first we've found."

Petyr was a sorcerer and one who'd likely had more interactions with Nightmares than most. He would almost certainly be fine, but Ashleigh was worried for Raven. He'd never so much as *seen* real magic before the conference, and with all he'd experienced with the Draug blade . . .

Ashleigh just hoped they'd find him in time.

~~~

His throat was raw, and he could taste iron on his tongue. Still, Raven kept screaming. He didn't know how to stop. Everything around him was pitch dark, and he felt the scratchy wooden walls of his coffin closing in on him. All over his face, a hundred thousand tiny legs scuttled in and out of his mouth and nose and across his eyes, which were frozen open in terror.

He expected it to get better, for him to eventually get *used* to the fear, but every time he felt himself growing complacent, something else would be added to the mix—the smell of burning flesh, the taste of rotting food, the sound of footsteps too distant for his screams to be heard.

But now, the footsteps got louder. They hadn't done that before. And then there was the sound of digging and cracking wood. Then a hand reached through and pulled him out.

"Ashleigh!" Raven exclaimed, taking the first breath of fresh air in what seemed like a lifetime. "You came back for me!"

"Of course, I did. Now, take your sword, and let's go." The sword Ashleigh held out to Raven was red and angry and hummed with the music of the Draugar.

Raven felt his mouth water as he stared at the blade hungrily. "I . . ." He hesitated.

"Take it."

"I'm just not sure I should, Ashleigh."

"*Take it*, Percival!"
~~~

Raven reached to his side and found *his* blade, the blade of green metal forged and enchanted for his hand specifically. He drew it quickly and brought it to the throat of the creature wearing his friend's face.

"What are you?"

The red blade clattered to the ground and Not-Ashleigh raised his hands. "You know me. I am your friend, Percy."

Raven stepped forward, bringing his sword closer to the creature's throat. "That's not my name. The *real* Ashleigh would know that."

The creature's look of surprise and betrayal quickly morphed to one of sick satisfaction.

"You've caught me, little dragon." It chuckled darkly.

"Do not mock me, creature. You will release me, or I will kill you."

The Nightmare laughed, its neck extending just slightly farther back than it should've been able to. "You truly think I mock you, don't you? You do not even know your own blood!"

"Shut up!"

"Oh, but I *know* things. Fear is an old power, older than your gods. I can show you things no other god could know."

Raven shook his head. "Nice try, but I'm not falling for any more of your tricks." He raised his blade and, with one clean swipe, removed the Nightmare's head from its neck.

~~~

When the rest of the group finally found Petyr, he was sitting at a small wooden table across a pale pink wisp laughing and chatting over a bowl of what looked like some kind of beef stew. He looked up and finally noticed his astonished onlookers.

"Oh, there you all are." He dropped a spoon full of stew and wiped his mouth. "Sorry, Giddy and I just got carried away."

"Giddy?" Hawthorn raised an eyebrow.

"It's a friend of my wife's. We were just catching up on how she's been."

"What about the Nightmare?" Tessia stared at him, bewildered.

Petyr shrugged. "Orphne's worked with a couple of them before. They felt they owed her a solid, I suppose." He looked back at the
~~~

spirit. "Lovely catching up with you, Giddy. If you see Orphne, send her my love, would you?"

The pink spirit turned to a deeper scarlet in response and then vanished in a cloud of rose-smelling smoke.

"Right. Let's go kill whatever is in charge and get out of here."

~~~

There was little time for a reunion, as soon as Raven found the others they were face to face with something beyond comprehension. On some level, everything in Phantasma defied comprehension, but the Dreadbeast existed on another level altogether. The creature was a megalith, ten times the size of a Great Wyrm and a hundred times as monstrous. It's limbs were beyond counting, and it had twice as many eyes as that covering every inch of its grotesque bulbous body. It was every fear come to life. It was the master of the region of Phantasma that they had stumbled into and exercised total dominion over the spirits and Nightmares who resided there.

Behind it was their only hope to escape Phantasma. It was a tiny rip in the fabric between realities, but if enough magic was brought to bear, it could be widened enough to facilitate their escape.

Raven felt sick. He wanted to throw up, but more than that, he wanted to run. He wanted to run more than he'd ever wanted to do anything in his life. But then he looked to his right and saw Petyr, a man with everything to lose, standing there resolutely with his staff at the ready. Then he looked to his left and saw Ashleigh, a man with seemingly nothing to lose yet was willing to fight for a world that would never thank him.

Then he looked ahead to Tessia Suncrest. She was a woman who came from means, who'd had a life most sorcerers could only dream of. She could've left the Legion of the Gods, returned to her family in Eastwell, and lived out the rest of her days as Tyr's chosen prophet. Instead, she stayed and became their general, the leader of the armies of the faithful. And now here she stood, staring down the Nightmare that wanted nothing more than to eat her memories and swallow her fear, and she did not flinch. All around them, imps, servants of the Dreadbeast, swarmed down the walls to meet them.

"On my signal," Tessia said, exhaling heavily, only just loud enough that those closest to her could hear, "make for the portal.
~~~

Cut down as many Nightmares as you need to, but *do not* engage the Dreadbeast. I'll keep it distracted and then follow once you're all through."

All at once, the group tried to protest, but she cut them off before they had the chance.

"This is *not* a matter of discussion."

Her eyes flashed with bright iridescence, and the rest went silent.

"As you say, Your Eminence." Ashleigh nodded.

Something in the way he said it, something about the *look* he gave her, made Raven doubt his sincerity, but if Tessia had any reservations, she didn't show it. Lady Suncrest smiled, and then the signal went off. The "signal," in this case, was a massive sphere of pure arcane energy shooting through the air and past the beast. It connected with the rip, causing a magical explosion of fractal colors that set the thing off balance.

"Go!" she shouted.

And they did.

Raven could hardly see what was in front of him through the limbs and viscera that went flying with every Nightmare they cut down, but he didn't stop moving. He kept his eyes on the iridescent glow just ahead of them. It got closer and closer until finally . . .

"We made it!" he exclaimed breathlessly, stepping up to the blinding light.

He turned to look for Ashleigh, but he wasn't there. Before he had time to call his name or seek him out, a hand closed around his arm, and he was pulled through the portal.

~~~

Tessia was getting tired. She could feel her magic reserves depleting. It didn't make sense, she was in Phantasma, the very *source* of magic. It was like running out of water in the middle of the ocean.

"Suncrest!" Petyr called. He was beset by a particularly aggressive Nightmare, swiping at him with claws bigger than his head.

Tessia glanced toward the portal and watched as Hawthorn dragged Raven through.

Good, they're safe.
~~~

Petyr's Nightmare fell when he was joined by Dragonguard Umber, sword burning with radiant light as he pulled it from the creature's skull. Then Petyr shouted something, but Tessia didn't get the chance to hear what it was because it was at that moment that one of the Dreadbeast's massive legs connected with the back of her head. She went out cold.

Within moments, Petyr was at her side. He lifted her up and hoisted her over his shoulder. He called out to Ashleigh, "Dragonguard!"

Ashleigh looked grim, more so even than he usually did. He nodded his head toward the portal. "Get Lady Suncrest to safety. I'll keep that creature occupied as long as I'm able."

Petyr looked like he wanted to argue, but instead, he just sighed. "You're a good man, Ashleigh. I won't let them forget that."

Ashleigh smiled weakly, but it didn't quite reach his eyes. "And when you see Raven, tell him . . ." There were so many things he wanted Raven to know, so many things he never had the words to say. "Just tell him I'm sorry."

Petyr nodded. Then he turned on his heels, Lady Suncrest's limp body slung over his shoulder, and he ran.

~~~

Back in the courtyard, there was a flash of light, and Petyr stepped out of the portal, carrying Lady Suncrest's limp body in his arms.

"Tessia!" cried Minthe, pushing her way through the crowd to get to her.

"She's all right," Petyr reassured her. "Just got a knock upside the head. I doubt there'll even be a bump."

That didn't seem to assuage her fears much, as she continued to fuss over the unconscious Tessia.

Raven pressed forward through the assembled Dragonguards, pushing aside anyone he needed to in order to reach the front. He was followed closely by Hawthorn, who was scolding him about moving so soon after he'd been seen by a healer. But Raven wasn't listening. He was drenched in Nightmare ichor, blood, and sweat. His braid was matted into a sticky mass by the stuff. He was certain if his mother could see him now, she'd die a second time.
~~~

He watched expectedly as the portal crackled and fizzed and then, with far less ceremony than with which it had opened, snapped shut. And Petyr still stood alone.

"Where's Ashleigh?"

PART II

CHAPTER SEVENTEEN

He had expected it to be raining. Wasn't it usually supposed to rain during these kinds of things? But no, the sun was shining, and there wasn't a cloud in sight. It was a beautiful day. Raven struggled to remember if he'd ever seen a more beautiful day. It was midday, and the light reflecting off the surface of the Sea of Shadows was breathtaking, to say the least. The docks of Aegisfjord were empty. No bannermen had come to mourn the fallen general.

"You are Prince Percival, correct?"

A woman, probably a few years older than him, approached from his side. She was dressed all in black, which contrasted sharply with her fair hair and skin. She wore a simple golden tiara with a small red teardrop-shaped stone in the center.

"Queen Elspeth." Raven jumped, quickly stepping back and bowing his head in deference. "Yes, Your Grace. That's me. But I usually go by Raven nowadays."

The queen smiled slightly. "Of course. My apologies, Your Highness."

He almost corrected her. He wasn't a "Highness" anymore, but then he thought better of it. Instead, he just smiled and nodded.

Raven's hair fell loose over his shoulders. He'd tried to braid it. He spent nearly an hour trying to do so. Eventually, he gave up. He couldn't bring himself to cut it. He was dressed in ceremonial Dragonguard armor. It was the kind that Dragonguards wore when they attended formal functions, usually at the behest of a nobleman who wanted someone to entertain his guests with grotesque tales. It was cheaper than hiring most bards and held a higher sense of prestige.

The Watchtower's seneschal thought it was appropriate for the occasion. However, it felt stuffy and tight, and Raven couldn't quite breathe if he slouched even slightly. It didn't feel right. Ashleigh would've *hated* the whole thing—the pomp, the ceremony, everything. But of course, he didn't have the chance to "hate" anything. He was dead.

Raven didn't want to blame Tessia—he really didn't—but it was hard not to. Why couldn't she have stayed? Why did it have to be *him*? It was a selfish and cruel thought to have, but he really couldn't bring himself to care, not today anyways.

He cleared his throat. "I'm sorry, Your Grace. Might I take my leave?"

The queen nodded. "Of course. I should go see to the preparations. I will see you tonight, Prince Raven."

It was dark out now.

Funny. When had it gotten so dark?

Raven was sitting on the docks, staring out at the endless black sea. The tide was low, and the slow waves crashing against the side of the dock were constant and consistent. It was almost soothing in a way. It was still clear, though, perfectly clear without a cloud in the sky. The sky was a tapestry of stars, like pinpricks in black velvet. It was offset only by the presence of the brilliant full moon over the horizon.

There lights from the keep—a feast, he assumed. According to the queen, it was an Aethic tradition to have a feast at a funeral. Raven had planned on going; it was just that the time got away from him. In truth, he didn't want to be around all those people. There were a couple of token Dragonguards from the Watchtower and a dozen nobles just there to ingratiate themselves to the queen.

This was wrong. This was *all* wrong.

And then Raven noticed he was shaking. When had he started crying? He couldn't remember. But now that he'd started, he realized that he couldn't stop. He brought his knees up to his chest and buried his head in his lap. He couldn't breathe. He couldn't think. Everything hurt, and he couldn't fucking breathe.

"It's not fair," he whimpered quietly to himself, shaking his head as tears continued to roll down his cheeks.

Just tell him I'm sorry.

"You stupid, *stupid* man!" He lifted his head and pounded his fist on the dock.

He was so damn angry with Ashleigh. And with Tessia. And with himself. He shouldn't have run. He shouldn't have let that damned elf drag him through the portal. He should have stayed. He should have waited. He could've stayed behind if he had to, instead of Ashleigh.

Ashleigh was a general, and a damned skilled one at that. The legion needed someone like him. They didn't need someone like Raven. *Nobody* needed someone like Raven.

"Hello, Dragonguard."

Raven jumped at the familiar voice. He leaped to his feet and drew his blade. Like his armor, it was purely ceremonial and not sharp enough to cut through butter.

He narrowed his eyes and glared at the intruder. "What are you doing here, Hawthorn?"

The end of Hawthorn's lip curled up. "And where do you imagine 'here' is, precisely?"

"Aegisfjord, obviously."

As Hawthorn smiled, Raven frowned.

"Gods save me! What're you—" He threw his sword to the ground as it hit him. The metal clattered loudly against the dock but not as loud as it should've been. "By the Wayfinder, Hawthorn! This is a dream? Why didn't you say that earlier, you ass? I don't even remember falling asleep." It wasn't uncommon for sorcerers to communicate with one another by weaving the Phantasma through dreams, but it was far beyond anything Raven had ever experienced.

Hawthorn's smile widened. He was clearly struggling to hold in a laugh. "You seemed to be having a contemplative moment. I did not wish to interrupt."

Raven rolled his eyes. "Fine. Where are you then? I mean in the *real* world, not in dreams."

Hawthorn sighed. "Her Eminence has brought us into the Deep Kingdoms in search of the Harbinger's base."

The Deep Kingdoms was the ancestral homeland of the Dwarves. Centuries ago, the Empire of Wyveria had strong trade relations with the dwarven city of Salok and had maintained trade routes that ran under the surface. Even long after the empire's fall, these trade routes were often used by smugglers because of their labyrinthian scale and the difficulty in properly policing and maintaining them. They stretched for miles and miles, and even now, the dwarves were still discovering long buried or hidden ways.

"Oh, shit."

"Indeed."

Raven crossed his arms. "Is there somewhere else we could go? Somewhere less…" *Depressing? Lonely? Cold?* "Aethic?"

Hawthorn chuckled. "It's your dream. We can be somewhere else if you wish."

Raven closed his eyes, and when he opened them, he was no longer in Aegisfjord. He was standing at the docks of Eastwell. It was probably around midday, and the port was bustling with activity. There were workers moving cargo onto ships, noblemen fussing over their luggage, and even a group of sorcerers huddled together like schoolchildren. The air smelled like expensive perfume and fish and tasted salty on his tongue.

"Is this Edelheim?" Hawthorn frowned. He looked very out of place among the crowd, but nobody seemed to notice them at all. Dream logic.

Raven shook his head. "No. Eastwell. We came through here on the way to the conference."

"It's . . ."

"It's awful. I was terrified when I arrived. I thought I was going to throw up before I even got on the ship." Raven laughed.

And then he blinked, and they were in the hallways leading up to the throne room in Edelheim's palace.

"I thought about bringing Ashleigh here, you know—after everything was done, I mean—to let him meet my brothers. I've got three of them, you know."

"This is your home then?"

"I . . ." Raven paused.

It *was*. He was certain at one point that it had been. But now? Standing in the building he'd grown up in and walking the halls he used to run through while chasing his brothers with little carved sticks, it didn't feel like home anymore. He felt like a stranger in his own house. The last time he'd truly felt at home was in the Mirewoods.

He opened his eyes, and he was standing outside the smuggler's den, with rain coming down hard. In the distance, a faint glow drifted off the lake. The portal hadn't been closed yet, and the corpses were still coming. Yet he couldn't have felt safer.

"I remember this place," Hawthorn said. "You and Dragonguard Umber lived here for a while, did you not?"

"Yes, I . . . wasn't in the best state of mind at the time. I'm not certain how long it was, but it must've been a few months at least."

Raven stepped into the cave and ran his hand along the length of the cold stone wall. It felt solid; it felt real. He wasn't certain if he'd ever had such a vivid dream before. He suspected it probably had something to do with the sorcerer on his heels. The end of the path opened up to a large chamber, but it was bigger than he remembered.

All the maps of the Red Wastes had been replaced with various maps from all over Nymor—Valmera, Dejar, the islands of Fjell, even a few of Orcanum. The books on blood magic had instead become historical texts and adventure stories.

A fire crackled quietly in the corner, and a small black dog slept on a rabbit fur rug in front of it. The scene was perfect, exactly how he'd imagined it in the dead of night when he'd woken from another corruption-fueled night terror, only to find Ashleigh at his side to comfort him.

But now Ashleigh was gone. Raven would never again feel the touch of Ashleigh's hands as he braided his hair with more gentleness and care than one would ever expect from a man who'd seen so much war and bloodshed. He'd never again feel Ashleigh's breath on him as he helped him wash the blood from his face. He'd never . . . He'd never feel *him*.

"This isn't quite as I remember it," Hawthorn said.

"No." Raven didn't look at him. "It's not."

He opened his eyes, and they were back on the dock, the wine-dark sea stretching on and on before them.

"I thought I'd feel better after this. Isn't that how it's supposed to happen? You explore your grief, and then you feel better?"

Hawthorn shook his head. "No. I'm afraid it doesn't happen as easily as that."

Raven sighed. "I know."

"It's going to keep hurting. It might not ever stop. But you will learn to live with the hurt, learn to breathe with it. It may feel like you are drowning, but you *will* learn to swim against the tide."

"You know grief."

"As an old friend, Dragonguard."

Raven exhaled deeply. "Thank you, Hawthorn. You've given me—I don't know—something better than what I had. Not quite hope, but something close. I think I'm ready to wake up."

CHAPTER EIGHTEEN

Jon's Rest had been abandoned for centuries—so long, in fact, that no one even knew who the eponymous "Jon" was anymore. Either way, it was highly defensible and unclaimed by any of the nobles who held land in the area, so it made the perfect headquarters for the quickly expanding legion. The ambassador, Lady Alcàntara, had been accommodating, as much as she could be.

Raven hadn't seen anything of the spymaster, Isadora, though he supposed that probably meant she was doing her job. Commander Edric Royce hadn't spoken a word to him. He hadn't even looked him in the eye when he came to discuss the legion's progress with the Dragonguard with Lady Suncrest. Raven didn't blame him, obviously, but that didn't make it sting less.

His quarters were small. He didn't expect them to be large, of course. In all honesty, he didn't expect Tessia to let him enlist at all. He assumed she'd send him away to serve with the rest of

the Dragonguard in fighting Nightmares and the Harbinger's forces across Valmera. Raven had stopped feeling sorry for himself, stopped feeling for his sins the shame that did not serve him. Even so, he wasn't sure if he deserved such grace.

There was a small desk in his room, covered in half-written and unopened letters. There were a few from Petyr, likely updating him on the situation at the Watchtower. There was one from Queen Elspeth and one from two of his brothers. All of the half-drafted letters were addressed to the same person—his father, who'd been teetering at the edge of life for the last few months. With Raven's removal from the line of succession, once their father died, his younger brother

Meliodas would become king. Meliodas was only twenty-two and already a widower. He wasn't ready to rule, but he'd have to be.

Raven sighed and stood up from his cot. It was stiff and cold, and the blanket he'd been given was coarse and threadbare. But it wasn't the worst he'd had. It was better than a pile of straw on the floor of a prison cell, at least. He ran his hand across the desk. It was polished oak, sturdy and strong. He paused on the letter from his middle brother and frowned.

Bedivere was eighteen, and the last Raven had heard from him, he was studying art and poetry at the university in Windhollow. Bed was always the most artistic of the family, his mind always overflowing with brilliant ideas and fantastical schemes. He was a romantic, simply put. Then why, Raven wondered, was his seal emblazoned on simple goat-skin parchment, as opposed to his preferred lamb-skin vellum? His brother had always been particularly anal about that kind of thing.

Raven quickly grabbed the letter, broke the seal, and unrolled the parchment to reveal the message within. It was just five words—five words that made his blood run cold.

The Harbinger sends its regards.

Along with the message was a single lock of Bedivere's curly black hair, stained with blood from where it had been cut from his scalp.

"Fuck you!" Raven spat, teeth bared.

The commander sighed. "The legion's forces are occupied enough as it is. We can't just send them off searching for someone with no leads—"

"Then *find* some leads, Gods damn you! They have my fucking *brother*."

Edric's eyes softened slightly. "I understand your distress—"

"You understand *nothing*," Raven hissed.

Edric looked like he wanted to argue, but Raven didn't give him the chance. He slammed his fist onto the desk, knocking something (he didn't see what) off and causing Edric to jump slightly.

"If you won't help me, I'll find someone who will." Raven stormed out of the office and slammed the door behind him. He hoped that whatever he had knocked off his desk was important. He hoped it held sentimental value. Then maybe the commander could understand a *fraction* of how he felt.

If Raven actually believed their forces were stretched too thin, he might've had more sympathy for the commander's situation, but they'd just won the allegiance of the Valmeran Dragonguard, and their armies continued to grow by the day. Moreover, Lady Suncrest had sent a battalion through the village of Farfeld for Minthe's sake, in search of the elf's wayward father. So this refusal from the commander wasn't about resources. It was about *him*; it was about his brother being punished for *his* crimes. Raven was not a true member of the legion; he would *never* be a true member of the legion. And he was fine with that. But to punish his family? That was something he couldn't forgive.

His hands were shaking. He thought he'd gotten better about controlling that but evidently not.

"Dragonguard?"

Raven jumped. "Gods, Hawthorn! You need to stop *doing* that. You're going to give me a heart attack!"

Hawthorn chuckled. "It is not the fault of mine that you so often find yourself consumed in your own contemplation."

Raven rolled his eyes. "Do you need something? I'm busy."

"Yes, I heard."

"You heard?"

"You were quite loud while shouting at the commander—justifiably so, I might say."

Raven frowned. "You seem to be the only one who thinks so. I've asked Tessia, Lady Alcàntara . . . I even tried to ask the spymaster, though she wouldn't see me. Edric was my *last* hope of finding my brother."

"I could help."

"How?"

"I could search Phantasma, with your help. Our experience in Aegisfjord showed that you have incredible control of your dreams, especially for one without magical aptitude. With your connection to your brother, I believe I could help you locate them—if not to an exact location, then at least an approximate region."

Raven's eyes widened, and before he knew what he was doing, his arms were around Hawthorn's neck. But then Raven quickly realized his mistake and stepped back, clasping his hands awkwardly behind his back.

"Sorry, and thank you. Sorry . . . I'll go. Thank you. See you tonight. Thank you." He was babbling. Gods, he was twenty-five years old, and he was *babbling*. He turned on his heels and walked away.

Sleep found Raven more easily than it had in years. Even before he underwent the initiation, it often eluded him, but tonight was different. The rough sheets offered nothing less than a warm embrace, and his straw-filled pillow made him feel like he was sinking into a downy cloud.

He was going to save his brother without the help of the legion or any of them. He decided to ignore the fact that for all intents and purposes, Hawthorn was also a representative of the legion. Semantics. He closed his eyes, and when he opened them again, he found himself in a memory he'd thought all but lost to him.

His youngest living brother, Elyan, had just been born. He must've been around nine or ten. They were in the nursery of their summer home just outside Arc-en-Ciel, near the village of Bellevides. Meliodas was seven at the time, and Bedivere had just turned three a few months prior. The two were off in the corner, play-fighting with wooden swords, so Percy had been left to watch the baby.

Their mother wasn't there. She was hardly there at all since Claudin had passed six years earlier. Despite both Elyan and Bedivere being born in the interim, their mother had never managed to pull herself out of the darkness the loss of her child had caused her to fall into.

The children's governess, an elf named Leuce, hovered over Percy's head, ensuring he held the baby correctly.

"Support his head, child. He's not a doll."

"I know he's not a *doll*, Leu."

Elyan was so small. Little sprouts of white-blond hair had just begun to form on his head. His blue eyes were closed. He seemed so peaceful. Percy never really liked children, especially at such a young age, but at that moment, he knew he'd never let anyone touch a single hair on his brother's beautiful head. Or Meliodas's. Or Bedivere's. He'd protect them, whatever it took.

But when he looked back down at his hands, Elyan wasn't there. Instead, he held the eighteen-year-old Bedivere's head as he sputtered helplessly, blood leaking from his sea green eyes and from between pale dry lips.

"*Brother, help me . . .*" he gurgled.

Percy panicked, clutching his brother close and trying desperately to wipe the blood from his face. "Hold on, Bed. I'll get help. I'll call for a healer!"

Bedivere shook his head. The blood wasn't stopping. "*No, no. You don't understand! You need to help* me, *Percy! The real me!*"

"I don't understand. Where are you? Bedivere! *Please!*"

Bedivere opened his mouth, but only more blood fell out. He coughed a few more times, splattering blood on Raven's smock, and then he went still.

"It's not him, Dragonguard."

"Don't you think I *know* that, Hawthorn?" Raven hissed, not letting go of his brother's lifeless body. "But it *could* be him. The Harbinger *could* be doing this to him *right now*." He looked down at Bedivere's eyes, tears of blood running down his face. "We have to stop them."

~~~

Edric knew it was stupid to send Raven away. Of course, it was. He should've gone after him and explained *why* they couldn't help his brother, explain that Isadora *was* looking into it but that they had nothing to go off of. Nobody knew where the missing man was last seen. He'd disappeared from the university at Windhollow months ago while supposedly chasing after some "muse." He could be anywhere in Nymor by now, and they couldn't very well send the legion's forces to scour the countryside with nothing to go off of. But of course, he didn't explain that.

It was because the moment he looked at Raven, all thoughts of strategy were forgotten, and all he could think about was what Raven had done, the people he'd hurt, and how he didn't seem to be suffering for it at all. Raven was just able to walk around Jon's Rest
~~~

as if nothing had happened, as if Raven had the right to be alive at all when so many good men and women had died.

Edric quickly banished those thoughts from his head. They were unbecoming of a man of his station and history. He sighed and bent over to pick up the item the Dragonguard had knocked onto the floor. It was a carved wooden soldier, a gift from a child in Darkwater whom he'd rescued from a rogue sorcerer. It was one of the few things he'd done there that he was still proud of. Back then, he had been so . . . *angry* and so righteous. He believed in the paladins. He *believed* in Lord Paladin Helaena. But now? Now he wasn't sure what he believed.

He believed in Tessia, but he also saw her for what she was—not a divine hero, just a woman trying to do what she believed was right. He didn't always agree with her decisions, not even most of the time if he was honest with himself. But she listened to his counsel, and she trusted in his expertise when hers fell short. He respected her, admired her even, but he didn't view her the way he did Helaena at her peak.

To him, Helaena was a shining beacon in the shithole that was Darkwater during his time on the island. She understood him, understood what sorcerers were capable of better than almost anyone else. In the early days after he'd just been transferred from the Aegisfjord Arcane College, she was the only one who seemed to take his concerns about dark magic seriously.

He ignored her more fanatical views, and when she went too far, he justified it however he needed to. And in exchange, he rose up the ranks until he was second-in-command, one of the most powerful people in Darkwater. When he saw what the paladins did to their charges, he turned a blind eye. He ignored the abuses of the sundered. He ignored the invasions of privacy. In his mind, it was all justified. They were *protecting* Darkwater. He thought he loved her, in a way.

And then Petyr stood against her. He was a sorcerer and yet had never hesitated to help anyone in need regardless of their affiliation. He'd saved Edric's own life multiple times already, and seeing him standing there, *begging* Helaena to lay down her arms and stop the bloodshed before it was too late, was enough to shake even the most devout man's confidence. And Edric was not the most devout man.

He stood against his commander, something he could never imagine himself doing ten years prior, and watched her madness consume her in the most literal way imaginable. Then, the Darkwater College collapsed, leaving the sorcerers to be transferred to other colleges in the Isles or on the continent. The paladins order split off from the Covenant of Light, and Edric was left alone and adrift in a world without the purpose that had driven him for so long.

"Commander Royce!"

His reverie was interrupted by the entrance of a scout, a young man called Jim who seemed to always appear at whatever time was the most inopportune.

Edric sighed and placed the toy back on his desk. "Yes, what is it?"

The scout's face went beet red. "Well, it's the Dragonguard, sir. This new one, not—" "Yes, what about him?"

He swallowed. "He's left the keep, sir, along with the elven sorcerer. They were last seen leaving the village at the foot of the mountain. No one knows where they're going."

Edric cursed under his breath. "Well, what're you just standing there for? Inform the spymaster. Find them!"

By the Gods, what has he gotten himself into this time?

Chapter Nineteen

Bedivere awoke from a restless half-slumber to the sound of metal scraping against stone. He craned his neck up, attempting to identify the source of the noise. His entire body ached, and he couldn't remember how he got to where he was. It was dark, and it was cold—cold enough that he knew if it wasn't so dark, he'd be able to see the breath in front of his face.

"Well? Is he awake?" It was a man's voice, deep and distinctive.

"He's been in and out but not fully conscious," replied a woman, younger than the man. Her voice was like silk, honey on her tongue.

"Good. As long as we keep him dreaming, his brother should be able to track him down."

Brother? Bedivere racked his brain. He had a brother, didn't he? Were they talking about him?

"Our spies indicate he's left Jon's Rest along with Lady Suncrest's elven sorcerer."

The man grunted. "I suppose it was too much to hope he'd come alone. No matter. The elf will be dealt with as well."

Bedivere felt himself struggling to remain conscious, and his head lolled to the side. His vision was hazy, but he could just make out the two people. The woman was holding a torch, and the firelight was flickering slightly and illuminating their faces. The man's face was drawn and thin, the skin pulled taut over bone. His eyes were sunken and red, and his face was lined with angry protruding veins. The woman, in contrast, was dressed in robes covered in ancient looking insignias that Bedivere didn't recognize. Her pale hair was neat and pulled back into a tight plait behind her head. Her eyes were ice blue, and she had a look of significant authority about her. Her eyes flashed to him, and Bedivere closed his, trying to play that he was still asleep.

"Looks like the princeling is awake, Oryan."

Heavy footsteps sounded, accompanied by metal sounds, and then a gauntlet-clad hand gripped Bedivere's jaw. His head was forcefully jerked upward, jerking his neck painfully.

"Hello, Prince Drake," the general said. His breath was sharp and sour, like old blood and rot.

Bedivere didn't respond, keeping his lips a thin pink line on his face. Then he felt a fist connect with his face, and he tasted blood. He coughed and opened his eyes to look at the man.

"There we are." The man smiled. His teeth were yellow and cracked, and a couple of them were clearly wood.

"Wha—" Bedivere's head spun, and he struggled to form words.

"I'm sure you have questions, but I'm afraid you won't be getting any answers from me. Except for this, I'll tell you where you are, and you'd better remember."

Bedivere's eyes widened, and then his brows furrowed.

"You're in a fortress called Ishmael's Reach in southwest Valmera. We're heavily fortified, and there's only one way in or out. So you won't be pulling the kind of trick you used at Dinas Fridd."

"What?"

"Oh, I'm not talking to you anymore." The man looked into Bedivere's eyes, but it was more like he was looking *through* him. "So come get him."

Chapter Twenty

Raven shot up in a cold sweat. He was shaking violently, and his breath was uneven and forced. He couldn't breathe. He couldn't think. He pulled open the flap of his tent and stumbled out into the cool mountain night. He took a deep breath, feeling the grass between his toes.

"Dragonguard?" Hawthorn peeked his head out of his own tent, rubbing his eyes. "Are you all right?"

Raven nodded. "Yes, I . . ." He let out a shaky breath. "A dream, I think."

Hawthorn frowned and then crawled out of his tent. "A dream?"

"I saw Bedivere and that man . . . Saddler. They mentioned him before, I think, when the paladins captured me and interrogated me about that Gods-damned sword."

Hawthorn stepped carefully over to him and placed a hand on his shoulder.

"He . . . *spoke* to me through Bedivere," Raven continued. "I think he knows we're tracking him through his dreams. He told me where to find him."

"So it's a trap."

Raven sighed and then ran a hand through his hair. "Yes, though I think I knew that from the start. This just confirms it."

"We should go back. Perhaps if they know Saddler is involved—"

"No!" Raven pulled away from him, turning to look him in the eye. "No. Knowing it's a trap won't make them help me, knowing where they *are* won't make them help me. They won't help me because they don't *want* to help me."

Hawthorn looked like he wanted to argue, but Raven didn't give him the chance as he stormed off to sulk. At the moment, the two were camped at the base of the Bulwark Mountains, not far from Arc-en-Ciel. They had made their way down from Jon's Rest, stopping only briefly to pick up some supplies in the small village at the foot of the fortress.

Hawthorn sighed, made his way over to Raven, and took a seat next to him on the ground. "All right," he said. we'll do it without them. Together."

Raven didn't look at him, but he didn't try to hide the smile that crept across his face either.

Hawthorn looked past him, over the horizon. "We should get moving. I saw some clouds on the horizon that I believe to be a snowstorm. It would be advisable for us to get off the mountain before the storm reaches us." Hawthorn looked around them stiffly, his pointed ears straining to the horizon.

Raven sighed. "All right, all right, don't get yourself into a twist. I wasn't planning on sulking forever, you know. If I'm right, we should be just about to reach the Valmeran border."

Hawthorn brushed off his tunic, pulling his jacket tighter around him against the chill. "Right, Arc-en-Ciel isn't far. With any luck, we'll be there before sundown."

Right. *Luck* seemed to be a resource that was in abundance wherever Raven went.

~~~

Meanwhile, at Jon's Rest, Edric paced the hall leading up to Lady Suncrest's chambers. He didn't know why he was hesitating, why every time he reached out to knock on her door, his heart leapt into his throat. Was it shame? Perhaps.

She had only just returned from an expedition into the Deep Kingdoms, following rumors of Draugar activity, but completely failing to find any sign of the Harbinger. And now he was about to bring her even more foul news. He considered waiting, giving her a few days to relax and recuperate before he spoke to her, but in that time, Gods only knew how far Hawthorn and the Dragonguard could have gotten. Isadora's birds could only fly so far. He sighed
~~~

and steeled himself. He'd faced Nightmares and homunculi and mad sorcerers alike. How much more difficult could facing one former noblewoman be?

"Lady Suncrest?" he called out, rapping his fist on her sturdy wooden door.

"I swear to Astraea and Tyr, if you interrupt us right now, I will set your desk on fire, Edric."

Us? He heard giggling through the door, along with the unmistakable sound of a stifled moan. *Oh, "us."* His face went beet red and he straightened up, turning and walking away as fast as would seem proper without breaking out into a full-on run. He was going to need a drink. Maybe two. Or four.

The tavern at Jon's Rest was as lively as it always was whenever Lady Suncrest returned from one of her quests. Most had no idea what she had done or why she was back, but the men often took advantage of any opportunity to get drunk and have a good time— not that Edric faulted them, naturally.

He remembered when he first joined the paladins. He snuck out almost every Friday to drink with the other recruits—until their supervisor found them, of course. That was a beating he'd never forget. After that, drinking lost some of its appeal as a means of entertainment. It wasn't a bad painkiller, though, or a memory killer in this case.

Edric caught sight of Dame Nestra, who was nursing a dark ale in the corner, and he made his way to join her. She was an older woman, probably in her late forties, much older than most other orcs Edric had encountered, and she'd been with the paladins almost her entire life. She offered an interesting perspective, and Edric welcomed her input, even if it was often unorthodox.

"Commander," she greeted him roughly, only slightly raising a dark bushy eyebrow in recognition.

"Dame Nestra," he greeted her back. "I noticed you're not taking part in the festivities."

She scoffed, "Speak for yourself. I'm doing exactly what everyone does if they manage to return from the Deep Kingdoms— gettin' drunk and tryin' to forget all about it." She cocked her head slightly, eyeing Edric's mug of ale, a dark almost bluish liquid.

"That's stronger than your usual swill, isn't it? What're *you* trying to forget, Royce?"

He chuckled. "Believe me, you do *not* want to know."

"Cheers to that, Commander." Dame Nestra lifted her cup and emptied it with one swallow.

Edric didn't even try to imitate that display, so he only took a long sip of his own drink. The orc was right about one thing. It certainly *was* stronger than what he usually drank. He'd just asked Laila to pour him her strongest drink, and it seemed she did not take such a request lightly. It burned like dragon fire down his throat, and he had to resist the urge not to wretch as it hit his tongue. It seemed he wasn't able to hide his disgust as well as he'd hoped, as Dame Nestra burst into raucous laughter.

"Oh, Fennir's shit! Laila gave you her special reserve, didn't she? That'll burn for *days*, Royce." Tears pricked at the edges of her eyes as she smacked him on the back.

He coughed loudly. The back of his throat felt suddenly bone dry. "What"—he coughed painfully—"what's *in* that?"

She shrugged. "Laila's secret recipe, though I hear she's got a dwarven contact in Kelimbor that can get the *real* shit."

Edric cleared his throat, pounding his fist on his chest.

"So . . ." Dame Nestra said, her jovial demeanor disappearing. "Why don't you tell me why you're *really* here, Commander? It's about the Dragonguard lad, isn't it?"

Edric narrowed his eyes. "What do you know about it?"

"More than you, I suspect."

"How?"

"Because nobody *likes* you, Commander."

Edric paused for a moment, frowning. "I beg your pardon?"

She sighed. "Nobody wants to talk to you, Royce. You intimidate people, so they don't come to you, even when it's important."

He took another swig of his drink, glaring down into the dark amber liquid. "I am their commander, not their friend. They are *obliged* to speak to me, whether they want to or not."

Dame Nestra rolled her eyes, crossed her arms, and leaned on the table to look into his eyes. "Do you want some advice?"

"No."

"Tough luck." She sighed. "Your men will never follow someone into the Abyss that they don't love. The people of the legion follow Tessia because they *love* her, they believe in her and what she's doing. But most of them won't get much more than a glimpse of her from across the courtyard. *You* are her representative to them. If they don't love you, then they won't love her."

He chuckled dryly. "A tall order for one man, don't you think?"

Her eyes became serious for a moment. "Then just imagine the weight on *her* shoulders."

Edric went silent, his gaze once again going to the glass in front of him. Dame Nestra's chair creaked across the wooden floor of the tavern as she stood up. Then she looked down at the Commander.

"Just . . . think on it. You're a good man, Edric. You just need to show them that." She began walking away but paused and turned back to him. "Oh, and Raven and Hawthorn were last seen by some hunters headed west toward Arc-en-Ciel."

Chapter Twenty-One

As it so happened, luck actually *was* on Raven's side for once. He and Hawthorn managed to make the rest of the trip down the mountain with no delays or interruptions. By the time they reached the great gilded gates of Arc-en-Ciel, the sun was beginning to set, but the city was just coming alive. Even from the other side of the walls, they could hear the music that flooded the streets and see the illuminating light of the streetlights as they were being lit.

They were stopped by a guard at the gate, halberd in one hand, the other resting on the hilt of his sword. Raven wondered how many times the guard actually had to use either weapon. Arc-en-Ciel was the most highly defended and fortified city in Valmera, if not all of Nymor, and hadn't been attacked since King Marcus's rebellion almost thirty years ago, and this guard looked far too young to have seen that conflict.

"Halt. What brings you into the city at this hour, citizens?"

Hawthorn opened his mouth to answer, but the guard cut him off.

"I wasn't talking to you, elf."

Hawthorn's jaw clenched, but he didn't say anything. Raven found it strange. He had never seen Hawthorn back down from a fight before, especially where ignorant bigots were concerned.

"*Both of us* are members of the legion. You should treat us with some respect, sir." Raven crossed his arms

The guard looked them up and down. "Even *if* I believed that, which I don't for the record, everyone entering the city past sundown has to pay a tax."

Raven frowned. "A tax? For entering a city?"

The guard shrugged noncommittally. "Hard times. You know how it is."

Raven glared at him, internally debating how much of a scene he was willing to cause with this idiot. Hawthorn placed his hand over Raven's clenched fist and shook his head.

"It's fine. We'll pay the tax. Let's just go."

"But—" Raven started to protest.

"Raven." Hawthorn's voice sounded pleading.

Raven sighed and then nodded. He reached into his bag and brought out a handful of coins. The guard smirked. "Your pet elf is smart. You should follow his lead once you get inside. We don't like *troublemakers* here."

Raven's fist tightened, but receiving one sideways look from Hawthorn, he loosened it. The guard's halberd moved aside, and the massive gate began to creak open. The two men exchanged a look and then walked into the city.

Arc-en-Ciel was a fortress, and some said it was even older than the Valmeran Empire itself. Over the centuries of its existence, it had fallen only three times.

The first time was the night that construction of the Château d'Ivoire, Empress Juanna D'Mer VII's palace in the city, was completed over a thousand years ago. Officially, the fault was placed upon a servant who had let the fire in the empress's chambers burn for just slightly too long, though there were rumors of nobles conspiring to assassinate the empress after the exorbitant cost it took to build the castle. Fortunately, the empress had been delayed by bad weather, so she arrived the next day to find the diamond of Valmera in ashes.

The second time was during the Seventh Cataclysm, when the hordes of Draugar surged over the walls of the city, staining the streets red with blood and viscera. Emperor Françoise D'Montagne XI and his family were present in the city at the time, and their heads were found on stakes along the walls of the city when the army arrived days later.

The final and most recent instance of fire's destruction of the city was during King Marcus's rebellion. The occupying forces of Valmera had been forced out of Aethel, and King Marcus had decided to march on the capital city of the enemy. It was a bold move, and countless died that day, soldiers and civilians alike, as the Aethic rebels sought revenge against their oppressors. The king never expressed any regret about his course of action, but many others who were instrumental in it did, one of whom was Ashleigh Umber.

Raven's eyes were wide as he took in his surroundings. Ashleigh had described the city to him once—the smell of burning flesh that never seemed to leave him and the plume of black smoke that could be seen a hundred miles away. He told him how a woman carrying a small child had run past him down an alleyway, only to be cut down by a man on horseback and left to bleed out in the street. He told him about how, for the first time over the course of their friendship, he had looked at Marcus and didn't see his friend but a king—great and terrible and everything a good king must be—and how it scared him.

Raven was pulled from his mind by the sound of running footsteps as a group of young children dashed past him, waving brightly colored ribbons behind them as they laughed. One of them tripped on a loose cobblestone, only barely managing to catch himself before his nose hit the pavement. Raven expected him to cry or at least pout for a bit. But one of the children just grabbed him by the hand and pulled him off, and they continued laughing into the night.

"Are you all right?"

Raven jumped as he felt Hawthorn's hand on his shoulder, gentle but firm. "Yes, sorry. I've just never been in a city so . . ." He trailed off, unable to find the right word.

"Valmeran?"

He laughed. "Yes, *Valmeran*."

Hawthorn smiled softly, clearly sensing that there was more to it but not wanting to press the issue.

After a bit of confusion, with neither of the pair being particularly familiar with the geography of Arc-en-Ciel, they eventually found their way to a small inn on the far wall of the city called the *Cerf et Lapin*—or the Stag and Rabbit. As soon as they entered, the smell of sweat and liquor was overwhelming. It wasn't the nicest inn, but it would allow them to go unnoticed.

The whole front room of the inn was full of interesting characters. There was a man in a dark hood, sitting in the corner and smoking a pipe. Over at the bar, there were two orcs arguing in their strange guttural tongue until the barkeep shooed them away. Most notably, there was a group of five men in faded paladin fatigues who were sitting around a table in the center of the room, loudly and drunkenly rambling.

"The only thing those knife-ears are good for is their wenches!" one of them slurred loudly, the drink in his cup sloshing over the edge and splattering onto the ground.

Another man, older than the first, snorted. "Aye, Sir Graham, there's nothing better than elven tits. If I had my way, we'd go down to their rookery by the water and slaughter all their men so we could keep the whores for ourselves!"

The table erupted into raucous laughter, and Raven felt his fists tightening.

Hawthorn placed a hand on his shoulder. "Raven, let's go get a room," he muttered, keeping his eyes downcast. Raven hadn't noticed when they entered initially, but now he realized that Hawthorn had pulled up his hood to hide his pointed ears.

"Someone needs to put those men in their place," Raven growled lowly.

Hawthorn shook his head. "It's just talk."

"It's bullshit."

Hawthorn sighed. "I'll talk to the innkeep. Stay out of trouble. Please?"

Raven gritted his teeth but nodded, and Hawthorn left his side, weaving through the huddled crowd to find them a room for the night.

"You know," one of the men sighed, "it's been too long since I've had myself an elven whore. Maybe we should go down there tonight and take us some, hmm?"

Raven opened his mouth and then closed it. Hawthorn was right; it was just talk. These drunk men were just trying to sound tough with empty words and empty promises. One of the other men, the older one from before, leaned forward and lowered his voice. Despite himself, Raven strained his hearing and began inching closer to them.

"Now that you mention it, Sir Hugh," the older man ran his tongue over his yellowed and chipped teeth, "I do have a friend in the guards. He had a particular appetite for young mages, and he owes me a favor or two. He could be convinced to look the other way—for the right price, of course."

The rest of the men began muttering among themselves, a general sense of agreement rising between them. Raven felt a sense of unease growing in his gut. Idle talk could turn into more if given the right spark. His eyes scanned over the men, noticing how their twitchy fingers hovered over their sheathed blades.

As the older man, the leader, began to stand up, Raven put his hand down on the table. "Good evening, gentlemen." He smiled, tensing his muscles under his leather armor.

The older man sat back down, raising an eyebrow as he examined him closely. "Good evening, sir. Sir Cender Doyle, at your service. How may we help you tonight?"

"I was actually hoping *I* could help *you*. Making threats of violence in a crowded tavern can be bad for your health, you know."

Doyle narrowed his eyes. "You're no guard. What gives you the authority to threaten me?"

Raven shook his head. "No, I'm not, but what I am"—he quickly grabbed on to Doyle's hand, twisted it, and slammed it on to the table, causing him to cry out—"is someone who gives a single shit about the elves."

The man from before—Sir Hugh, based on Doyle's words—stood and drew his blade. "Unhand him, craven, or you'll be losing that hand, I swear to you."

Raven grinned, dropping Doyle and drawing his own blade. The viridian metal glowed with potential and magic, and he saw a few of the men step back at the sight. But Sir Doyle and Sir Hugh didn't falter.

Doyle stood to his feet and shook his aching head, mumbling to himself. "Well? What are you waiting for? Get him!" he barked to his men.

Then all at once, they all came at him.

The first to strike was Hugh. He was fast and strong but out of practice, and it was clear that like with many paladins, he was only used to taking on opponents much smaller and much weaker than he. Raven was smaller, but as his blade clashed against Hugh's, it was painfully apparent that Raven could easily match Hugh in strength.

Raven pushed him back and quickly brought up his blade to block the attack of another man. Then he swiped with his sword, drawing a red line across Hugh's cheek and causing him to stumble back.

Then came Sir Graham with a short and jagged dagger. He was better than his compatriots, even managing to slice across Raven's armored stomach, but like the rest, he was rusty. When he ducked low, Raven grabbed a fistful of his hair, which was long and unkempt, and Graham screamed as Raven's hand came away with a bloody clump of the stuff.

Finally, all that was left was Sir Cender Doyle. He growled at Raven, baring his old teeth, and lunged. Raven expected him to be slow, given his age and apparent fragility, but such was not the case. Doyle struck like a viper, his long curved scimitar swiping not a hair's breadth from Raven's throat.

Raven scrambled back, only barely managing to bring his sword up to block each relentless blow. Finally, Doyle had him backed against a wall. He swung at Raven's head. As Raven ducked, Doyle's blade thudded heavily into the wood off the wall. Doyle struggled to pull his blade loose, and Raven, breathing heavily, managed to just barely slip under Doyle's arm and swing around to place his blade under his throat.

"Do you yield, Sir Doyle?" he said breathlessly.

"That's *enough*."

They were interrupted by the entrance of the innkeeper, an older human man with a fleshy pink face and a red nose that seemed to take up the majority of it.

Raven breathed a sigh of relief. "Thank you. I was just—"

"You!" The innkeeper glared at Raven, small black eyes burning like embers. "You need to get out of my inn this instant. *Allez!*" he barked.

"But those men were—" Raven tried to protest.

"Sir Doyle and his men are paying customers. What they do outside their time here is no business of mine, nor is it yours. Now, are you going to leave, or shall I have the guards come and drag you out?"

Raven matched the innkeeper's gaze and slowly lowered his blade, returning it to its sheath. "I can see myself to the door." He growled and let his hands fall to his side. And then, as he turned to leave, he heard the innkeeper call out to him.

"Oh, and don't forget your little friend. You didn't really think I didn't see you come in with your little knife-eared *pet*, did you?"

Raven felt his blood boil, along with a dark urge he thought he'd buried with the Draug blade. It frightened him, and his grip on his blade loosened. He hadn't remembered grabbing it again, and that frightened him even more. He turned back to the innkeeper, Doyle, and his men, noting the sickening gleam in their eyes. He looked around the room and stopped when he made eye contact with Hawthorn, who glared at him.

Raven lowered his gaze before calling out. "We're leaving, Hawthorn. Let's go."

They'd made their way down the road a bit but had come to a fork in the path. One way led down to the lower part of the city and the docks, and the other led off toward the opposite edge of the city, near the guards' barracks.

Raven kicked the dirt, scowling down at his boots.

"You're a child," Hawthorn scoffed.

Raven looked up and glared at him. "What?"

"You're a petulant *child*, Raven."

Raven growled. "You just expected me to let those men speak that way?"

The elf crossed his arms, straightening his posture so he stood over Raven. "Yes. I did actually expect for you to not act completely like a rash idiot for once, but I suppose I was mistaken."

Raven stepped forward, stabbing his pointer finger into Hawthorn's chest. "Don't you *dare* speak to me that way! I am not a fucking child, Hawthorn."

"No, you're right. A child can't be expected to know any better. You should."

"Hawthorn, that's not—"

"Not what? Not *fair*? What's not 'fair' is how you treat elves like maidens that need protection." His red eyes flared, and his fists balled. "You don't actually care about us. You just do it to fuel your own ego, to absolve yourself of the murder of that woman." Hawthorn pushed

Raven away and then turned his back to him. "You are a murderer, no matter what you do, and your arrogance blinds you to that."

And with that, Hawthorn stormed off towards the docks, leaving Raven dumbstruck in his wake.

Raven eventually found himself in another inn. Well, perhaps "inn" would be an overly generous way to describe it. In reality, it was barely even a bunkhouse. It consisted of one main congregation area with a bar and a few tables, and a secondary area off to the side that reminded him of the hold of the ship that had brought him to Aethel in the first place. It was filled to bursting with tightly packed beds and hammocks, making the whole experience intensely claustrophobic. Raven was fairly sure the place *had* a name, but he was three cups into a strange dwarven beer the proprietor had offered at a discount, so he couldn't quite remember what it was.

He couldn't stop replaying the argument with Hawthorn over in his head. How could he *possibly* see him that way? Raven knew he was many things—a killer, a liar, a thief—but *arrogant*?

Raven was yanked from his thoughts by the feeling of a firm hand on his shoulder. "Hello again, little prince," a voice rasped in his ear.

The voice was familiar, so tantalizingly familiar, but staring down at his empty glass, Raven just *couldn't* quite place it.

"Just grab him, and let's go," said a woman's voice, soft as spider silk and familiar as well.

Then, like a flash of light, a memory came. It was not quite his own, but it was like he was watching through someone else's eyes. He watched the woman stand behind General Saddler, pale eyes gleaming as she glared down at Bedivere, who was lying helpless before the two of them.

The memory jolted something in Raven, and he leapt to his feet, instinctively going for his blade. But he was clumsy and sloppy and only just barely managed to brace himself upon the bar.

"Aww . . ." The man tutted. "The little prince can't handle his drink?"

They put something in the beer, Raven thought as the edges of his vision began to fuzz.

"Now that's not the Percy Drake *I* remember."

"What?" Raven tried to say. But before he got the chance, a leather-gloved fist connected with his cheek, and suddenly, he was on the floor. He spat and saw red.

Fuck. I'm really starting to get tired of this.

"Stop playing with him." The woman crossed her arms, tapping her foot on the ground like a mother scolding an insolent child. "We need him *alive*, remember?"

Raven felt a boot connect with his ribs and heard a loud *crunch* followed by a curt laugh from the man.

"Eyre!" the woman hissed.

Eyre? No, it can't be.

"Janus?" Raven groaned.

The last he'd seen of his former mentor and guardsman, he'd been . . . lost. His eyes were vacant and he'd moved like a marionette on strings. But now his eyes were the clearest they'd been in all the years that Raven had known him. He looked younger too—his face less lined and his hair with less grey—but it was unmistakably him.

Janus was looking down at Raven with more hateful fury than he'd ever seen in another single human being.

"Janus, I don't unders—"

And then Janus's boot connected with Raven's nose, and everything went black.

Chapter Twenty-Two

The starless sky reflected off the surface of the Lac du Lys, a featureless black mirror that stretched as far as Hawthorn could see. The lake was situated just outside the city, and it was the largest on the continent by far. He had made his way down through the lowest part of the city, the elven district, also known as the "rookery." He tried to avoid large cities whenever he could, especially large human cities. He'd been to the dwarven capital, Salok, years ago, but compared to Arc-en-Ciel, it was practically a hamlet.

The moment he stepped through the gates, every one of his enhanced elven senses was assaulted by the violent colors and lights and sounds. The stench of humanity was everywhere, like mold in food, and no matter where he went, Hawthorn couldn't escape it—except in the rookery. The humans seemed to avoid the elven district like the plague—when they weren't going on drunken raids, of course.

The paladin that Raven had provoked had evidently not decided to follow through on his plans, so that night was one such quiet night. The rookery had noise, of course, but it was a softer noise. The scent of sage and eucalyptus, the soft reds and yellows faded from lack of upkeep and splattered with muddy handprints, the sound of the pan flute on the breeze—these all reminded him of growing up in the Unsettled Wilds. They reminded him of home.

The anger he felt toward Raven had cooled somewhat, leaving an aching void in his chest. Raven was a fool. He'd proven that time and time again. But there was never any malice in his actions—a great deal of anger, yes, but never evil. Hawthorn had seen men like him burn out before, consumed by a rage that could only take them so far. He often saw that rage in Raven's eyes, as he saw it in his own. It was rage against the injustices his people faced, rage against rulers who didn't care for their people, rage against a world that shunned and feared magic in all its primal beauty.

And this rage scared him. All sorcerers knew what undirected emotion could wreak, and it never ended well for the sorcerer. Perhaps he envied Raven in that way. He was not burdened with magic, burdened with the responsibility that came from having such a power. Hawthorn stared out across the lake, clenching and then relaxing his fists a few times, feeling the electricity crackle between his fingers and palm.

Then something broke the stillness of the lake. A flickering light, like a candle flame, was moving across the surface of the water. Hawthorn crossed his arms and narrowed his eyes. The light was moving too quickly and too close to the surface of the water to be a boat but was moving with too much purpose to be a lampyridae. The light shifted, and suddenly, it was headed straight toward him. He felt his fingers tense but made no move to summon his magic, not yet. The spirit appeared in front of him and then shot up suddenly, taking an ephemeral humanoid form, pale and flickering.

"Why are you here, spirit?" Hawthorn asked evenly, his tone and expression betraying no emotion.

"Help," it said. Its voice was small and high, like that of a child, but he knew that the spirit was older than the mountains.

"Why do you need help?"

The spirit's featureless face shifted and then became reptilian and angular. Its eyes flared, and it bared its teeth.

Hawthorn shook his head. "I can't help if you don't talk to me."

The visage shifted again, taking a more concrete form. This time, when it spoke, the words dripped out like smoke through a dragon's fanged mouth.

"The dragon cannot reach the sky," it growled.

His eyes widened. "The dragon? Do you mean Drake?"

It seemed impossible the Raven could've reached out to a spirit, let alone brought one *physically* from Phantasma. But Hawthorn had seen first-hand how much control Raven could exert over his dreams, and if the danger was sufficient, it wasn't impossible for a non-sorcerer to be capable of such a thing.

The spirit's form shuddered, its hand shooting up to cover its mouth like it had just said a swear word. "Old blood of old masters," it whimpered, the dragon's maw melting like wax over a flame.

Hawthorn sighed. "Just tell me where he is, spirit."

The spirit opened its mouth, but instead of words, it spoke in sounds. Carriage wheels on cobblestone, hoofbeats on the road. Then not against cobblestone, but on a dirt road, rolling across uneven stone and the snapping of twigs under the pressure.

"He's left the city."

Heavy breathing and then the sound of metal sinking into flesh.

Hawthorn swallowed. "He's injured. Where are they taking him?"

The spirit covered its eyes, the dragon's face falling away entirely and leaving behind the face of a scared child with familiar grey eyes. "They tried to Reach divinity, but it was denied to them."

They're taking him to Ishmael's Reach. Hawthorn nodded and bowed his head respectfully. "Thank you, spirit." He raised his hand in a closed fist and waved it over the spirit's form. "I release you from service."

The spirit mirrored him, bowed its own head, and then vanished in a small hail of golden sparks.

~~~

Raven felt the cloth covering his eyes and the rope wrapped tightly around his wrists, but besides that, he couldn't feel much else. Janus and the woman had been all but silent over the course of the journey, and try as he might, he couldn't distinguish where they were. He could tell they'd gone off the main road, but he wasn't nearly as familiar with Valmeran geography as he should've been. Even if he was, there was no way he could know how long he'd been unconscious or how long they'd been traveling for.

Someone shifted beside him, and his whole body tensed. Janus's voice was low and rough as he chuckled and reached over to lace his fingers through Raven's hair.

"We can tell you're awake, boy. There's no need to pretend." Janus yanked Raven's head back, slamming the back of his skull
~~~

into the hard wood of what Raven had to assume was the interior of a carriage.

"Where are you taking me?" Raven gritted his teeth, turning his head slightly toward the source of the voice.

"Ishmael's Reach," the woman said. By the sound of her voice, she was sitting across the two men. "The Harbinger cannot afford to wait any longer."

"All of this for a damned *sword*?"

When the woman laughed, it was shrill and made his ears ring. "You really think this is still about Ignos's Edge? My, my, I thought Sir Eyre *exaggerated* when he described what a fool you were, but I can see that's not the case!"

She leaned forward, and Raven felt her breath on his face. It was hot and acrid, like overripe fruit. She placed her fingers under his chin, and he could hear the smile in her voice.

"No, my dear," she said. "We have something *much* better than a simple sword."

Suddenly, the carriage jolted to a stop, and the woman was thrown off him and onto the floor of the carriage.

"Kalaya!" Janus called, his voice losing some of its assuredness.

"I'm fine," she growled, the wood of the carriage shifting slightly as she stood to her feet. "Go investigate. I'll watch Drake."

Janus grunted in agreement, and then his fingers untangled themselves from Raven's hair, letting his head drop forward. Raven gritted his teeth to avoid crying out. The carriage shifted slightly, and then he heard the door slam as Janus made his exit.

Most likely, whatever had stopped the carriage wasn't good—bandits if he was lucky, rogue paladins or a fallen tree if he wasn't. Either way, it was a distraction. The woman, Kalaya, hadn't been carrying a weapon in either of the times Raven had seen her—neither in Bedivere's memory nor when she and Janus ambushed him.

She was tall and well built, but if he could get the jump on her, none of that would matter. Of course, there was the problem of being bound and blindfolded, but the carriage didn't seem to be especially large. Raven knew if he could just get his hands on her, he could get his arms over her neck and then—

The carriage shook with the force of something hitting the side. It leaned dangerously off-kilter and then slammed into the ground with great force. Raven slammed into the wall and felt a sharp, throbbing pain in his shoulder where it connected. He grunted in pain, and Kalaya let out a string of curses in what sounded like elven. Conveniently, in the commotion, Raven's blindfold was knocked off from his eyes. However, what he saw unfortunately dashed any hopes of overpowering Kalaya.

Her meticulously braided hair had come loose so that some strands dangled in her face, and her eyes burned as she stumbled to her feet. Somehow, she'd been injured when the carriage was knocked over, so a trickle of deep red blood ran down her arm. She balled her fists at her side, and then something happened.

At first, Raven couldn't explain it. It was as if the air itself was shaking around her, vibrating in such a way that her form was distorted. And then he realized just what she was doing. Tiny lightless specks began to float up and around her and then congealing into lightless voids circling around her head.

This was sciomancy, the forbidden art of dark magic.

Kalaya blinked, and her eyes were completely enveloped by the void. "I am surrounded by *morons*," she muttered to herself, her voice taking on an echoey quality that reminded him far too much of when the Harbinger spoke at Dinas Fridd.

Kalaya threw out her arm and opened her palm, and the shadows shot away from her and into the door, which now sat above their head. She then brought her hands back down, and like a cannon from a barrel, she shot up and away.

Now left unattended, Raven took his chance and began struggling against his bindings, which were tight. He could tell, however, that Janus had been the one to tie them, and if he was correct in that assumption . . . He twisted his wrist, ignoring how his shoulder throbbed when he did so, and began tucking his finger into the knot. No one in the Isles made it very far without knowing how to tie at least five different kinds of fishermen's knots, and sheltered noblemen were no exception. In fact, Raven had been taught by none other than Janus himself.

Finally, he managed to get his finger looped through the rope, and he tugged. The entire thing came loose, and he shook out his raw wrists. They were encircled by angry red welts, and his shoulder still throbbed. But aside from that, he was, by some miracle, uninjured. They had disarmed him, but he wasn't willing to stick around and look for his sword. This was his chance to escape.

Raven pulled himself from the wreckage, and as he fell down onto the soft grass, he let out a small sigh of relief. That relief was quickly dashed, however, when he realized he'd landed at Janus's feet.

"*You*," he growled, bringing his sword down toward him.

"Shit!" Raven just barely managed to roll out of the way, the sword thudding into the soft dirt right next to his head.

He scrambled up to his feet, instinctively going for his blade.

Shit, right.

But there was one trick he hadn't learned from Janus, one that Ashleigh had taught him. His hand quickly went for his boot, finding his extra throwing knife still secure where he'd left it. He took it out, and Janus laughed.

"Learned some new tricks, did you? Too bad I *know* you, Percy. I know you're still that pathetic little boy from Edelheim who's too scared to speak out against his weakling father."

Raven growled, lunging for him with the blade. "Don't you *dare* speak about my father!"

Janus blocked the blow easily, bringing his sword up to parry and push him away. "You don't even *know* your father, boy. But I did. I *do*. I know exactly what kind of man he is. Your father is a coward, too afraid of the world to even look outside his window. And you would've become the same kind of man if Tristam and I hadn't framed you for High Cleric's murder."

Raven froze, and once again, he was a young man standing in front of his father's advisors and doctors, being told he'd never be allowed to see him again. Once again, he was a little boy, wondering why he couldn't see his new baby brother and wondering why his mother hadn't stopped crying for hours. Then, once again, he was himself, on his knees, begging Petyr to admit he was lying, begging him to say Ashleigh wasn't really gone.

His hands dropped to his sides, and Janus laughed and stepped forward. He held his sword to Raven's throat and dug into his flesh.

"We would've preferred to take you alive. The Harbinger says your blood is the most potent as it's been in centuries. But once we gather up all your brothers, they should have enough between them to suffice." He lowered his gaze and smiled. "Any last words, Percy?"

As Janus smiled, so did Raven, and Janus stopped smiling. Raven had stabbed his blade into Janus's belly, and now he twisted it deeper, between the chinks in the older man's armor. He brought his hand up to wrap around Janus's head and pulled him closer.

"That's not my name, and you're not getting anywhere *near* my brothers."

Raven pushed him away, and Janus stumbled back, his hand going for his stomach before falling to his knees. Raven reached down and yanked away Janus's sword from him. It was a sturdy Damascus steel, forged in the heart of Edelheim by King Regnant Sagramor's own smiths as a gift to Janus for his long years of fidelity to the family.

"I was wrong about you." Janus gurgled, blood spilling from his lips as it filled his lungs. "You really are—"

He wasn't allowed to finish that sentence, as his head was disconnected from his body by a sweep of the blade.

"No!" A voice boomed, loud enough to shake mountains and wake sleeping giants.

Raven looked up to see Kalaya hovering at least ten feet above him, black eyes wide and wild.

"You'll pay for that, you worthless maggot!" she screamed hysterically, then hurled a dagger of black void at him.

Raven only just managed to deflect it with Janus's blade. And then he didn't think; he just ran. With sword in one hand and dagger in the other, he shot off and toward the tree line. All around him, clumps of dirt and grass shot up with every one of her reckless attacks, but he didn't look back. He was close, so close to the tree line, just a few more feet . . .

Suddenly, he felt something sharp in his thigh and screamed. As he fell to his feet, he lost his grip of both of his weapons. He looked back and, seeing a massive shard of black magic jutting from his leg, whimpered at the pain.

Kalaya drew closer. She was cloaked in darkness that seemed to pulse and grow, like a blister that was ready to burst. Her hands were covered entirely in darkness that dripped from her like ichor.

"Don't worry. I'll make sure this hurts."

~~~

Hawthorn entered the clearing to find Raven on his back, staring up at something he initially mistook to be a Nightmare. But as the figure raised its fist, Hawthorn caught the barest bit of pale pink flesh under all that shadow, and he realized it was a sorcerer.

"Raven!" he called out, hoping to at least distract her long enough for Raven to get away.

It worked. The woman's head jerked toward him.

There was a reason sciomancy was outlawed and forbidden even among the most skilled of sorcerers. It was what the original Archons of Wyveria had used to bind the Great Wyrms and conquer nearly all of Nymor. It was powerful but came at a cost.

The woman he was facing now was proof of that cost. The flesh off her face had been seared, leaving nothing but musculature that was coated in a thick layer of pitch-black ichor. She growled and lashed out at him with her magic, screaming at the same time as it stripped a little more of her away.

Hawthorn reacted quickly, throwing up a barrier that shattered like glass when her magic hit it. He stumbled back slightly, glancing over at Raven, who was still on the ground. It was hard to tell at this distance, but it seemed like Raven was injured.

So running is out of the question then.

Hawthorn jumped out of the way as another sharp of cold black magic was hurled toward him, leaving a gash in the earth that caused any plants within a few feet of it to suddenly wither and die. The woman lunged toward him, screaming like a banshee and looking the part as well. Hawthorn countered with a spell of his own, a jet of ice magic that connected with her shoulder.

She didn't seem hurt at all by it, or if she was, she didn't care. But it did at least alter her trajectory, causing her to career off course and land a couple dozen yards away from him.
~~~

"Hawthorn!" Raven shouted.

Hawthorn glanced over to see Raven on his feet, using a sword as a crutch.

"Keep her busy. I have a plan!"

Hawthorn was about to respond, but before he had a chance to do so, he felt a whisper on his ear and a change of air current and just managed to step back before another of the woman's spells hit him. Magic, as he understood it, was life, light, and warmth. Sciomancy was anything but, yet he couldn't help but marvel as the beam of freezing cold darkness shot past him and hit a tree on the other edge of the clearing, reducing it to a pile of rotted wood and lichen.

"I'll kill both of you, and then I'll eat your souls!" The woman laughed maniacally.

Hawthorn threw up another barrier, and this time, when she cast a spell, her entire arm melted away from the force of it. The barrier fell, and he felt the magic searing his skin. It felt like the burn of frostbite but hurt a hundred times worse. He turned away, his back taking the brunt of the attack, but he managed to remain standing.

But the woman didn't stop laughing. He looked back to see her holding up her remaining hand, a massive sphere of darkness in her palm.

Spirits! She's going to destroy the whole clearing!

Hawthorn's eyes widened, and he braced himself, hoping that whatever Raven did, he would do it soon.

The woman laughed and laughed, and the laughter was intermixed with an equivalent amount of screaming as the hand that held the sphere melted away until the sphere floated autonomously in front of her. The laughter faltered, however, when the sphere began to grow.

"No! Stop that! No!" she shouted, scolding the ball of volatile magic as though it were a puppy that had just chewed her favorite slippers.

Unlike a puppy, however, the sphere refused to acquiesce. It burned into her flesh and seared away everything remaining that made her mortal. Her screams suddenly stopped, and just as it did, the sphere of energy sputtered out and faded away, having lost its tether and source of energy.

"Well, that went better than expected!" Raven quipped, limping out from behind the overturned carriage. "Thanks for that, by the way."

"Raven!" Hawthorn gasped, quickly rushing to his side and supporting him. "That was quite something. Was that your plan?"

"What? No. I was just going to try to stab her while her back was turned." Raven cringed, looking over at the pile of mangled ichor that had once been a formidable sorcerer. "Astraea preserve us! She was mad as a bat, but . . ." He swallowed.

"Indeed." Hawthorn nodded. He looked over at the carriage. It had been upturned when he arrived, but he hadn't noticed the headless corpse in copper and red. "What . . . happened here?"

"Long story," Raven grunted. "But first, would you mind?" He gestured down at his leg, at the leg of his trousers quickly being stained with deep red.

"Spirits! Of course." Hawthorn carefully helped him to the ground and then sat down beside him on the grass and got to work gingerly unveiling the wound. He used a small knife to carefully cut off the trouser leg, ignoring how Raven hissed as the fabric was pulled away from the quickly drying blood.

"This might sting a bit."

Hawthorn placed his palms over the wound, and they began to glow slightly. Unlike Tessia's golden healing magic, however, his was a shade of pale green. Raven gritted his teeth and leaned back. After a few minutes, Hawthorn was magically exhausted, and he pulled his hands away.

"There. It will be painful for some time, and I wouldn't suggest you do any fighting for at least a couple days. But you needn't use a cane to walk, at least."

Raven nodded. "Thank you, Hawthorn."

"Now, will you tell me what happened?"

Raven nodded and explained as best as he was able, though by the end Hawthorn was frowning, deep lines drawn in his brow.

"Stop. So the carriage was attacked *before* you escaped? And you weren't injured at all before that?"

Raven shrugged. "Janus knocked me around a bit, but there wasn't any real damage, no. I assumed the carriage was *your* doing."

"No. When I arrived, you were prone on the ground." He shook his head. "And what about the spirit? Do you recall entering Phantasma while you were unconscious?"

Now, it was Raven's turn to frown. "A spirit? No, nothing like that." Hawthorn sat back, crossing his arms. "That is . . . troubling." He hummed.

"Right, well." Raven slapped his hands on the ground, pushed himself up, and stood to his feet. "Janus was an insane bastard who betrayed my entire family, but he had one thing right."

Hawthorn raised an eyebrow.

"My father is weak, and he's a fool. You know that my house's motto is 'A dragon flies alone.' My father is *obsessed* with keeping Edelheim independent. He thinks Drakes don't need allies." Raven reached a hand down, which Hawthorn took, and pulled him up to stand beside him. "Well, maybe he's right about that. But I'm not a Drake anymore, and I *do* need allies. We can't do this alone."

Hawthorn placed a hand on his back, looking unsure. "Are you certain? We know this isn't about the blade anymore, and we know the Harbinger is expecting you. That hasn't changed."

"No, it hasn't, but they'll be expecting us to come alone. They'll be expecting me to do exactly what I've been doing."

"So what do you suggest we do?"

Raven smiled. "We prove them wrong."

Chapter Twenty-Three

A dozen different tomes were spread out in front of Tessia, detailing hundreds of magical rituals from all over Nymor—rituals for power and wealth, rituals for summoning Nightmares, even a few fringe theoretical rituals on how one could fuse with a Nightmare to gain their insight and power.

"None of it makes any sense," she muttered to herself, running a hand through her dark hair. "Glad you're finally getting my view of things." Minthe snorted, peeking over the cover of her own book.

The two women, along with Isadora, the spymaster, had gathered in the library of Jon's Rest and were currently poring over its contents. The Harbinger's forces had been heavily impacted by the assault on Dinas Fridd, but it wasn't going to give in that easily. Isadora's spies had discovered a massive operation of dwarven lepidolite smugglers who, once questioned, admitted to supplying the Harbinger. Along with lepidolite, it had been amassing a number of other odd and esoteric materials, including various artifacts from the ancient Empire of Wyveria, vast quantities of sulfur and mercury, and most unsettling of all, a large number of human and elven slaves. All these were ingredients used in a number of powerful rituals.

"That's not what I meant, Min." Tessia sighed. "Nothing matches up, not perfectly anyhow, and we still don't know exactly what it's using the slaves for."

Minthe wrinkled her nose and looked down at her book. It was an adventure story written by a popular dwarven author from the Dejari city of Espar. Minthe was mostly there for emotional support.

"I think I've found something," Isadora said, emerging from behind a bookshelf with a large black tome held in both hands.

Tessia frowned. "I thought we had all the magical books already."

She shook her head. "Not quite. This is one from the keep's original collection, penned in the Twilight Age by one Yon Penthras."

Minthe giggled, setting down her book and folding her arms over her chest. "What? You're saying this book belonged to *Jon himself?*" She joked.

Not a woman of high humors, Isadora just nodded.

"Shut up." Minthe's jaw dropped.

Despite herself, Tessia snorted. Minthe just had that effect on her, she supposed.

Isadora ignored them and opened to a random page. The book was written in a strange script, clearly a very old form of the common tongue with a few symbols Tessia recognized as ancient Wyverian. She traced a finger over them, frowning at the feel of the letters on the page.

"What is it?" Isadora raised an eyebrow, her carefully trained insight quick to pick up on Tessia's apprehension.

"It's just . . ." Tessia hesitated. "The words—they're not written in ink."

"What are they written in then?" Minthe peaked around her, both of her hands on her shoulders.

"It's written in magic—sciomancy, I think."

Minthe took a large step back, her hand going to the dagger on her belt.

Isadora, in contrast, stepped forward, a look of keen interest in her eyes. "Can you read it?"

Tessia nodded. "I . . . I think so, yes."

She looked down at the page, splaying her palm open to drink in its energy. It was old magic, older than anything she had ever experienced or even heard of. It was said that the Arcane Colleges were old, their protective magic weaved into the very foundation, but this . . . this was centuries beyond anything at the Eastwell College at the very least.

As she focused her energy further, the words on the page began to move and shift, forming into recognizable shapes and then melting into letters and words. She squinted, just beginning to make out the first sentence. Her eyes skimmed across the page, skipping over paragraphs and paragraphs of meticulous preparation, noting only the key ingredients: sulfur and mercury, a large amount of blood sacrifice, a symbol of the supplicant's house, and a sample of the supplicant's blood.

She frowned at the last two. *The supplicant?*

The wording was esoteric and hard to understand even with the magical translation, but it soon became clear that the entire tome was a copy of a much older manuscript, the entirety of which was dedicated to detailing one extremely complicated ritual. Tessia gasped and slammed the tome close, causing Isadora to flinch slightly and Minthe to draw her dagger and aim it at the book.

"What? What does it say?" Minthe backed up, not taking her eyes—or her blade—off the closed book.

Tessia looked between the two of them, her eyes wide and flecked around the edges with tiny black specks. "I know what the Harbinger is trying to do. He wants to resurrect an Archon of Wyveria."

~~~

As soon as Raven and Hawthorn arrived back at Jon's Rest, the work of planning began.

With the information they'd gotten about where the Harbinger was holding Bedivere, along with Tessia's newfound insight into its plans, it didn't take much to convince Edric to view it as a priority. Actually, that meant it wasn't hard for Tessia, Hawthorn, and Isadora to convince him.

Raven still refused to speak to him. He still felt the sting of his refusal to help too freshly. Whenever he looked at him, he could see nothing but the vision of Bedivere's bleeding face as he begged for help.

A plan was quickly devised, largely through the help of some of Lady Alcàntara's contacts in Espar at the University of Dejar who had copies of the original blueprints of Ishmael's Reach, which was built all the way back at the end of the Black Age at the height of the Empire of Wyveria.

Isadora had a copy of said blueprints spread out over a large oak table, the edges held down by various books and heavy knick-knacks.
~~~

"Here, the front entrance." She pointed to a spot on the page. "This is where Raven will attempt to enter. It's where they'll be expecting him and where they'll be the most fortified."

Edric frowned. He stood behind the spymaster, his hand resting on the hilt of his blade. "We're sending him alone? Are you sure that's wise?"

Isadora shook her head. "No, but the only one he was seen traveling with was Hawthorn, and we need all the sorcerers we can afford focusing their magic here." She pointed to a spot on the opposite side of the fortress, a plain wall marked with a red *x*. "This wall was built on an unstable foundation, but the Magi of Wyveria compensated for that by weaving magic into the stone, much in the way the towers of the Arcane College are built but in a more primitive form.

It will take a lot of energy, but if our sorcerers can unravel the enchantments, the wall should come down."

Raven shook his head, unfolding his arms and stepping toward the table. "What about the Harbinger's dragon?"

Tessia sighed. "No one from Aethel to Dejar has seen any sign of it since Dinas Fridd. It's possible Fontaine's spell was enough to actually mortally wound the beast."

Raven felt a twang of sadness at the idea that such a majestic beast could've been killed so easily by someone like Fontaine. He knew how valuable dragon remains were. If it flew somewhere away from Dinas Fridd to die, its body would've been quickly picked clean by bandits and poachers.

"And once the wall comes down?" Edric leaned over the table, his arm brushing lightly against Raven's and causing him to tense slightly.

"That is when you come in, Commander. While the Harbinger's forces are distracted, you'll send fifty of your best men in to secure the castle."

"Fifty?" Tessia frowned. "Will that be enough?"

Edric nodded. "A fortress of this size won't have more than two hundred men garrisoned there. The Harbinger suffered greatly after the loss at Dinas Fridd, so I'd wager it won't have more than a hundred in total."

Raven moved around the table, tracing his hand over the map. "And the Harbinger itself?"

"It's a sorcerer, or it used to be at least." Tessia pointed at a spot in the map labeled "great hall." "It's powerful. We've seen that much. But that means it likely has an ego. Here is where we'll most likely find it, and the circular shape of the room makes it perfect for performing the kind of ritual it's going to attempt, which"—she bit her lip—"is where things get complicated."

"What do you mean?" Raven frowned.

"I've read through the tome that details the ritual a hundred times, and I believe that once it begins, we won't be able to stop it. So we *have* to stop the Harbinger before that happens."

"There's more, I assume?"

Isadora nodded. "Indeed. My sources, along with Lady Alcàntara's sources at the university, believe that the Harbinger is using a lost form of sciomancy, a *stable* sciomancy that won't burn itself out. It's entirely immune to most forms of magic, and it's unlikely that any blade could injure it either."

"Right. So how do we kill it?"

Tessia shook her head. "We don't."

"What? But I thought you said—"

"We have to *stop* it. Hawthorn and I have been working on a binding ritual that should hold it, at least until we figure out a way to disrupt its magic."

Edric hesitated. "I know you find it . . . unseemly, my lady, but this is what the Rite of Sundering was made for. It was designed to stop sorcerers like the Harbinger."

She swallowed. "It's never been performed on a creature like it before. We don't know if it will even work." She sighed. "But you're right. The Administrator of the Arc-en-Ciel Arcane College should be able to get the components for such a ritual within a day or so."

Edric's eyes softened slightly, and he nodded and stepped back from the table.

Tessia placed a hand on Raven's arm. "Are you sure about this? It's going to be dangerous. You might not make it back."

He nodded. "As long as we get Bedivere out of there, it doesn't matter what happens to me." But because he was looking at Tessia, he didn't see the look of sorrow and then confusion that flashed across Edric's face before it was gone.

Raven was packing, carefully selecting enough spare clothes and other supplies for the journey. He had actually learned a few things from the first time he did this, though the comparison did make him chuckle. He thought back to the last time he had packed like this—the night he had fled, the night he had killed that boy. Jaime, he had been told his name was.

Raven made sure to remember that as he thumbed the fabric of his spare shirt, carefully examining the stitching to ensure it wouldn't tear during the trip. He sighed as he carefully folded it and put it into his pack.

There was a knock at the door, followed by a voice.

"Raven?"

Raven stood to his feet, ambled over to the door, and opened it groggily.

"Hello, Commander," he said, yawning.

Edric looked at him, then quickly looked away and up at the ceiling. "If now is a bad time, I can come back—"

"What?" Raven frowned, then looked down at himself. *Oh.*

He realized slowly that he wasn't wearing a shirt. He might've been more embarrassed if he hadn't also been enjoying some elvish honey-wine, a welcome-back present from Laila.

He laughed airily. "Shit, yes, one second—"

"Wait." Edric frowned. "Where on earth did you get *those*?" He glanced down, dark eyes widening as he saw the series of large pale scars on Raven's lower stomach.

"Oh, right." Raven chuckled, as if remembering an inside joke. He turned back to grab a top from the floor, where his clothes were scattered. "Back in the Mirewoods, Ashleigh and I had a run-in with some Nightmares. We took care of them, but . . . well, it was close."

Edric stepped into the room. He carefully examined Raven, who was slipping the shirt on, noting the identical scars on his back. "How . . . how did you survive *that*? I've seen men *crippled* by injuries less severe."

Raven paused, pulling the shirt down to cover his back. *There isn't any point in hiding it, right?* "The sword—Ignos's Edge, I think the Harbinger's woman called it—it . . ." He looked back at the commander, huffing in frustration. "I don't know how to explain it, but it was like it was able to cure me after it tasted my blood. And then with every Nightmare I killed with it, it . . . grew in power somehow."

Edric's mouth opened, then closed, and then opened again. "What? The blade *healed* you?"

Raven cocked his head slightly. Making his way over to the desk, he poured himself another cup of honey-colored liquid out of the bottle. "Yes? Is that unusual?"

Edric nodded, a completely bewildered look in his eyes. "I should think so, yes. I've never heard of any object, even something like an artifact from the First Cataclysm, being able to do anything like that."

Raven rolled his eyes, taking a sip from his glass. "What does it matter? I got rid of it."

Edric stepped forward, back to gaping like a trout unceremoniously pulled from a river. "What do you mean you 'got rid' of it? Did you destroy it?"

"No, I just . . . It's somewhere it can't hurt anyone, all right? Let's just leave it at that." Edric narrowed his eyes. "Fine, but something like that is dangerous—"

"I promise you that I am *not* someone who needs *that* explained to me."

Edric's lips made a thin line. "You're right, and I'm sorry. This . . . isn't how I planned this conversation going."

Raven nodded. He pulled the chair out from the desk and sat down. "Right. What did you need then? If you're just here to wish me a safe journey, it could've waited for the morning."

"I . . ." Edric swallowed. "I just wanted to see you."

Raven sighed heavily, leaning his head back over the chair. "I'm not much in the mood for games tonight, Commander. Whatever you're going to say, just come out and say it, all right? I've got things to do, a brother to save."

The bitterness in the last sentence was not lost on Edric.

He stepped forward, balling his gloved hands into fists and then letting them go. "I just wanted to apologize for not looking into your brother, for being cold to you."

Raven's eyes widened. "Apologize?"

"I . . . I cannot *forget* what you've done, the people you've hurt. But I let that cloud my judgment. I swore to myself that after Darkwater, I would not be ruled by hatred any longer, and I broke that oath." He looked down at the floor.

"I'm . . . I'm glad you see it that way, Commander." Raven's eyes softened. "And for what it's worth, I'm sorry too, sorry for the people I've hurt, sorry for running."

Edric's throat bobbed, but he didn't look at him. "I have seen darkness, sorcerer's lost to madness and consumed by nightmares. Paladins who forsook their vows to the covenant, men and women who threw everything away for nothing more than hatred or greed. When I look at you, Raven, I don't see that darkness. You have stumbled, but you have not fallen."

Raven looked at the commander from his chair, studying him carefully. Edric's eyes were still firmly trained on his two feet, covered by well made leather boots. He stood up, stepping towards him carefully. He smelled the honey-wine on his own breath, and lifted his hand. He hesitated for a moment and then, while Edric was still distracted by his boots, gently cupped his cheek. Edric froze, and then, after a moment, leaned into the touch.

"You're not broken either, commander." He smiled softly. "You're stern, and you don't have much of a sense of humor–"

Edric's face curled into a frown at that, but Raven continued before he could protest.

"–you notice people, you care about the men under your command, and you're gentler than you'd like to admit."

The frown fell, and Edric looked up, finally bringing his dark eye's to meet Raven's pale ones. "Your eyes are different, from Sanctuary. I'm sorry, I don't know why I didn't notice until now."

"A lot has changed since then." Raven agreed. "But some things stay the same."

Edric swallowed and his cheeks turned red, and Raven felt the heat under his hand. "Like what, for example?" Raven might have imagined it, but was that a tiny bit of hope in his voice?

"I still want to kiss you, for one."

Edric's breath caught. "That sounds like the wine talking."

He shook his head. "It's not."

Raven didn't expect it, but Edric was the one to move first. Raven's eyes widened as Edric's lips crashed against his, slightly chapped and tasting of ginger. Then, both of Raven's hands were on his cheeks and he was pulling him against him. Raven's back hit his desk, and it clattered, sending the glass of liquid shattering against the floor. Edric pulled back, looking as though he was going to apologize, but Raven didn't give him the chance. He swept everything left on the desk onto the ground. And then they were together again, bodies holding one another, Raven's bare chest against Edric's clothed one, breaths labored, blood pumping. They held one another close, and between the heat and the haze, for the first time in longer than Raven could remember, he felt safe.

Chapter Twenty-Four

Ishmael's Reach was a good two weeks' trip by foot, but the lot of them traveled by separate roads and ways so as to not raise suspicion.

Raven traveled alone along Valmera's Imperial Highway, stopping to rest only when he was forced to. He had no way of knowing the progress of the others and no way of contacting them to let them know of his progress. About halfway through the trip, he managed to find a good horse, a black and white palfrey with large brown eyes and a short cropped mane. Five days after acquiring the palfrey, Raven was outside Ishmael's Reach.

Positioned at the very edge of the Unsettled Wilds, Ishmael's Reach was much smaller than Dinas Fridd. It was originally built as a scouting post when the Empire of Wyveria attempted to expand into the Wilds but was largely abandoned after the empire's collapse at the end of the Black Age. Now, from afar at least, it appeared as little more than an overgrown ruin. Deep viridian foliage covered nearly the entirety of its surface, save for the stone turrets that peaked out over the nearby forest and the large reinforced gate, clearly a much newer addition as the original would've already rotted away centuries ago.

On the battlements, Raven could see a number of men patrolling. Most of them were dressed in dark armor that resembled chitin with the silver symbol of Wyveria on their chests, but there were some in Dragonguard fatigues, the few who had remained loyal to the Harbinger after its true intentions had been revealed.

Raven took a deep breath, carefully dismounted his steed, and tied it to a tree a few hundred feet from the entrance. He raised his hands over his head so that sentries could plainly see that he had come unarmed without a sword (though he had, of course, thought to keep a dagger in his boot).

"Harbinger!" he called out, voice echoing across the clearly. "I've come for my brother. It's me you want, not him."

He noticed some of the men on the battlements shifting, the sound of some conversation washing over them, too far away for Raven to make out any of the words. Then one of the sentries nodded, and the gate began to creak open, loud enough that the men Raven hoped had gathered on the other side of the fortress would know he was being let in.

All according to plan.

The gate didn't open completely, just enough so that a retainer of the Harbinger could slip through to lead the way. It was a man dressed in hooded robes that covered his face entirely. At first glance, they appeared black, but on further inspection, they were made of a deep multi-shaded purple with tiny embroidered stars running all through the fabric.

The man did not speak, simply motioning for Raven to raise his hands in front of him. Raven hesitated at first but still complied. The man then stepped forward and put a pair of heavy iron shackles around Raven's wrists.

"You . . . follow . . ." the man grunted, his voice sounding strange and forced, like it hurt him to speak.

He led Raven through the door and into the courtyard, and were it not for his tight grip on the shackles, Raven would've frozen where he stood. There, curled up in the fair corner of the courtyard, in an area that seemed to have been entirely cleared of foliage and was blackened by soot, lay the dragon. Its massive head was resting on its tail, and while it seemed to have been asleep when they entered, by the twitch of its nostril and the black smoke that was beginning to pour from its nose, it had since woken up. It raised its head, and its black eyes opened, staring directly at Raven.

"You . . . move . . ." the man grunted, yanking on the chain and forcing Raven to move forward.

Raven didn't take his eyes off the dragon, though, even as they passed through the courtyard and into the antechamber of the fort. And the dragon didn't take its eyes off him either.

The interior of the fort was sparsely decorated. Everything of value had already been stripped away in the centuries since its operation, except for a large mural on the far wall depicting a group of men kneeling before a multicolored five-headed dragon made of gold, silver, emerald, sapphire, and ruby. The men before it were dressed in the same purple robes worn by his guide except that their faces were uncovered, revealing them to be painted in black and white, resembling a death's head. Despite the mural's obvious age, it had avoided losing any of its original luster; even the original gold leafing on the dragon remained.

Past the antechamber and through a short hallway was the great hall—and "great" it was. Raven sucked in a breath as they entered. The entirety of it was filled nearly floor to ceiling with various artifacts. Most were rusted or blackened with age, leaving them completely unrecognizable, but a few had been polished or maintained enough to resemble something. One item, in particular, made his heart jump into his throat. Left like trash leaning against the wall was a deep black blade with red gemstones embedded into the hilt. Wisps of red drifted off and away from it, but the blade remained blissfully silent.

All the items in the room were ancient, but they all had something else in common as well—they were all distinctly remnants of Wyveria. The only place in the room that wasn't covered in detritus was a small circle in the center, where sat the strangest remnant of the long-dead empire.

The Harbinger had its head bowed low to the ground, hands clasped in prayer as it knelt before a black stone brazier that crackled gently with black flame. It had stripped itself of the robes it had worn at Dinas Fridd, leaving its dark glassy skin fully exposed. The only article of clothing that remained was the circlet. Now that Raven was able to get a closer look, he could see quite plainly that the metal was embedded into the creature's very skin, like a brand.

"Har-bing-er . . . Drake," Raven's escort croaked painfully.

The creature's head nodded, and it stood to its feet with unnatural fluidity. "Thank you for coming." Just like at Dinas Fridd, its mouth didn't move when it spoke. The only sign of life on the thing's face was the occasional blinking of its eyes. "And what of your elf? I had heard you traveled with company."

Raven gritted his teeth. "We had a disagreement. He wanted to involve the legion. I disagreed."

The Harbinger's thin lips turned up slightly, revealing a row of sharp black teeth. "A pity. My master did always enjoy elven blood. It would've made for a pleasing breakfast."

"Your master?"

The Harbinger turned away, waving a large clawed hand behind it. In response, the cloaked man shoved Raven forward and to his knees before the brazier.

"Hey, you bastard! What about my brother?" Raven cried out.

The Harbinger stopped, turning its head slightly. "Ah, yes. The whelp." It glanced to the side, making eye contact with a Dragonguard sorcerer who was busying themselves with some sort of preparation. "Retrieve it."

The sorcerer nodded and then left. Shortly after, he returned dragging a man in dirty rags. His black hair had been cropped at odd angles, and his face was bloodied. But nothing could stop Raven from recognizing his brother.

"Bed!" he called out.

Bedivere raised his head slightly, but before he had the chance to respond, the Dragonguard threw him to the ground before the Harbinger. Once again, Raven caught a glimpse of those horrible teeth. The Harbinger knelt down and tangled its knife-like fingers in Bedivere's hair, dragging him to his knees. There was a flash of black metal, and suddenly, the Harbinger had a dagger to Bedivere's throat.

"Wait! Stop! You don't need him. I'm the one you want!" Raven struggled against the manacles, which were still being held by the man who had escorted him inside. Despite the man's unassuming stature, he was strong and didn't allow Raven to move an inch.

The Harbinger tutted. "I sent my generals to retrieve you. What happened to them?" Raven remained silent.

"Just as I thought. You took something from me, and now I shall take something from you. 'Tis only fair." The Harbinger dug the knife into Bed's throat, causing a fresh dribble of blood.

"Please! I'll do anything!" Raven felt tears coming to his eyes, but he didn't care. He hadn't come all this way just to watch his brother die in front of him.

"Percy . . . no . . ." Bed groaned weakly as blood pooled at the corners of his mouth.

The Harbinger's grip on the knife loosened. "Swear it."

"What?"

It pointed the knife at Raven, holding Bedivere with only one hand. "On your blood. Swear it, Percival."

Raven nodded. Just a little longer. He just needed to stall a *little* longer. "I swear it. On my blood, I *swear* it."

Despite its massive size, the Harbinger was surprisingly fast. In a moment, it had discarded Bedivere and now stood before Raven, holding one of his hands in its own. Its black teeth flashed, and then it drew the black dagger across Raven's palm, causing him to cry out. The moment the metal made contact with his skin, though, he felt a rush of heat. The blood from the cut shot out like a freshwater spring. It gathered in the air and swirled around the dagger before melding into the edge.

With one movement from the Harbinger, the dagger cut through the chains, and they shattered like glass. Raven's whole body shook, and he felt like he was going to wretch.

The Harbinger turned its head slightly and held the dagger over his head. "Now, kneel."

To Raven's horror and entirely without his permission, he sank to his knees and bowed his head before the Harbinger. It placed the dagger below his chin, angling it up so that he was looking into its small red eyes.

"Good boy," it purred.

Then it dug its claw into his hair and lifted him up. It brought the dagger low, and Raven was certain it was about to kill him. Instead, the Harbinger took a handful of his hair and cut close to his scalp, leaving a patch of short cropped hair on the back of his head.

"Now, let us commence."

No, no, no! It's too soon. The others won't have brought down the walls yet. Not enough time, not enough time!

Then there was a great rumbling sound, which momentarily reignited Raven's hope that they'd be able to stop the ritual from happening. But the rumble didn't come from farther in the fortress but from directly about them.

Still on his knees, Raven craned his neck to look up. His eyes widened when he saw the deep cracks forming along the ceiling. But instead of collapsing, the cracks began to widen. He realized they weren't cracks at all; they were lines. Through some lost magic or technology, the roof began to *open* to the sky, revealing the dragon hovering overhead.

Raven felt its black eyes on him, and more. He felt its hunger—deep, primal hunger. There was also that sense of familiarity, but there was something else there too. A tether. Like a fishing line, it was translucent in the light but not invisible. As Raven glanced at the Harbinger's dagger, he felt the tether strengthen.

The Harbinger must've used the same magic to bind the dragon that he used on me.

He reached out, pushing out and out with his mind like he'd done in Phantasma, feeling for something, *anything*, to latch on to.

The Harbinger stood over the brazier and dropped the clump of ash-blond hair, and a plume of black smoke rose from the black flames. It was chanting in what Raven could only assume was ancient Wyverian, but he wasn't listening. His eyes were closed, and he was focusing on his heartbeat—and a deeper, louder heartbeat somewhere behind it. He had no idea what he was doing, but if he could just break the Harbinger's connection with the dragon for a moment, maybe it would fly away; it was just an animal deep down, after all. He didn't even know if such a thing would be possible, but as he felt his fingers against the cold stone floor, he knew he had to try.

Ba-dum, ba-dum, ba-dum.

Raven felt his heartbeat, and he felt the beating behind it. He let out a breath, and the two beats became one—two hearts as one. One heart. One blood. Then he felt something snap, and when he opened his eyes, he wasn't on the ground anymore.

CHAPTER TWENTY-FIVE

As he soars over cities, meadows, and villages, people below him look like ants, running as fast as their tiny legs can take them. But he's faster, faster than them, faster and higher than any bird, soaring and soaring. With the sun on his scales and the cool air around him, he is far, far above the clouds. He looks down and sees nothing but white and blue forever. There's a heat in his belly, the taste of brimstone on his tongue. He is fire. He is fire. He is light. He is power. He is the blood of the gods and the stone of the earth. He is a dragon, and he is *eternal*.

Chapter Twenty-Six

When Raven returned to his body, he could feel it, like metal that had been bent to its breaking point and then shattered. The Harbinger's hold over him was broken, but a new bond had been formed. It was a blood magic older than even Wyveria.

Raven glanced up and noticed how the dull red glow had faded from the dragon's scales. Now, they were pure black, like deep polished onyx. The dragon glanced down, and Raven felt the connection between them. It was no longer as thin as a fishing line, but neither was it a chain. He felt his breath leave his lungs at the same pace as the dragon's, and he knew that when he moved, it—or *she* would follow.

The Harbinger brought the dagger over its head, presenting it to the brazier. The black flames grew in intensity in tandem with the chanting until finally it reached a crescendo. Raven braced himself for a scream or a blast. Instead, when the Harbinger brought the dagger down, plunging it into the embers, the entire room fell silent. No sound could be heard, not even the flapping of the great beast's wings that hovered above them.

Then the whole fortress began to shake.

Two men dressed in Wyverian chitin burst through the doors, swords drawn.

"Master! The legion's forces, they're here! The western wall has fallen!"

As soon as the man spoke, he fell, an arrow pierced through his windpipe, and revealed behind him was the cavalry, charging with swords and bows drawn as they cried a mighty battle cry.

Minthe was at the back of the group, shooting arrows at any man in black she could see and swiping with a long curved dagger at anyone who managed to get past the barrage of crystalline ice that swirled around her. Ahead of her, face coated in sweat and still shining like a beacon, Tessia strode forward. Motes of ice and light hovered around her head, shooting out and freezing any of the Harbinger's men who got too close.

Hawthorn and Petyr weren't far behind, looking similarly exhausted but unrelenting with their assault on the enemy. Hawthorn cried out as he shot a bolt of lightning from his fingers, illuminating and then incinerating a man lunging for him with a blade. Finally, there was Edric, his blade glowing with holy light. Raven recognized that blade; he had held that very blade in his hands. The runes shone with radiance as they pierced the body of an incoming Nightmare.

Safeguard the Light.

Raven glanced up at the dragon hovering above them and smiled. "Now!" he cried, suddenly leaping to his feet.

He knocked away the man behind him, sending him sprawling in his back and causing his hood to fall away. His black hair was thinning and patchy, and his skin was so pale it was nearly translucent, exposing the dark purple veins underneath.

General Saddler looked up at him, and when he opened his mouth, Raven could see why speech had been such a struggle. The lining of his throat was entirely covered in blackened grape-sized boils that oozed thick brown pus. Raven curled his nose in disgust and kicked the man away, causing Saddler to cough up spoiled black blood and curl in on himself.

Startled, the Harbinger staggered back, almost knocking into the brazier. "But how—"

Before it had a chance to finish its thought, however, there was a great cry from above them, and the dragon dove down. Her eyes burned with intensity as she opened her mouth, a massive orange fireball forming in her throat. The Harbinger threw up its hands, forming a rippling barrier. As the dragon's fireball hit it, thousands of tiny hairline fractures formed across its surface, but the barrier still didn't shatter.

Raven grinned. *Maybe we can actually kill this thing.*

The Harbinger strained against the force of the dragon fire, beads of blood-like sweat rolling down its jaw until it seemed very close to losing concentration.

And then something went wrong.

The air around the flames began to ripple and shudder, and an iridescent sheen washed over it like a mirage in the desert. A hand, wrinkled and thin and the color of the sky over the sea during a storm, reached out from the flame of the brazier and wrapped its boney fingers around the back of the Harbinger's throat. Its expression went placid, and with one jerk of the boney wrist, the Harbinger's neck snapped.

As the sound echoed through the hall, the chaos of the legion's assault came to a sudden halt.

The boney hand crumbled to the ground like a broken statute, and then the pieces began to rise and reconstitute themselves into something new, into *someone* new.

First, the rest of the arm formed. Then that was connected to a torso, followed by long thin legs, and finally, a head. The features were indistinct. It looked like little more than rotted necrotic flesh pulled taut over a skull, but one thing was very familiar—the stormy grey eyes that formed in the deep sockets. They were the eyes Raven saw every time he looked in the mirror.

Then this man-creature-ghost thing looked at Raven, and time broke.

He didn't have any other way to describe it. The dragon froze where she was, her deep black scale covered in an iridescent sheen of magic, the next plume of hot orange fire frozen in her throat. All sound and movement left the hall in a moment, and the only breath that remained was Raven's.

The man, the ghost, the corpse stepped out of the fire, and his body was suddenly cloaked in deep-wine-colored robes that dragged along the floor behind him. He smiled, and his teeth were yellow and chipped. The longer he stood there, the more human he looked, the more *real* he became. Flesh began to fill his cheeks, along with a healthy color, a rosy warmth that seemed alien in this cold and ancient place.

"Hello, my boy." When the man spoke, his voice was low and hoarse but had a gentle quality to it that reminded Raven of the few memories he had of his grandfather.

"What are you?" Raven stepped back, stumbling slightly when his foot hit the paralyzed Saddler on the ground behind him.

The wrinkles on the man's face smoothed away with every step he took. He laughed, and his voice had a song-like trill to it. "Oh, my sweet boy, haven't you figured it out already?" He bowed dramatically. "Archon Ignos Drake."

Where once there was a shriveled purple corpse, there now stood a young man around Raven's age. But that wasn't where the similarities ended. Along with those same stormy eyes, he had the same sharp features as Raven—the same thin nose, the same lightning-shaped scar on his cheek. The only difference between the two was that the man had sable-black hair.

"H-how? That's not possible."

Ignos laughed. "You have no idea what is possible." He glanced up at the petrified dragon. "Though it seems even still you have the capacity to surprise me. That creature's binding blood magic was strong, but this . . ." He clicked his tongue. "That's soul magic, my dear boy, far older than even my Old Gods."

Every time he moved, the air rippled and displaced around him, like the portals to Phantasma. He was an anomaly, an aberration. He *shouldn't* exist.

Ignos's eyes darted to the side, to Raven's sword, Ignos's Edge. "And that . . . Well, I truly have much to thank you for. A man separated from his blade is hardly a man at all. Thank you for returning it to me, Percival."

"What? But I never—"

Ignos laughed, harsh and wild, and when he looked into Raven's eyes, there was a mad gleam in them that made Raven's breath catch in his throat.

"You threw it into Phantasma, right?" Ignos asked.

Raven's stomach dropped.

"Oh, I'm sure you thought yourself quite clever at the time." Ignos held out his hand, and the Edge began to rise from the pile of other Wyverian artifacts, hovering vertically at least two feet above it. "And the price to recover it was"—he looked down at Saddler, a look of disgust on his face—"substantial. Poor Oryan had to make a deal with a rather sadistic Nightmare of pestilence, but it all worked out. And now . . ." He put his hand under Raven's chin, pulling him toward him slightly. "There's only one last thing I need."

Raven swallowed, his jaw tightening. "And what's that?"

Ignos leaned forward, his lips just brushing against the crest of Raven's ear. "*You.*"

Raven growled, pushing him away, "You're insane!"

"Look around us, Percival." Ignos laughed, gesturing to the great hall.

And Raven did just that.

All around them, the edges of the room were starting to crack—just a bit at first, dust crumbling off and falling to the ground. But then larger chunks of stone started dropping and shattering, and behind them was nothing, just pure white void. As pieces of the wall and then bits of the piles of detritus fell away and into the void, they were unmade, disintegrating into spots of empty blackness that then lightened into the bright emptiness.

"What's happening?"

"I can't exist here. Just look at me."

The lightning-shaped scar, identical and mirroring Raven's own, started out the same pale pink as his but then began to turn white. First, there were hairline fractures like on ancient pottery, and then the entirety was pulsing with empty white light.

"I need you, Percy."

"Why would I ever help you?" Raven clenched his fist, preparing himself to go for the knife that was still hidden in his boot.

"Because I can give you the one thing you desire more than anything in the world."

Ignos waved his hand, and Raven felt his resolve weaken. There, hovering in his palm, was a vision, memory, illusion. It was of Ashleigh, who was entrenched deep in the heart of Phantasma, coated in red blood and black ichor still fighting for his life against an onslaught of Nightmares.

"That's not real. He's dead. He's . . . he's been dead."

He tutted. "For you, in your time, yes. But Phantasma exists outside of time. A powerful enough sorcerer could easily reach in and pull him out at the moment before his demise. All I would ask in exchange is you. A life for a life. A fair trade, is it not?"

"Ashleigh wouldn't want—"

"What does it matter what he'd *want*. He'd be alive, wouldn't he?" Ignos said quickly, cutting him off with a low hiss.

The white cracks on his face were growing. He stepped forward and grabbed Raven by the throat. His grip tightened, and his nails, suddenly sharp and claw-like, dug into the tender flesh of Raven's neck.

Then Ignos sighed and turned his head slightly, his black pupils gleaming with something almost like sympathy. "Wouldn't it be so much easier to just . . . let go? You fight *so hard*, my sweet boy. Day after day, you struggle. Haven't you had enough?"

Raven hesitated. For just a split second, less than a moment, he hesitated, and as he did so, the Archon smiled. His grip on him loosened, and Raven dropped to the ground, landing hard on his knees. His hands hit the stone floor and found himself staring into his brother's eyes. Bedivere's face was bloodied and frozen in time in a mask of fear, but there was more behind the fear, something into those deep ocean-colored eyes of his.

Raven's own eyes softened when he recognized it—*hope*. Bedivere was always so full of hope. Hope for a new world, hope for a *better* world. And Raven knew that hope would die with the return of Wyveria. If anything in the world mattered, that hope *mattered*. He balled his fists, pressing the palm of his other hand into the ground. His body began to shake with barely contained sobs.

"Come now, my boy. It won't be so bad, letting me make use of your body. I'll take perfect care of it, and ensure those mortals have a place under my new regime." Ignos tutted, a small smile spreading across his lips.

Raven looked up at him, face streaked with tears. "No."

"No?" Ignos's smile fell ever so slightly.

Raven's hand went quickly to his boot, and he stumbled to his feet. "No, Ignos. I won't be your puppet."

Ignos laughed and caught Raven's wrist mid-thrust. Then he yanked it up and squeezing tightly. The dagger clattered from Raven's grasp and landed on the ground, and Ignos kicked it into the crumbling reality around them.

"Did you really think that trick would work on me? *Me?* I am Ignos Drake, Archon of the great Empire of Wyveria. I have razed kingdoms that would not kneel before me. I have bathed in the blood of thousands of slaves and sated my thirst on the blood of dragons older than the gods. Did you really think any metal forged by mortal hands could kill *me?*"

"Maybe not," Raven grunted, lifting his free hand up and holding it out beyond the Archon's line of sight. "But I'm really hoping this will."

He closed his fist, and there was a short sharp whistle as something moved through the air. Ignos made a wet choking sound and dropped his hold on Raven, his grey eyes going wide. He glanced down, and Raven grinned up at him, ignoring the soft warmth building in his gut. The blade, black as night and coated in red, shot out from Ignos's stomach, the tip piercing into the space just below Raven's chest plate.

"How—" The Archon gasped, hot red boiling up from his lungs.

Raven pulled him closer, reached around, and grabbed hold of the sword's hilt. Then he twisted it. "You've been gone a long time, Archon. It seems you've lost your edge."

The whites of Ignos's eyes burned, and cold light emanated his mouth, opened in a silent scream. With his last bit of strength, he reached up and dug his fingertips into Raven's head, digging and digging and digging.

As Raven screamed, the white light grew, and then it swallowed them both.

Chapter Twenty-Seven

When Raven opened his eyes, he wasn't—he wasn't standing, he wasn't sitting, he wasn't lying down. He simply *wasn't*.

Stretching on and on and on as far as he could see in every direction was a plane of white light. Like a mountain of chalk blanketed in snow during a blizzard or a flame burning hotter than passion or rage, there was nothing but dazzling white light.

This must be Phantasma, as it truly is not altered by mortal perceptions. He marveled. He had no idea where the revelation came from, it simply appeared in his mind like it had always been there. Raven doubted even Hawthorn had ever seen anything like this.

He took a step and suddenly felt himself falling. There was a flash, not white, but almost. He saw something behind his eyes and behind his ears and beyond him. The space in front of him cracked, and through the crack, he saw a woman.

Tessia stood in an elegant floor-length gown the color of buttercups with golden embroidery and diamonds sewn into the collar. Her dark hair was braided with golden thread and tied up in an elegant plait, and her eyes were painted with kohl and dusted with gold. She held in her hand a half-empty glass of pale wine, and a cordial smile played on her dark lips. She was talking to someone, but the person's face was obscured by a pale fog that seemed to hover around the room. Raven tried to call out to her, but when he opened his mouth, no sound came out. Despite that, her ears perked up, and she frowned.

"Pardon me. Will you excuse me a moment, my lord?"

The faceless man nodded, and Tessia turned away from him and stepped toward the crack in reality.

Raven tried to call out her name again, and this time, her eyes widened, flashing with something approaching recognition. He held out his hand to her, and she reached back, taking hold of his hand just as something began to flood behind her. There was a plume of red fire, and then rocks crumbled around them. Tessia just barely pulled herself from the blast. Raven felt her hand slip from his grasp and watched helplessly as she fell back and cracked her head on the now collapsed ruins of the Temple.

The crack snapped shut, and then there was another flash, another snap.

Crack.

Another portal opened up in front of him. Raven saw a shape, like a candle flame made humanoid, flickering in a dark space. He opened his mouth, but instead of his own voice, he heard Hawthorn calling out to the spirit.

"Raven!"

The spirit looked up, its visage shifting from a blank slate to a bird and then to a dragon. It nodded and then vanished, and he was falling again.

Nothing was real in this place, nothing except him, and he knew that because when he looked down at his stomach, he was still bleeding. He groaned, reaching out for another crack, another way out. The space between his fingers cracked. He hissed as he felt a jolt of electricity through his fingertips. He shook his head, ignoring the searing heat between his ribs and the sharp bite on his fingers. He reached out once more, and the space in front of him began to rip. Like poor tailoring tearing at the seams, it opened until he was looking into a clearing in the woods.

A carriage rumbled through the clearing, and Raven gaped at the storm cloud forming above it. He clenched his fist, and the storm cloud fizzled with electricity.

Phantasma, the birthplace of magic, where anything is possible. Of course!

He smiled and forced his fist down. A massive bolt of lightning struck the space in front of the carriage, causing the horses to rear up and the coachman to be thrown to the ground by the force of the blast. The tear snapped shut, and when it opened again, a grey-haired soldier was standing outside of the carriage and scratching his beard. Raven brought his hand down again, and this time, the lightning struck the ground next to the carriage, causing it to tilt and careen to the side before the cloud vanished into a bluebird day.

The crack snapped shut, but he didn't see it. His eyes were closed, and he was falling and falling. He could feel his warm blood spreading over his stomach and staining the tunic he wore beneath his armor, but even so, he felt the chill begin to come to the tips of his finger and his toes.

Bedivere was safe; everyone was safe.

A soft voice in his head whispered to him that now he could rest, that now he could go to the Gods with a clear conscience, that now he could have peace. He recognized the voice. It was the voice of his mother before he'd lost her, before she'd lost herself to drink and sorrow.

"It's time to come home, Percy," she cooed.

He could feel her breath on his cheek, the gentle caress of her hand on his shoulder, her soft lips on his head, and he smiled sadly.

"I'm sorry, Mother, but I'm not done yet."

He didn't hear a response, but he felt her presence leave him. When he opened his eyes, all he could see around him was darkness. Then he stopped falling, his back hit something rough and cool, and consciousness slipped from his grasp.

Epilogue

Raven held out his arms as a man put a coat over his shoulders. He was surrounded by countless attendants, all fussing over various aspects of his appearance.

"Is this really all necessary?" He puffed out his chest, allowing a stout dwarven woman on a stool to affix a pin to his lapel.

"For a coronation? Yes, m'lord, I believe it is." She laughed, and he rolled his eyes.

She hopped down, allowing him the space to look at himself in the mirror. His hair was cropped short, almost to his scalp, but that was compensated by the nearly full beard he had managed to grow. It was strange, and the hair was curlier than that which grew from his head. But Bed said it made him look more mature, and who was he to argue with that?

He was dressed in deep royal blues and silvers with a waistcoat the color of the sea at twilight and a jacket with buttons polished to resemble the stars. His pants were well tailored, and he had a pair of sturdy black boots, along with a belt that held an empty sheath designed for a ceremonial sword. His hand rested on an ornate silver cane with a black dragon's head for the handle. He looked like all the paintings of all the kings that had ever come before.

"Are you ready?" Hawthorn stepped out from behind the partition.

He was dressed more modestly in comparison, but it was still a far cry from his usual garb. He wore a deep hyacinth-colored robe with copper-colored fastening, denoting his status as a highly respected sorcerer of the court. His white hair was pulled up into a simple topknot tied with a purple thread.

Raven smiled softly and nodded. "Let's not keep them waiting any longer."

The throne room of Edelheim's palace was bustling with activity. No coronation since that of his great-aunt Hippolyta had been such an event, in no small part due to the attendance of the Suncrest noble house. This was because if House Suncrest was there, then obviously House Castillan and House Javik had to be there as well. If the Castillans were there, then obviously House Cabelle had to be there, and obviously, if the Cabelles were there, House Yarlan had to be there. And so on and so forth. As a result, the docks of Edelheim were so overwhelmed that some of the visiting dignitaries had to drop their anchors farther out and row to shore.

Raven smiled, looking out over the crowd. He caught Tessia's eyes and then Petyr's. Tessia's hair was shorter than when he'd last seen her, cropped so that the dark coils were almost flush to her scalp. She'd created quite a scandal when she'd announced she was bringing an elf as her paramour, but no one would dare speak out against a woman chosen by the gods, and looking at the two women holding hands in the aisle, Raven wasn't going to correct them on that.

He'd spoken to Tessia after he'd recovered, told her what he'd seen, but they'd both come to the conclusion that it was better to let the people believe she really had been rescued by an aspect of Tyr. And maybe in a way, she had been. The Gods did work in mysterious ways after all, and who could say how their will would manifest itself?

Petyr had brought his wife as well, an elf-blooded dwarf with dark skin and pale patches near her eyes around her mouth, and on the knuckles of her fingers. Raven hadn't had the pleasure of meeting Orphne yet, but looking at the woman talking to her husband, he knew he wouldn't get away without doing so. Along with them, Lady Alcàntara had attended with her family, and Dame Nestra with hers. Raven had also extended an invitation to Isadora, though he also knew that if she had come, he most likely wouldn't be seeing her. Queen Elspeth and King Harold had sent a dignitary in their place, an elf-blooded human called Alastair. He seemed a good man, if a bit unfocused.

Finally, standing vigilant as ever at the back of the hall, was Edric Royce. He stood with a woman with eyes similar to his but hair like dark mahogany. She was mussing his hair and he was glaring daggers at her.

His sister, Raven concluded.

Edric was dressed in a red doublet with dark brown stitching in the shape of two swords. His hair had been combed back, and his face was clean shaven. He looked nice; he looked clean. Raven was tempted to go and speak to Edric, but he knew the ceremony would be starting soon. He didn't have a moment to waste.

As if summoned by his thoughts, the bell rang, and all the guests took their assigned places. Hawthorn shot him a smile before he moved to stand beside Lord Pernam.

As Pernam opened his mouth, a hush fell over the entire hall.

"My good ladies and lords, people of Edelheim, and those who have come from your far-flung places to witness this glorious day," he spoke, his ancient voice booming with authority, "after thirty-six years of good stewardship, our good King Regnant, Sagramor the Fair of House Drake, first of his name, has passed."

Raven swallowed, lowering his eyes respectfully at the mention of his late father.

Pernam continued, "But the time for mourning has passed, and today is a day for celebration. Today, we crown our new King Regnant. Today, we welcome the reign of King Meliodas, first of his name and rightful King of the Isle of Edelheim!"

Raven raised his eyes and watched as the doors at the end of the hall swung open, revealing his brother in all his glory. He was dressed from head to toe in fine silks and velvets, along with the furs of animals he'd hunted and those that had been passed down for generations. Behind him, holding the trail of his blood-red cloak, were Elyan and Bedivere.

It had taken months, but Bed had finally regained the strength to walk, and to see him beaming with pride now, you'd never know what he'd been through.

Meliodas's eyes, so much like their mother's, were determined and set ahead of him as he stepped forward and up to the dais before Lord Pernam, who held the Drakes' ancestral crown. Meliodas let out a shaky breath and glanced over to Raven, who shot him a reassuring smile.

Raven knew when he became a Dragonguard that he would never be king of Edelheim, even if he managed to clear his name. Meliodas would make a good king, and Raven couldn't be more proud to stand before him now.

"My lord," Pernam said, stepping aside and gesturing to Raven. "Would you do the honors?"

Raven bowed his head and stepped forward. "I would love nothing more, Chancellor." He placed his hand on either side of the crown and lifted it up. Then he held it over his brother's head.

"You're going to do great things, Mel," he said quietly to his brother.

Meliodas let out a deep breath, and the tension fell away from his shoulders as Raven delicately and gingerly placed the crown on his golden locks.

"I give you . . . King Meliodas!" Raven cried, drawing the ceremonial blade and raising it high.

From the crowd came a great cheer, and he was joined by dozens of other men and women raising their blades in solidarity. Meliodas then turned to face the crowd. Even though he was facing away from him, Raven could feel the light of his brother's smile radiating like the light of Astraea's own stars, and he smiled too.